A LOVELY ~~SEDUCTION~~

"My Lady," Maude said heavily, "Did no one teach ye about the bedding?"

"Aye—Nay." Emma laughed. "My father told me my husband would share my bed."

"And that is all? Oh, my Lady! Ye should have told me. I could have prepared ye."

"'Tis all right," Emma assured her with a wry smile. "I am prepared now. 'Tis why I took the hops and willow. All will be well tonight. I will forbear."

"Nay! My Lady." Maude started urgently, only to snap her mouth shut when Lord Amaury stepped in. She hurried from the room.

Amaury watched Maude go, then turned to his wife. It was more than obvious to him that she wore nothing beneath the black linen wrapped around her.

Amaury felt his throat closing up as his gaze wandered over that body. It appeared that he would not be gaining satisfaction anytime soon. Not if his wife was ailing.

"You are ill. I wish to know what is ailing you, wife."

"Nothing, husband."

"You will tell me what is ailing you. 'Tis your duty as my wife."

Emma frowned at him. She had no idea why he would think her ill, unless he had also somehow learned of her taking the white willow bark and hops. If so, she definitely did not wish to explain her reasons to him. Deciding that distraction was needed, she managed to gain her feet without losing her balance, then dropped the linen to the floor. "Do I look ill, husband?"

LYNSAY SANDS

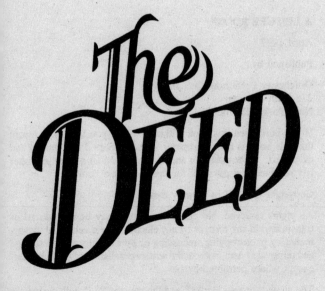

The DEED

LEISURE BOOKS **NEW YORK CITY**

For
Maggie Willan
You gave all the love, support,
and encouragement that a mother can.
I wish that you were here to see what came of it.

A LEISURE BOOK®

April 1997

Published by

Dorchester Publishing Co., Inc.
276 Fifth Avenue
New York, NY 10001

Printed in the United States of America.

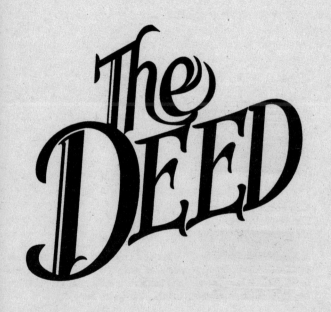

Prologue

Leicestershire, England, May 1395

Emma peered surreptitiously over her companions in the antechamber. Some were pacing off nervous energy, others sat stiff and still, but every single one seemed tense and alert as they awaited their appointed visit with the king.

Glancing down, she noticed that she had begun to shred the hankie she held, and quickly eased her hold, crumpling the piece of cloth in her hand to hide this sign of her nervousness.

It had taken a great deal of begging, nagging, and pleading for her to get her cousin, Rolfe, to arrange this meeting with Richard II. It was not often that women were granted an audience at court. Popular opinion was that any issue they might bring forth would be of little import and therefore better seen to by their husband or father. But Rolfe was one of Richard's most favored dukes. He had also been raised with Emma, loved her like a sister, and was prone to let her have her way whenever possible. Despite her refusal to explain what her complaint involved, Rolfe had agreed to request an audience for her, and—unfortunately—the king had been in the mood to indulge him.

Tucking her shredded hankie up her sleeve, Emma settled her hands in her lap and tried not to fidget. A difficult task. Now that she had gained what she had worked so hard for, Emma was beginning to regret the impulsive plan she had come up with. Unfortunately, she hadn't stopped to consider it thoroughly before pursuing it with her usual dogged persistence. She had conceived it and struck out to make it happen without thinking about it too much. That was one of her failing sins. She was too impulsive and stubborn in her approach to the problems in her life. Even she could see that. It would see her in Hell some day. At least that was what Father Gumpter constantly told her.

"Lady Eberhart."

Emma gave a start, then paled at the sound of her name. It was time for her audience with the king! Oh, sweet Saint Gabriel! This was a mistake.

"My lady?" When the steward raised one eyebrow at her hesitation, Emma silently cursed her sudden cowardice and got promptly to her feet. Like it or not, she was here now. By her own request. She had no choice but to go through with her plans and hope for the best.

Straightening her shoulders, she approached the steward, then followed when he turned smartly on his heels and led her through the door people had been walking in and out of for the past hour. Well, most of them had walked in and out, she thought now. There was that one poor unfortunate fellow. Emma wasn't sure what he had said, but he had apparently displeased the king. At least that was the opinion she had arrived at when the guards had dragged the terrified man out by his heels and hauled him away. Probably to the tower, she thought nervously as she was led into the audience room and up to the chair where the king was seated.

A cleric of some sort stood on the king's right, while Archbishop Arundel, Lord Chancellor since Bishop Wykeham's retirement, stood on his left. Emma tried to staunch the unpleasant thoughts that ran through her mind on seeing the prelate. She did not care for the new chancellor. He seemed far too arrogant and sly to her. Her opinion was not softened by the expression on his face as he took in her presence now. It seemed he did not even need to hear her complaint before deciding it a waste of the king's time.

Emma was working herself into a fine temper over that fact when she suddenly realized that what she would say would most likely prove him correct. B'Gad! This had indeed been a mistake.

"Lady Emmalene, Your Majesty."

Grasping at the distraction, Emma turned to watch the steward leave after he announced her, then immediately wished she had not. This was her first visit to court. She was completely ignorant of the proper etiquette in most things, so she had been simply following the example of those around her. However, the steward was bowing his way backward out of the room, leading her to believe she would be expected to curtsy her way backward out of the room as well. If that were the case, she very much feared she would make a horrible bungle of it.

"Lady Emmalene?"

Giving a guilty start, she turned abruptly to the three men before her and dropped a curtsy, staying in that pose until the king bid her rise.

"You are Rolfe's cousin?" The king's voice was gently

curious as he looked her over.

"A-aye your majesty." Emma shifted nervously and swallowed the little ball of apprehension that had lodged itself at the back of her throat. She briefly considered discarding her plan and excusing herself, but feared such behaviour might find her being dragged out of the room by her feet as the earlier unfortunate had been. A most distressing image. Rolfe would be horribly embarrassed.

"Lord Rolfe asked that I grant you an audience?"

Emma bit her lip and nodded.

The king waited patiently for a moment, then raised his eyebrows slightly. "What did you wish to see me about, my lady?"

Feeling a blush bloom beneath her skin, Emma let her gaze skitter over the two men flanking him. She had never considered that there might be someone else present at her audience. Truthfully, she hadn't really considered the audience itself at all; she had simply determined to persuade Rolfe to acquire one for her. Now she stood before the king and these two other men with little in her poor addled mind but horror over what she had gotten herself into. She was nervous, of course, and had no problem at all in determining where to place the blame for it.

It was the archbishop's fault, she decided, giving that man a firm glare now. While the king was peering at her with nothing more than gentle inquisitiveness and the cleric looked simply curious, Arundel's expression was becoming more scathing with each second that she delayed. It made her nervous.

"My lady?"

Emma's gaze slid back to the king at once. He really was not at all what she had pictured. She had known he was not very old—being perhaps four years older than herself—and despite living so far away from

The Deed

court and all of its gossip, she was aware of the stories of his sadness and gloom over the loss of his wife this past year. It was said he had loved Queen Anne deeply. A rarity in made matches. Still, she had expected him to have more presence. Truthfully, Emma found the archbishop much more formidable. That gentleman's expression at the moment was enough to shrivel her up.

A flicker of movement drew her gaze back to the king to see the impatient way he was now tapping his fingers on the arm of his seat. Emma drew herself up and spoke. "I apologize, Your Majesty, but I wish to speak to you of . . ." She paused, flushing slightly, a pained expression crossing her features. " 'Tis a delicate matter, Your Majesty," she told him unhappily.

The king's expression immediately became sympathetic. "Pray, take your time, my lady," he said gently.

Nodding, Emma glanced down at her wringing hands, sighed, took a deep breath, opened her mouth to speak, then shook her head helplessly. " 'Tis most difficult."

The king nodded, but raised an eyebrow in question and Emma sighed. Deciding there was nothing else for it, she plunged into speech. "My lord, you know that I am married to Lord Fulk, the Duke of Eberhart?"

Richard II inclined his head solemnly. "Aye, my lady. I am aware of this. Does your request for an audience have something to do with your husband?"

Emma nodded helplessly again, silently berating herself for her foolish plan. "Aye . . . well, I. . . . You see, the marriage took place, but to date his lordship has not seen fit to . . . um. . . . well. . . ." She frowned slightly, aware that her face was now completely red. It felt on fire.

The king raised his eyebrows curiously even as the archbishop's brows drew down in unpleasant suspicion.

11

Lynsay Sands

"He has not seen fit . . . ?" the king murmured now, letting the question trail away, a small frown of concern marring his lips as he leaned forward in his seat. Despite the displeasure evident on his face, the holy man was leaning forward as well, as was the cleric.

Emma gazed slowly over the three men and wailed despairingly, "He has not bedded me since our wedding, Your Majesty!"

All three mouths dropped open at her announcement. The archbishop was the first to recover, his mouth snapping shut in a firm line of definite disapproval. Catching the motion, the king straightened a bit more slowly, his lips easing back into an uncomfortable line. The cleric, however, continued to gape at Emma as if she had just stripped off her clothes and suggested a game of chess.

Doing her best to ignore the servant's rude behavior, Emma caught her hankie as it slid from beneath her sleeve and twisted at it miserably as she awaited the king's pronouncement. It was a long time in coming.

Shifting, he cleared his throat, scratched his head, then glanced at a spot vaguely over her shoulder to ask, "I take it this . . . er . . . situation . . . displeases you?"

He didn't sound totally certain of that even as he said it, and Emma frowned slightly. She supposed his confusion had to do with the fact that ladies were not generally thought to enjoy the marriage act. At least that was what Father Gumpter had told her when she had approached him. Personally, she did not see what all the fuss was about. She did not like or dislike it herself. However, enjoy it or not, she was aware of the facts of life and there was no other way that one might beget a child.

"I would like very much to have children, Your Majesty," she said firmly, then added, "That is after all what the Church says a wife's duty is, does it not? I wish to

12

do my duty and bear an heir to carry on my husband's name." Her gaze flew to the archbishop as she spoke, and she saw the frown he had been regarding her with up until now fade, to be replaced by a blink, then the beginnings of approval as he nodded.

"Ah." The king nodded solemnly, his hand moving to cover the lower part of his slender face. Holding his chin thoughtfully, he nodded repeatedly, wisely, and silently. Emma was beginning to think he would sit their nodding all day when he suddenly shifted, a frown flickering briefly across his face before he suggested, "Mayhap his lordship has been busy with affairs." He paused abruptly to glare at the cleric when that man giggled nervously at his unfortunate choice of words. The cleric sobered at once, and the king amended his words. "Estate affairs."

"For two whole years?"

The three men before her goggled in unison again.

"Do you mean to say, my lady, that your husband has not . . . ?"

"Aye," Emma admitted grimly.

The three men sucked in their breath in unison. Emma shifted under their glances, aware that they were now inspecting her for flaws. After all, why else would a man refuse to bed his bride for two full years? She ducked her head in shame, afraid of what they would see. Many was the time she had peered into her own looking glass, trying to fathom why her husband turned away from her. She did not consider herself a raving beauty, but surely she was not a hag either?

Her hair was honey blond. Her skin pale but flawless. It was true her eyes were perhaps a bit large for her face, her nose turned up just a bit too much, and her lips just a touch too large. And aye, she was not fashionably thin, but she was not fat either. She was well shaped and buxom. And certainly not that ugly, she thought dismally as she once again wondered why her husband had refused to even step into her room since their wedding night.

"What do you wish that we do about this, my lady?"

Emma blinked at the question, surprised by it. The answer seemed simple enough to her. "Why . . . order him to, my lord."

"Order?" The king nearly choked on the word.

He truly looked taken aback at that, Emma noted with a frown. "Of course, my lord. You must explain that 'tis his duty . . . to you as well as to me."

"To me?"

If he opened his eyes any further, surely his eyeballs would fall right out of his head, Emma thought now, and sighed patiently as she explained. "Aye, my lord. He is your servant, and as such he should continue his line so that his sons and grandsons might serve you as faithfully as we do."

The king blinked at that, then glanced at the archbishop who bobbed his head from side to side slightly, then nodded with a small shrug as if to say it was a plausible argument . . . almost. Leaning closer to the man, Richard murmured something Emma couldn't hear. Now it was her turn to lean forward as the holy man responded. She only managed to catch the last of that as well, however.

"Whatever the case, sire,'twould certainly seem a sin to leave such . . . er . . . ripe fruit on the . . . er . . . vine to waste. Or for someone else to pick," he added grimly.

Sighing, King Richard turned back to her, eyed her silently, then sighed again, pursed his lips and leaned forward in his seat, a pained expression coming to his face. "My lady . . ." He paused to frown as he realized that he had almost whispered the words, glanced to each side with irritation to see that the archbishop and the cleric had leaned forward to hear what he said as well, then glanced beyond Emma and glared.

Following his gaze over her shoulder, she saw the guards at the door straighten abruptly from their bent-forward positions. They too were curious to hear the king's words.

Shaking his head, he tried again. "My lady, you said he had not . . . er . . ."

"Seen to his conjugal duties," the archbishop offered softly.

"Aye, seen to his duties since your wedding night. Are we to take it then that he did at least . . . er . . . ?"

"Consummate," the holy man murmured.

"Aye, did he at least—" He waved toward the archbishop.

"Consummate."

"The wedding?"

"Aye," Emma said.

He scowled at her expression. "You do not appear too certain, my lady."

Emma frowned slightly now herself. Truth to tell, she was not sure. She really had no idea what consummation included. Her mother had died in labor—along with the long-hoped-for son she had been trying to bear—when Emma was just six. Her father had raised her on his own after that, and while he had been an excellent father, he had not been a mother. When it had come to preparing her for her wedding night and all it entailed, he had hemmed and hawed, his face flushed red, and told her gruffly, "Your husband will be sharing your bed now, girl."

"Aye, Father," Emma had murmured, and awaited further instruction. But he had merely tugged at his collar, nodded, then patted her shoulder and escaped.

"Perhaps if her ladyship could describe her wedding night," the archbishop suggested delicately when Emma simply stood lost in thought.

Her head came up at once. "Describe it?"

"Well, not all of it." Flushing, the holy man peered helplessly at the king.

Suddenly impatient, Richard II muttered under his breath and glared at her. "My lady, did your husband share your bed on your wedding night?"

"Oh, aye." Emma smiled her relief. She had been consummated. "Aye. His men undressed him and put him there, my lord. He made quite a racket, I can tell you. I thought his snore would lift the roof."

"Aye, but did he touch you?" the archbishop put in impatiently.

"Touch me?" Emma looked uncertain again as she tried to recall. For a moment she was quite concerned for she could not recall if he had and judging from their expressions it was quite important, but then she smiled again with relief as she remembered. "Aye, my lord, he rolled upon me in the night. In fact, he near suffocated me." She lowered her voice as she confessed. "He was quite sotted, my lord. He did not even wake up when I rolled him back off."

Rather than being pleased by this news, the archbishop and the king both straightened with disgust. There was a moment while both men were busy grimacing at each other as if in pain; then the archbishop asked wearily, "What happened in the morning, my lady?"

"In the morning?" Emma frowned slightly once more. It had been two years ago, after all. "Well, as I recall, my lord, I woke up first. Aye. Aye, I did. I woke up and got dressed behind the screen. When I came back out, my lord husband was . . . Why, as I recall he had been playing about with his dagger in the bed and cut himself," she told them with surprise at the memory.

"Cut himself?" the archbishop asked, his eyes narrowed suspiciously.

"Aye." Emma nodded. "Perchance he was still a bit tipsy from the night before? Whatever the case, he wiped the blood on the sheets. I was about to get him a cloth, for I knew the blood would surely ruin the sheets, but then there was a knock on the door."

"And who was at the door?" the king asked in a world-weary voice that suggested he already knew the answer.

" 'Twas my father, Father Gumpter, and Lord Fulk's cousin, Bertrand."

"What did they do?"

Emma shrugged. "They simply wished us good morrow. Oh, then my father saw the sheets and ordered them taken away and hung above the hall. I think he thought that airing them would save the stain from setting, but of course it did not work. My lord, why are you shaking your head? Have I angered you?"

"Nay, my lady," the king said grimly before turning to his cleric. Unfortunately, he was otherwise engaged in ogling Emma at that moment. It seemed by his suggestive leer and the way he was waggling his eyebrows at her that he found her husband's neglect not the least bit detrimental to her attractiveness. In fact, Emma was getting the distinct impression that he would be most willing to offer himself up as sacrifice in place of her husband "to pick the ripe fruit."

All of his posturing and posing disappeared like smoke in the wind when the king snapped his name sharply.

"Aye, my lord." The cleric's head dropped at once to the book he held, his hand at the ready to write.

"Send a message to the effect that His Majesty the King desires Lord Fulk to see to his . . . er . . ."

"Conjugal duties," the archbishop murmured.

"Aye, conjugal duties, else . . ." He hesitated, seemingly at a loss.

"If I might suggest," Emma murmured, and the king turned to her hopefully. "You might fine him . . . oh . . . say . . . sixty sheep? His lordship is quite fond of sheep. At least there are hundreds of them around the castle. Though we have yet to have any served up to dinner," she added with a perplexed frown.

"A hundred sheep!" the king snapped. "Nay, every last blasted one of them will be taken should he not attend his wife forthwith."

Emma beamed at the man, relief adding to her gratitude. "Oh, thank you, my lord. I will name our first child after you," she announced, grabbing his hand and kissing it swiftly. A glance at the archbishop as she did showed him looking alarmed and shaking his head feverishly. Flushing again, Emma released the king's hand at once and dropped into a deep curtsy.

"Aye, well . . ." King Richard cleared his throat and straightened in his seat. "That's very . . . nice, Lady Emmalene. Now, if we have dealt with everything?"

"Aye, Your Majesty. That was all." Emma said at once, glancing up from her curtsy.

"Very good." He gestured toward the men by the door, and Emma glanced back to see them opening the doors for her exit.

Biting her lip, she hesitated as the picture of the steward backing out in a bow came to mind.

"My lady?"

Emma took in the king's raised eyebrows and sighed. Forcing a smile, she began to scoot backward still in a curtsy. It was a very awkward move to perform. Much more awkward than a backing-out bow, she was sure. Emma was rather proud of how well she was succeeding, when she managed to get halfway to the door before stumbling, and that was just a small stutter in her step.

"My lady!"

Emma paused and glanced up at the alarm in the voice. The king looked torn between dismay and laughter, the cleric looked flabbergasted, and the archbishop was definitely amused. Coughing suspiciously into his hand, the prelate gestured for her to get up.

Flushing, Emma straightened slowly, hesitated, then bowed as the steward had done and backed out of the room so that she was facing the doors as they closed.

Chapter One

"Damn ye, Alden! Go give your ears a shake! Did I not say my green tunic?!"

"A-aye, my lord." Alden cringed and took a nervous step backward.

Dressed only in hose and braies, his wide chest bare, Lord Amaury de Aneford looked just as fearsome as he did in full battle dress. Especially now in the foul temper he was in.

Alden had only been with the warrior for a matter of two weeks. Despite this short length of time, he did not think his lord's present mood was natural. At least not to de Aneford. He based his judgment on the reactions of the other soldiers and the exasperated amusement Lord Blake had been showing over the man's behavior. Alden wasn't exactly sure what had brought about the man's displeasure, but knew it had something to do with the king's message. A courier had brought it to Amaury as he had been concluding his business with

Lord Chesterford the day before. The warrior had paled as he had read the missive, then crumpled it into a ball, tossed it into the fire, and stormed out of the keep bellowing for his horse to be saddled. Seconds later he had cancelled the order, stormed back indoors, and proceeded to get drunk.

He had been behaving thusly ever since. Storming and rushing about, then pausing to get drunk and dally. His antics were beyond Alden's young comprehension, and made him terribly axious in the man's presence.

The slap of material against his face as the tunic was tossed back at him in disgust drew Alden out of his thoughts and sent him stepping backward to trip over a boulder. Scrambling quickly back to his feet, he began sidling away. "I-I will f-fetch the g-green one, my lord. Forthwith."

Amaury watched his squire go with narrowed eyes, then turned back to peer at the cold lake he had just left.

"You should not vent your anger on the boy."

Amaury glanced over his shoulder at those laughing words, his displeasure obvious as he eyed his friend. "He is a clodpole."

"He is afraid of you," Blake countered, smiling easily as he clapped his friend on one bare shoulder. "He will be less clumsy once he is more confident."

Amaury grimaced at that. "He will ne'er become more confident."

"Not if you continue to take your anger out on him."

The warrior frowned over that but remained silent, his gaze returning to the placid lake.

Blake followed his gaze, then sighed. "Refuse to marry her," he suggested for the hundredth time since this trip had begun.

Amaury snorted at that, just as he had every time the suggestion had been made. "And give up the opportunity to be lord of mine own estate?"

Blake smiled slightly and shook his head. "Fine. Then marry the wench, but if it is what you want, why be so surly with everyone about you?"

" 'Tis not what I want," Amaury countered at once. "It is what must be done to get what I want. Who in his right mind would wish to be married to an ugly old hag?"

"You have not even met her yet," Blake protested at once, and Amaury turned on him in disbelief.

"Are you not the one who told me that she had to petition the king to get her husband to sleep with her?"

"Aye, that is the gossip at court, but no one knows what she looks like save the king, and he refuses to discuss it. 'Sides, her husband died on the way home to perform his . . . er duty."

" 'Twas probably suicide," Amaury muttered grimly.

Blake hid a smile at that. "Then refuse to—"

"Nay!" Amaury turned on him, frowning. "You know I cannot." He sighed unhappily. "It may be my only chance to gain a home."

Blake nodded solemnly, then glanced to the side as Alden returned, a green tunic in hand. Smiling slightly at the boy, he strode forward and relieved him of the item. "That will be all, Alden. Mayhap you could have your lord's horse prepared. We ride shortly."

"Aye, my lord. Thank ye, my lord." Relief shone on the boy's face as he turned and charged back to camp.

It had only been midday when they had stopped the night before, a mere hour's ride from Eberhart Castle. Amaury had used the excuse of wishing to clean up from the trip before presenting himself to his new bride for the delay, but after making camp he had promptly set about getting dead drunk. For the first time since Blake had known the man, he had had to be carried back to his tent. Then he had woken late this morning and dallied as long as possible about his breakfast and bath. Now it was noonday again and he had yet to complete his dress.

No doubt he would insist on pausing for lunch before leaving as another stall tactic, Blake thought as he returned to his morose friend and held the tunic out.

"Thank you." Amaury accepted the tunic and shrugged into it quickly before walking to the rock where he had left his sword and vestments. "Mayhap we should have lunch ere we go on," he suggested with a frown as he belted the tunic. At Blake's burst of laughter, he turned to him with a frown. "What?"

"Lord Rolfe!" Sebert hurried down the steps of the keep as he recognized the fair-haired man dismounting at the front of the party baring the king's colors.

"Sebert!" Rolfe tossed his reigns to one of his men and clapped the steward on the back in greeting. "How do you?"

"Fine, my lord. And all is well with you, I hope?" he responded, his gaze moving curiously over the bishop and the king's guard that had accompanied him.

"Fine. Where is Em?"

"In the kitchens, my lord."

Nodding, Rolfe gestured toward the mounted men behind him. "See to the bishop's comfort, please, Sebert. I'll find my cousin."

Nodding, Sebert turned away as Rolfe continued up the steps and into the keep.

The heat that met him when Rolfe reached the door to the kitchens and pushed it open was enough to make him pause. It seemed to roll at him in waves. Swell after swell of the damp heat surged over him. It came from the pots by the fire. Three of them. Each big enough to boil a full pig in. Frowning, he squinted through the steam at the darkly garbed figures near the cauldrons, fancying for a moment that he had stepped into a witch's dwelling . . . then he recognized his cousin. She was the tiniest figure in the room. Had it not been for her voluptuous figure, Rolfe would have thought her a child as she carried her small stool from one pot to the next, set it down, then stepped up onto it to peer down into the cauldron.

A much larger woman stood by with an air of forbearance as Emma gave the pot a stir before moving on to check the next one. Expression exasperated, Rolfe stepped into the room and let the kitchen door swing shut behind him.

Emma never had been able to keep her nose out of the servants' business. He blamed it on her husband and her father before him. Cedric Kenwick had allowed his only daughter free run of the castle as a child . . . and Fulk, Emma's husband, had never bothered to stay around long enough to notice her, let alone bother about what she did.

Shaking his head, he moved up behind his cousin to tap her on the shoulder. A mistake. She was bent over the pot at the time. His touch startled her enough that she nearly tumbled into the vessel of boiling liquid. Catching her by the waist, he drew her back in the nick of time and sighed. "Em, can you not leave this to your servants?"

"Rolfe!" The petite blonde squealed and turned to throw herself into his arms as she recognized his voice. Then, remembering that she was in mourning, she stepped back and presented a suitably solemn demeanor. "How do you?" she asked more sedately.

"I am boiling to death, if you must know," he told her dryly, taking her arm. "Let us go into the next room and speak."

"Oh, nay, Rolfe! I cannot. I must see to the last of the blacking."

"The last of the . . ." His gaze shot to the pots, missing her proud nod.

"Every piece of cloth in the castle has been blackened," she informed him, moving back to the pots.

"Every piece?" Rolfe let his gaze drop down over his cousin's black gown. He recognized it at once as the one she had worn to her audience with the king. However, then it had been a pale blue. Suddenly recalling the somber weeds Sebert had been wearing on greeting him, Rolfe glanced instinctively toward the laundress, noticing only then that she too was adorned in black. It seemed his cousin thought the entire population of the castle should mourn Fulk's death.

"Aye. This is the last of it." She turned to stir the pot she had nearly fallen into. "The bed linens."

He goggled at that. "The bed linens? You even blackened the bed linens?"

Emma frowned over her shoulder at the disbelief in his voice. "We are in mourning, Rolfe. My husband died this last week."

"Aye, but . . . Faith, Em! You hardly even knew him! Good Lord, from all accounts, he hardly spent a week here if you put all the days together of the last year."

"Aye," she said unhappily.

"Surely you did not love him?"

She frowned at the question. "Of course I loved him, he was my husband. 'Twas my duty to love him."

"But . . ." He shook his head as he realized he was being distracted and took her arm once more, pulling her away from the pot. "I *must* speak with you. This is important, Em."

"So is this, Rolfe. I am in mourning now. I must show the proper respect."

"Aye, but this is *important*."

"Well, then talk to me here."

Rolfe opened his mouth to argue, then shrugged.

There was no sense fighting with Em when she got the determined set about her shoulders that she was showing just now. Besides, once he informed her of the reason for his visit, he would no doubt be able to get her out of the kitchen.

"I bring greetings from the king," he began staunchly, pausing when she whirled around again, excitement on her face once more.

"Really? Is that not exciting? It means he remembers me."

"Aye, well, I doubt he shall ever forget you," Rolfe commented dryly. "At any rate, he sends his greetings, his best wishes, and an order for you to be married."

"What?" She gaped at him briefly. "Married? Again? But my husband was just buried."

Rolfe considered her displeased expression, and decided the bishop really should be allowed in on this chore. Taking her arm determinedly, he steered her away from the pots and their heat. "Come. Bishop Wykeham accompanied me and is no doubt waiting impatiently in the hall."

"Bishop Wykeham is here as well?" Emma smiled with pleasure. She had met the Bishop a time or two and liked him. He was a kind and gentle soul who had managed to remain so despite his time at court as Lord Chancellor. It was her opinion that the church had lost a good man when he had retired.

"Aye." Rolfe looked uncomfortable. "He accompanied me here for this business of your remarriage."

"And we have left him alone all this time? Fie, Rolfe! You should have told me he was here," she chided, handing the stick she held to the laundress.

Rolfe smiled slightly as he watched her attempt to brush the wrinkles out of her slightly damp skirt and pat ineffectually at her hair. It was a wasted effort. Several strands of the golden glory had slid out of the chignon they had been placed in, and the heat and steam had managed to turn them into frizzy little ringlets about her face. In his opinion, the gossamer curls resembled a halo about her face and added to her charm, but then he supposed he was biased. He loved her dearly.

"Come," Emma said now with a sigh as she realized her appearance was beyond repair. "We cannot leave the bishop unattended so long. 'Twould be rude." Turning to lead Rolfe through the room, she asked over her shoulder, "Who does the king wish me to marry?"

"His name is Amaury de Aneford," Rolfe muttered, stepping around a pile of already dyed linens on the floor.

"Amaury de Aneford?" Emma paused at the door and repeated the name thoughtfully. "I have never heard the name, but then I fear I do not hear much news out here. We are quite out of the way of society."

"He has been newly lorded. He was a knight. His majesty titled him out of gratitude for saving him from assassins during the expedition in Ireland."

"He saved the king's life?" Emma peered up at him wide-eyed.

"Aye."

"Oh." Turning, she pushed through the door into the hall. "He must be a great warrior. Is that not nice?"

Rolfe rolled his eyes at her statement and followed her into the hall.

"My Lord Bishop." Emma held out her hands as she moved to welcome the man who stood patiently by the mantle. "How nice to see you. And how kind of you to come all this way simply to help my cousin tell me I am to be remarried."

The bishop's eyebrows rose at that. "But my Lady, I am not here to *inform* you of your marriage. I am here to *preside* at it."

27

Lynsay Sands

Emma blinked at him. "Preside at it?" She turned to glance at her cousin with a frown. "But . . . That cannot be so. I am newly widowed."

There was silence for a moment as the two men exchanged glances; then the bishop cleared his throat. "His Majesty is aware of the timing being poor, my lady, but he wishes that this marriage occur. Immediately."

Emma looked taken aback. "Well . . . that is simply not possible. Surely you misunderstood him. I have not been widowed even a sennight."

The bishop glanced at Rolfe, who threw him a warning look and stepped forward to say, "Aye, but Emma, he feels since you are so desirous of having children, you would wish to remarry . . . soon."

Emma bit her lip as she considered that. She *was* aging swiftly. Goodness, she was already two and twenty. Truth to tell, she had nearly reached the end of her childbearing years. "Aye, mayhap due to my age we might shorten the mourning period," she murmured uncertainly.

Rolfe and the bishop looked relieved.

"Aye," she decided with a nod. "Certainly we can shorten it. Three months should be acceptable under the circumstances. Do you not think?" She glanced at the men questioningly to see that the bishop was staring at her cousin wide-eyed.

Rolfe shifted uncomfortably, then sighed. "Emma, you do not comprehend. You are to be married as soon as de Aneford gets here."

Her eyes narrowed suspiciously. "When is that to be?"

Rolfe shifted on his feet, then sighed. "Today. We hope."

"Today?" Her eyes widened. "But . . . That is not proper. And . . . and I have nothing to wear."

The bishop turned to share an amused smile with

The Deed

Rolfe, thinking this the usual woman's cry, but his eyebrows rose in question when he saw the frown on that man's face.

"They just finished blacking everything," Rolfe explained.

"Well surely there is something?" He paused at the younger man's expression.

"Did you not notice that even the servants are in black?" Rolfe asked dryly.

The bishop glanced around the empty room at that. Truthfully, he had not noticed. He supposed he had been wrapped up in his own thoughts. Frowning now, he walked to the door of the keep and tugged it open to peer out at the bailey. His jaw dropped when he saw that every man, woman, and child was running about in black clothing. Slamming the door, he turned back to peer at Rolfe in mingled bewilderment and irritation.

"Emma had everything blackened," her cousin explained, suddenly finding the situation amusing.

"Everything?"

"Even the linens."

"Even the . . ." The bishop's voice faded away.

"It seemed appropriate," Emma said uncertainly now, feeling a bit foolish. She supposed it was going a bit far to include the linen, but truly, it had seemed appropriate at the time. After all, it was not just the mourning of her husband that had caused her to do so. It had been in honor of the mourning of her hopes of having children as well, all chance for which she had thought dead along with her husband. She was more than aware that at two and twenty, no man would have offered for her hand. Even now she was sure that had it not been for Rolfe's favor with the king, she would have been left to wither in this old castle as a childless widow.

Sighing, she shook her head. "It matters not. My husband, despite his neglect, deserves at least a short mourning period. I simply cannot remarry for at least three months," she announced firmly.

Frowning, Rolfe glanced at the bishop who murmured, "Mayhap this would be a good time to explain the difficulties to Lady Emmalene."

"Aye. Indeed," Rolfe said with a sigh, then turned back to his cousin. He opened his mouth twice to begin these explanations, then sighed and urged her to sit in the seat before the fireplace, positioning himself with his back to the mantle so that he could see the empty hall and all its entrances. It would not do for anyone else to hear what he had to say.

"Understand you, Em, this is a delicate situation. You see, due to your request of the king . . ." He hesitated, forehead furrowed, then caught his hands behind his back and paced before the fireplace some before turning again to where she sat patiently. "You see, Em, by requesting that the king order Fulk to . . . er . . ."

"Attend to his conjugal duties," the bishop supplied.

"Aye. Well . . . by doing that, you see, you made it public knowledge that your marriage was ne'er . . . er . . ."

"Consummated," the bishop murmured.

"Just so," Rolfe agreed, tugging at the top of his tunic and clearing his throat. "That being the case, there is the problem of Fulk's family. You see, Fulk's aunt and cousin are claiming that the marriage is null and void because it was ne'er . . . er . . ." His gaze slid to the bishop.

"Consummated."

"Just so."

Emma's forehead puckered. "But Rolfe, it *was* consummated."

Rolfe froze and turned to her in surprise. " 'Twas?"

"Aye." She scowled slightly. "I explained my wedding

night fully to the king. My husband and I shared a bed."

Recalling the king's words to him that Lady Emma was so naive she had not even realized the marriage had not been fully consummated, Rolfe shook his head. He briefly wondered how to explain things to her, then decided it was beyond him. Duty to the king notwithstanding, no man could be expected to—

" 'Tis true," Emma said, interrupting his thoughts. "That my husband ne'er repeated his . . . duties. Truth to tell, he neglected his . . . er . . . duties horribly. However, only the king knows of this, and he is aware that I did not wish it so. I cannot think that he would punish me because of my husband's lack of attention."

"Nay, Emma, he is not trying to punish you, he is trying to protect you. And himself. Fulk's aunt and cousin know of your husband's neglect. There is no heir. They know that. They are a bold, greedy pair. They can cause much trouble for the king, and trouble is the last thing he needs just now. They are claiming Fulk's neglect makes the marriage invalid, and are requesting that the land and title be turned o'er to Fulk's cousin Bertrand."

"Bertrand?" Emma frowned over that. She was not terribly surprised to hear that Bertrand sought Fulk's home and title. She had met him at her wedding and had not cared overly much for him. It was not anything he had said or done that had caused her dislike. He had not been rude or mean. In fact, if anything, he had been very gracious to her. Gallant even. Too much so. There had been something almost oily in the man's ingratiating manner. And his apparent chivalry had not hidden the avaricious gleam in his eyes. He had peered at the castle, everything in it, and even at herself, with an oddly greedy glitter in his eyes that had made her feel like a chest of gold he coveted. "He seemed overly ambitious," she murmured to herself at last.

"More than you know," Rolfe muttered, catching her words.

Emma glanced at her cousin curiously. "What mean you?"

His gaze slid warily around the empty room. Then he said quietly, "The king suspects Bertrand and a few other lords of plotting to depose him."

Emma gaped at that, and Rolfe nodded grimly. "He suspects the lord chancellor is involved as well."

"Archbishop Arundel?" Emma gasped, recalling the grim-faced man who had stood at the king's side throughout her audience.

"Aye."

"But why? What would they hope to gain?"

Rolfe sighed. "I cannot know what the chancellor hopes to gain. We are not even sure if he is allied with Bertrand, but Bertrand, I suspect, hopes to gain power."

Emma frowned at that, and the bishop explained, "As a boy, Bertrand squired and became quite close friends with Henry of Bolingbroke."

"The king's cousin," Emma murmured, her frown deepening.

The bishop nodded. "Should King Richard be deposed, Henry would be the most likely person to succeed him."

"And as a friend of the king's, Bertrand would be well positioned," Emma realized grimly. "So, Henry wishes to take his cousin's throne?"

The two men exchanged glances; then Rolfe shrugged uncomfortably. "There is no evidence of that, Em. Bertrand and the others may simply be using the king's cousin for their own gain. Henry has always shown himself loyal to his cousin."

"I see," she murmured, her gaze moving to the fire thoughtfully.

Rolfe allowed Emma her thoughts for a moment,

then added, "Knowing of Bertrand's greed for power, His Majesty does not wish to give him any means with which to increase it. Bertrand has a small holding which he inherited from his father, but 'tis nothing in comparison to the wealth and power he would wield should he gain this holding. Hence, Richard has arranged this marriage. On marrying you, de Aneford gains the title of Lord Eberhart with all it includes."

Emma grimaced at that. "That will not please Bertrand."

Rolfe shook his head. "Nay. No doubt Bertrand *and* his mother shall be quite displeased with this turn of events. However, by the time they approach the king with their complaint, it shall be done. Or at least that is his hope."

"By the time they approach?" Her eyes narrowed. "Have they or have they not made a complaint to the king?"

"Well . . ." He looked uncomfortable for a moment, then sighed. "Nay. They have not had a chance. The king heard gossip about their plans before they made a request to see him and he managed to delay seeing them until after arranging everything. We left the day before the appointed audience with the Fulks, which means they will be one day behind us."

"They?" Emma frowned.

"Lady Ascot and Bertrand."

"Lady Ascot is heading here as well? Oh, dear Lord, of course she is. She seems to go everywhere that Bertrand does, doesn't she?" Emma stood up, anxiety on her face. She could very well recall her husband's aunt from the last time she had suffered her presence. While his cousin had seemed as oily as a greased pig, his aunt had been a harridan of a woman, terrifying the servants. Emma had never met a more unpleasant woman. Cold, complaining, and just plain mean, the woman had actually started to beat one of the serving girls with her cane because she had not served her quickly enough. The last thing she wished was to see that woman return here, let alone have any power over the people who had served Emma so well. She would never enjoy another heartbeat of peace knowing that the people she had once led were suffering under Lady Ascot's rule. That being the case, she could only be grateful that King Richard had vexed their plans. But if he had, why would Bertrand and Lady Ascot be heading for the castle? Emma asked that now, and watched with suspicion as her cousin's discomfort grew.

"The king intends to tell them that he was unaware of their discontent and—"

"Lie."

Rolfe winced at her accusation.

The bishop looked disapproving. "Lie is a strong word, my lady."

Emma waved that away impatiently. "What else is he going to tell them?"

Rolfe hesitated. "He is intent on keeping the peace."

"Of course," Em agreed dryly. "And?"

"He intends on telling them that as it was so obvious to the court that you were more than willing to . . . er . . ."

"Do your duty," the bishop supplied.

"Aye. That being the case, he had not thought they would bring such a petty claim."

"He hopes to shame them into recanting their claim," the bishop pointed out with satisfaction.

"However, should greed win out o'er honor . . ."

Emma rolled her eyes at that. There was no doubt—in *her* mind at least—that given a choice between saving their pride and getting their hands on Eberhart Castle, greed would win out.

"Then he shall tell them that ne'er having considered

such a problem and having been concerned for the safety of the castle, its occupants, and yourself now that there is no lord, he commissioned the marriage between yourself and Lord Amaury. However, he will supply them with a letter to the effect that should they arrive before the wedding is accomplished and . . ."

His gaze swam anxiously to the bishop again, who sighed and supplied, "Consummated."

"Then they may call a halt to the wedding and reclaim the property."

Emma's eyes narrowed at that. The very thought of those two vultures gaining power over her people made her blood boil. Then she noticed the way Rolfe was suddenly avoiding looking at her. "And? What else?"

Rolfe turned his gaze unhappily away, and Emma found herself wringing her hands again as she waited impatiently. Finally, she took a step forward. "What else, Rolfe?"

When he could only look at her pityingly, it was the bishop who filled the silence. "Bertrand also wishes to lay claim to you, my lady. As his wife."

"What?" She turned on him in horror. "But I do not like him." A foolish argument indeed. Liking had little to do with duty and marriage. Besides, she had not even met Amaury de Aneford, but had not protested his possible suitability as a husband. Still, Emma was not thinking too clearly just then; she was a mite overset by the fact that Bertrand had even included her in his plans. It was astonishing to her. After all, Fulk had not been able to bear his husbandly duties, why would his cousin wish to saddle himself with her? Good Lord, this was a worry, she thought.

"Bertrand claims 'tis the only fair resolution," Rolfe put in dryly. "That way you shall not be 'deprived', as he puts it. Though we all know it simply is not true. He's commented to one and all that he would like nothing better than to get his hands on your—"

"Dowry," the bishop said with a sharp look at Rolfe.

"Aye, that too," Rolfe muttered. Eberhart Castle had been falling apart when Emma had married Fulk. Without her wealth it would have fallen completely to ruin. No doubt Bertrand and Lady Ascot would not wish to have to return *that*. If there was any left.

"The PIG!" Emma bellowed, surprising both men with her volume. She'd rather lie down with snakes than share her bed with Bertrand. Aside from that, the idea of having his mother here—for she would no doubt move in should her son become lord of the castle—gave her the vapors. The woman would take over. She'd run the place as if it were her own. She'd order Emma about like a servant, and most likely treat the servants like slaves. Emma could almost feel the beatings that would occur then. The spilling of a tankard of ale would probably bring about the breaking of bones. By God, she would not have it! "This will not do at all. We must . . . Where is my husband?"

"Your husband?" Both men peered at her in confusion.

"Amaury," she said grimly. "He is to be my husband, is he not? Well, where is he? Does he not realize the seriousness of the situation?"

"He has not been apprised of the situation as I understand," the bishop said carefully. "However, the king sent him a message to make himself available here forthwith to be married." He glanced at Rolfe, then back. "We actually expected him to arrive before us as he was only—"

"Well, where is he?" Emma demanded, then frowned suddenly as a thought struck her. "Mayhap he has been beset by bandits."

Rolfe smiled slightly at her suggestion. "I do not think a couple of pesky bandits would even slow down, let alone stop de Anéford. He's—"

"Then mayhap Bertrand had him assassinated."

"My lady," the bishop said soothingly, but Emma was in no mood to be soothed.

"SEBERT!" she roared suddenly, moving to the door.

"She has quite a set of lungs for such a petite woman," the bishop murmured with a mixture of awe and horror to Rolfe.

"Aye." Her cousin smiled crookedly. "I had quite forgotten about that aspect of her personality. She has not displayed it since our youth that I know of."

"Aye . . . well . . ." the bishop murmured, then winced as she bellowed for her steward again.

Emma had just reached the door when it burst open and the man presented himself. Alarm was written all over his face.

"My lady?" He peered briefly around to see that all seemed in order, and confusion immediately covered his face.

"Take a dozen men and ride out in search of my husband," Emma commanded at once. The steward goggled at her.

"But, my lady—"

"*Now*, Sebert. Or all will be lost."

Sebert nodded and started to withdraw, then paused and turned back, his gaze moving helplessly to the two men by the fireplace, before flying back to Emma herself. "But my lady, yer husband is dead," he pointed out miserably.

Emma rolled her eyes at that. "Sebert, why can you not be like other stewards and listen at doors?"

"I . . ." Sebert drew himself up indignantly, but Emma continued.

"Had you done so, you would be aware that I am to marry Lord Amaury de Aneford. Immediately. Before Lord Fulk's cousin and aunt can get here and Bertrand

37

can lay claim to the manor and myself."

"Lord Bertrand? And his mother?" Sebert looked horrified. He too recalled the wedding and Lady Ascot's cruelty to the staff.

"Just so," Emma said dryly. "Now do as I say and fetch some men and search for my husband. He is lost or something. He must be brought here forthwith. And in the future, do please try to be privy to such serious conversations so that I do not have to waste time explaining things to you."

"Aye, my lady," Sebert said at once, nodding and hurrying out the door.

Rolfe opened his mouth to try to calm his cousin once her unfortunate steward had fled, but Emma gave him no chance. Moving to the bottom of the stairs, she peered up and bellowed again. "MAUDE!"

The female servant presented herself at once, flying down the stairs as if demons were on her heels. "Aye, my lady?"

"Flowers. I must have a garland of flowers and a veil. And a fresh gown."

"A veil, my lady?" Maude's plain face became as blank as slate.

"Aye, Maude, a veil," Emma said between her teeth with forced patience. "I am to be married. I need a veil."

"Married?!" Maude gaped at her.

"You do understand the word, do you not?" Emma asked grimly.

"Aye. But my lady . . . your veils . . . all your clothes are—"

"Black. Aye, I know. Bad luck that. There is little help for it. See to my instructions, Maude."

Swallowing, Maude nodded, turned back toward the top of the stairs, hesitated, turned back, then threw her hands up. "Mavis!" she shrieked at last, and flew up the stairs. A moment later another female servant, a younger one, nearly as fair as the first had been plain, came flying down the stairs. Presumably, this was Mavis and she had been sent for the flowers while Maude apparently sought out the necessary clothes.

"If you will excuse me, gentlemen, I must change," Emma said now, with a calm that was in direct contrast to the uproar she had caused. "Go you to the church. We shall await my husband there."

The bishop watched her move sedately up the stairs with something akin to amazement, then turned to Rolfe. "Quite a . . . lady," he pronounced at last.

"Aye," Rolfe sighed, and moved to the table where a tray holding a pitcher of wine and three glasses sat. "A drink, Bishop?"

The holy man started to purse his lips in disapproval, then changed his mind. "Aye," he said heavily, moving to join him. "It may be just the thing."

Chapter Two

"My God!" Amaury glared resentfully at the armed men surrounding his own as Castle Eberhart came into view. "See you the gall of the woman?"

Blake hid a smile and shrugged. " 'Twould seem your bride would have you safely delivered."

"Safely delivered?" Grimacing, he shook his head. "She sends her men out to fetch me as if I am a stray cow."

"Surely she would not send so many for a cow?"

Amaury glared at his laughing friend.

Blake shrugged. "Well, I have said it afore and—"

"If you say once more that I should refuse to marry her, I will strike you down right here."

"You may try," Blake allowed with a small smile.

Grunting, Amaury decided to ignore him. It was obvious that Blake had no concept of the situation. How could he? *He* was not a bastard son with no hope of coming into holdings by natural progression. *He* had a legitimate father who would pass the reins of his estate on at his death. *He* did not truly know how hard Amaury had worked all these years to gain a place in the world. Marrying Lady Eberhart would give him everything he had ever dreamed and striven for. A home to call his own. The very idea was like balm to his hungry soul.

It was just a shame his soon-to-be-wife was a hag, he thought with a sigh. But then, perhaps he would get lucky and she would be too busy running after their children to pay him any mind.

That being the case, he would see to it that she was pregnant as quickly as possible. If he could bear the chore, he thought grimly. Then his gaze slid over the outer wall of the castle and he sighed.

It was the most beautiful castle it had ever been his pleasure to look upon. It was his. His! The thought made him straighten in the saddle. *His*.

Damn! He could lie with Medusa herself to make this his own. Amaury filled with determination as they rode into the bailey and his eyes slid across the towers, barns, and people hurrying this way and that. His people. His vassals . . .

A frown plucked at his mouth as he took a second look at those people. Then he turned to peer at the men escorting them.

He had not noticed before, but the men Lady Emma had sent to fetch him were all garbed in black. Amaury had been so angry at the action, he had not taken note of their garb. Now, however, he was hard put not to notice. It looked as if every single person within the walls was dressed in black, and he frowned at the oddity of it.

He had heard of castles where the people wore their colors, but usually it was reserved for only personal servants in the castle and men-at-arms. Here, everyone

41

seemed to wear black. Even the very littlest babies wore their color as they played about the bailey. If they were their color. He hoped this wasn't a portent of things to come.

A glance at Blake showed that he too had noticed the odd dress. He was frowning as he took it all in. Still being peeved at him, Amaury merely shrugged and dismounted when his friend finally turned to him questioningly.

"Sebert!" A plain-faced maid rushed down the stairs as they started up them. "Yer to escort his Lordship to the church. The bishop, her lady, and Lord Rolfe are waiting there."

"God's teeth," Amaury muttered under his breath to his friend, forgetting his determination not to speak to him. "They be waiting at the church."

" 'Twould seem the bride is eager," Blake said drolly as Sebert turned to them.

Ignoring him, Amaury continued up the stairs, announcing, "I shall have refreshment first."

The little serving wench immediately threw herself at the door, barring his way. "Nay! Her ladyship said ye were to—"

"I am the lord here now," Amaury began coldly.

"Not yet."

Turning slowly at those grim words, Amaury stared at the man pushing his way through the group of men at the bottom of the steps. Tall and well-proportioned, the man had an air of belonging about him that immediately annoyed Amaury. This was to be his castle, after all. No one but he should be so comfortable here.

"You are?" Amaury drew the words out dangerously.

"Lord Rolfe Kenwick." He gave a slight nod. "Lady Emma's cousin. And soon to be your cousin-in-law." He grinned slightly as he added that last sentence, knowing instinctively that while de Aneford hadn't refused, he

42

most likely wasn't comfortable being ordered to marry.

"I have had a long trip," Amaury said now. "I wish refreshment."

"Plenty of time for that," Rolfe said cheerfully. "The servants are busily preparing a repast even as we speak. However, at the moment, the bishop and my cousin are waiting patiently at the church. You took longer than expected."

Amaury shifted guiltily at those words, aware he had dallied as much as possible. That guilt was the only reason he allowed Rolfe to urge him back down the stairs. "I came soon as I got the order," Amaury muttered, glaring at Blake as if daring him to refute his words.

Coughing into his hand to hide his amusement, his friend remained silent and fell into step on Amaury's other side as they crossed the bailey. The hundred or so men who had accompanied them, soldiers who had followed him into battle on countless occasions and had elected to remain with him on hearing that he was to have his own manor, fell into line behind them.

" 'Tis sure I am you did. Quite sure," Rolfe commented dryly, patting him once more on the back. "I, of course, reassured my cousin of this. Several times this afternoon as we waited," he added a bit archly, then paused and turned to face Amaury as they reached the crowd of black-bedecked servants crowded around the church. "Treat her well, or I shall be forced to kill you."

His tone was so cheerful as he added that last thought that Amaury was left gaping after him as he moved through the people who even now were parting to allow them a path to the church.

"I believe you have been warned," Blake commented dryly as he watched the other man join the bishop and the woman at the door of the church, then his eyebrows rose. "Good God, she looks all fit for a funeral."

43

Amaury peered at the woman in question, and his jaw dropped once more.

"Well, at least she is not large . . . or rake-thin, for that matter. She appears quite voluptuous, in fact," Blake commented, looking again at the petite, rounded woman, then grimacing at the black gown and veil she wore. "However, it does appear I was wrong about her being eager. Think you she actually loved Fulk?" He glanced at his friend. "I suggest you close your mouth, my friend. I fear you are in danger of swallowing a fly."

Amaury's mouth snapped shut and he uttered between clenched teeth, "What is this? A joke? Black to our wedding? Waiting at the church? Have I lost my—"

"My lord," the bishop called impatiently from the front of the church, frowning in disapproval. "Do not tarry."

The woman, who had stood with her back to them up until then, turned now to peer curiously at them, giving them a fleeting glimpse of her black veil before she turned swiftly away.

"She must be truly ugly, Amaury. Mayhap that is why the rush to wed you. This way you'll not get the chance to see her face before you are wed."

Amaury swallowed grimly and considered simply mounting his horse and riding away, then stiffened his shoulders. *Get a hold of yourself, man,* he ordered himself grimly. Think of the manor. Sighing, he straightened and moved through the crowd, feeling like a man on his way to the gallows.

Emma forced herself not to turn again. She had spied several strangers standing at the edge of the crowd. They had stood out next to her own people, who were in their solid black garb. Her husband could have been any one of them, but judging by their stance and carriage, she knew that he was one of the two who had stood in front. That knowledge had been enough to unsettle her. Neither of these men had been what she expected in a husband. Both were giants. She herself was a bit below average size. Well, all right, she was short. It was the bane of her existence. Rolfe had teased her endlessly about it throughout their childhood. She barely came up to the shoulders on her cousin, and both these men were taller still. She doubted she would reach halfway up either man's chest. Add to that the fact that both men also appeared to be nearly as wide as they were tall, and she found herself swallowing in trepidation and considering the alternative.

Bertrand. And a point in his favor was that, like his cousin, he was much more delicate of form. However, that was the only point in his favor.

There was no question of her choice. Giant or not, her soon-to-be-husband could not possibly be a worse choice than Bertrand and his mother.

As she waited for him to join her at the door of the church, she set her mind to trying to figure out which of the two men was to be her husband. One had been as fair as the other dark. They had been too far away to make out any individual features really, but she had been able to tell that the fair one had been smiling, his face lit up with lighthearted amusement. The other had been as solemn and glum as death. Surely a man would not be so glum on his wedding day? Therefore, she reasoned, her husband must be the blond.

Emma sensed his presence when he finally reached her side. Swallowing, she clutched her bouquet of flowers tightly and stared steadfast at the bishop. She was almost afraid to look at the man who was to be her husband. She feared what her reaction might be were he unbearably ugly. She didn't like to be shallow, but truly it had been a relief to her that her first husband had been pleasant to look upon. Should her new husband be horrendously ugly, she might offend him with a sour reaction. There being little choice but to marry him, it seemed much more sensible simply not to look.

"My lady?"

Emma blinked at the bishop when he called her name. His raised eyebrows told her that she had missed something important. When he repeated himself, Emma swallowed, then echoed the words in a breathless voice. Her new husband, despite his size, spoke his words in much the same manner. When the bishop came to the part about kissing the bride, she steeled herself and turned to her new husband, closing her eyes lest she insult him by expression should he be ugly.

Amaury took a bracing breath, then reached resignedly and lifted the black veil of his wife. The sight that befell him made him freeze as the veil flew back over her head. Her eyes were closed, it was true, so perhaps he was not getting the full picture, but the woman before him was not the slightest bit ugly. In fact, she was quite pretty even. Her skin was flawless. Her lips were full, round, and inviting. Her nose was not the straight royal nose that would be considered attractive by most, but one with an endearing tip to it that suggested impudence. And she was young, too. Not an old hag as he had suspected.

A smile tugged at his own lips as her own turned down with slight impatience at his hesitation and he recalled himself to his duty. Grasping her by each shoulder, he lifted her clear off the ground to meet his lips. His relief made the kiss warmer than he had originally intended, so that the peck he had thought to grimly grace her with became instead a warm caress.

Emma's eyes opened in surprise at his kiss. That first surprise was compounded by his looks now that she was finally seeing them. It was the darker man. And he didn't appear the least grim now. In fact, he was smiling down at her with a warmth that left her slightly bemused. Mustering an uncertain smile, she flashed it at him briefly as he set her back on her feet, then whirled to face the bishop as he finished the ceremony.

Bishop Wykeham's voice flowed deep and smooth over her as he pronounced them husband and wife, but Emma hardly heard a word of it, and she certainly didn't really see his face as she peered at him. Instead, her new husband's face swam into view before her, floating there, smiling at her as he had done when she had opened her eyes.

Dark hair. A bit long, perhaps. Even a little shaggy, but perfect for the sun-warmed face it surrounded. Kind, dark brown eyes with small wrinkles at each corner that spoke of much laughter. A mouth that had been firm yet soft, charming in smile, and sweet against her own.

Emma sighed as the crowd surrounding them suddenly burst out cheering. The ceremony was over. They were married now. All was well. They were safe.

" 'Tis time you two retired."

Emma flushed brilliant red at the bishop's firm announcement. She had spent the last half hour in a sort of daze, eating the food placed before her and drinking the wine offered as she did her best to avoid staring at her husband. It was most odd being married to a stranger. Emma had been through it before, but still found it disconcerting.

She was aware that Rolfe and the bishop had pulled Lord Amaury aside and spoken to him as soon as they had returned to the castle. No doubt they had been informing him of the full state of affairs, and no doubt he was now aware of the urgency to consummate their marriage, but truly, to order them to bed seemed a bit much. They had not even spent three quarters of an hour in celebration.

" 'Tis not yet dark," Emma protested now, trying to ignore her blush.

"Aye, but the bishop is right," Rolfe announced, rising from his seat beside her. "The deed must be done."

Seeing his new bride's embarrassment, Amaury frowned at the two men and got to his feet as well. "Come, my lady, we shall retire. Never let it be said that the bishop and your cousin were more eager for us to be bedded than we were ourselves."

Smiling uncertainly, Emma rose beside him, her gaze flying over everyone else in the hall. Her own people had been updated on events this afternoon, not by Emma, but through the castle grapevine. They were looking on with obvious relief that the consummation was to take place forthwith, ensuring their future safety from the rule of Bertrand and his mother. Lord Amaury's men, however, were looking on with confusion. Some even appeared suspicious. The one called Blake, for instance, was frowning with great concern at the bishop and Rolfe's odd behavior.

Noting this, Amaury put a hand on his friend's shoulder. "Lord Rolfe will explain," was all he said before leading Emma silently away, aware as he did that Rolfe had moved to sit beside his friend to do just that. He could almost imagine Blake's consternation when he learned the reason behind this sudden rushed wedding. 'Twas the truth, neither he nor Blake cared for Bertrand. He was a greedy, selfish beast, and a coward to boot. Many a man had died needlessly in Ireland due to that cowardice and his poor leadership. Worse yet—though they had no proof—both of them suspected it was Bertrand who had betrayed the king in Ireland and smuggled the assassins into camp the night he had almost been killed. But perhaps that was simply their own prejudice against the man, Amaury thought now. He pondered the incident briefly, before realizing quite suddenly that they were halfway up the stairs on the way to . . .

Good God! They had reached the time for the bedding. His gaze dropped to the wee woman beside him and he swallowed anxiously, all thoughts of Bertrand fleeing.

Lord Rolfe had taken great pains to stress his cousin's innocence. As the rumors had suggested, it appeared she had not even been bedded once by her husband. Amaury could hardly believe Fulk fool enough to neglect her so, and was not sure that he was pleased at the knowledge. He supposed it was nice to know his wife had known no other, but Amaury had never taken a virgin. Being a bastard and knowing the trials of a bastard's life, he had been determined not to produce one himself, and had therefore lavished his attentions on camp followers and wenches, never virgins. Now, however, he found himself in a quandary. Never having bedded a virgin, he really had no idea how to proceed.

His gaze slid to his wife's face. She looked completely unperturbed by what was coming, but he had to wonder how long he could hope for that to last. Probably right up until the bedroom door closed, he decided. Then she would no doubt burst into rivers of tears and fears and look at him like he was an animal.

Sighing inwardly, he tried to remember all he had ever heard of bedding virgins from others. They were a fearful lot from all accounts. That much was certain. And the first time would hurt too, he'd been told. It was the maiden's veil, of course. A man had to ram through it. There was said to be blood sometimes, sometimes a great deal of it.

Swallowing once more, he felt a fine film of sweat begin on his forehead. How was he to approach this frail and petite lady with all of this? It was impossible. He would crush her with his very weight. Might crack her in half with his passion. He simply could not give her the tenderness she deserved, especially not when he had thought of little else but the consummation since their wedding. At least he had since he had lifted the veil and seen how comely a wench she was. Lady, he corrected himself. His wife was a lady and an untried one at that.

"My lord?"

Amaury glanced at her with a start to find her smiling at him ever so gently.

"This is my—our room," she informed him quietly.

"Ah." Clearing his throat, he reached for the door and opened it for her, then hesitated about entering. It had suddenly occurred to him to wonder if it would not be more seemly to allow her a few moments alone in their room to do whatever it was women did to prepare for bed.

Emma was halfway across the room when she realized that her new husband had not followed her. Turning back, she found he still stood in the doorway of the room. Neither all the way in yet, nor all the way out, he seemed deep in thought, his face pinched in concentration as he pondered whatever was concerning him. "My lord?"

Her new husband looked at her then, and Emma was amazed to see uncertainty on his face. Then understanding came to her. This was his first time, she realized, and felt her heart melt with understanding. Up until that moment she had been working herself into a fine lather, silently fretting over having to share her bed again. Despite knowing what to expect, it was still nerve-wracking being abed with a man for the first time. But now that she saw how fearful he was, she found herself feeling much better. After all, if he had

never been abed with a woman before, she was the
more experienced one. That being the case, she immediately found herself taking control of the situation.

"Come." Smiling gently, she held a hand out toward
him. "All will be well."

Realizing that his virgin wife was trying to comfort
him, Amaury shook his head in bewilderment and entered the room, pulling the door shut behind him.

As he closed the door, Emma turned to peer around
the room, her gaze landing on the screen Rolfe had
brought back to her from one of his travels. "Would you
like to use the screen to disrobe?" she asked when he
turned to peer at her.

"Nay, I'll wear naught to bed."

"Oh!" She flushed slightly, disconcerted at that, then
regained her composure and moved to the screen.
"Then I shall use it and you may use the room itself,"
she decided, moving out of sight behind the screen.

Amaury stared at the screen his young bride was hidden behind, then turned to survey the room. It was a
dark and gloomy room. The large bed was the first thing
he noticed. It appeared more than big enough to accommodate his unnatural height, he was happy to see.
But it was also solid black in color. Not the wood. The
wood itself was a dark mahogany, but the linens on it
and the drapes that had been pulled back to reveal the
bed itself were both as black as the clothes his bride
had worn to their wedding.

Amaury frowned as he took it in. From what he had
seen, his wife had an uncommon fondness for black.
He would have to see to that. The room would be much
cheerier with different bedding, he decided as he set
about unbuckling his sword from his waist. Then he
turned his attention to the rest of the room. A large fire
took up most of the wall opposite the bed. One chair
sat before it. He would have to see to another being

added. The idea of spending cold evenings comfortably in front of the fire with his wife had some charm to it, he thought with a slight smile. His eyes moved over the tapestries on the wall as a familiar chorus rose up in his mind. Mine. Mine. Mine.

Sighing his satisfaction, he slid his gaze over the screen behind which his wife changed. It was obviously foreign. He had never seen anything like it, but even so, the painted designs on it spoke of foreign lands and people. A rustle of material caught his ear just as his new bride slung her dress over the top of the screen, and Amaury swallowed, realizing that while he had been dallying, his wife had not. He could almost picture her standing behind the screen, stripping her clothes away one piece at a time.

Feeling the stirring in his nether regions, Amaury quickly shook the image away. It would not do to get excited already. He suspected he had a long stressful night ahead of him in wooing his virgin bride. He intended on making it as easy and bearable an experience for her as he could manage. With that intention, he began to quickly strip. He was unsure how she would handle seeing him in full nudity and thought it might be best to be already abed when she came out.

Best intentions aside, he had only managed to strip his tunic off before she stepped out around the screen and presented herself. Amaury's hands froze on the waist of his braies as he caught sight of her, his eyes widening in shock.

God's tooth, even the woman's nightgown was black! Did she not own a single item of cloth that was not? he wondered in dismay as he took in the voluminous folds of the gown that covered her from her neck to her very toes.

Emma took in her husband's wide-eyed face and tried not to fidget under his gaze. His expression merely assured her that she had been correct in assuming he was untried. Forcing a reassuring smile, she walked cautiously past him to the bed and crawled carefully beneath the bedclothes, then took a great deal of time and care straightening all the wrinkles out of them until they lay across her in a nice smooth wave. That done, she glanced furtively at her new husband, only to find him still standing where he had been, eyeing her with wide eyes. Frowning slightly, she started to speak, then realized he was probably shy.

"I promise I shall not look," she told him gently and to prove it, closed her eyes and covered them with both hands.

Amaury straightened at her action. Giving his head a shake at her odd behavior, he stripped his pants quickly off and moved to the side of the bed, lifting the linen and slipping beneath the bedclothes beside her.

Emma dropped her hands as soon as she felt the bed depress. Turning, she shone a bright smile on him. "There. That was not so bad, was it?" she asked gently. "Now, just lie back."

Amaury swallowed his shock as she pressed him gently back to lie on the bed, wondering what exactly was occurring. Was his wife truly taking control of the situation? His *virgin* wife?

Once she had urged him to lie flat on his back, Emma smiled sweetly, tucked the bedclothes gently about his neck, then lay back herself, pulled the covers up to her neck as well, and sighed.

Amaury lay silently beside her for a moment, then glanced at her curiously. His bride's eyes were closed, a serene smile on her face. "Lady Emmalene?" he asked uncertainly.

Her eyes fluttered open. "Aye?"

"What are we doing?"

"Consummating the marriage," Emma whispered

53

with a reassuring smile and closed her eyes once more.

"We are?"

Emma frowned at the perplexed tone in his voice. "Aye. We are sharing a bed, sleeping together, lying together."

Amaury groaned as her words tumbled out. His bride, it seemed, was more innocent than he had thought if she believed this to be consummating the marriage. How was he to tell her . . .

"My lord?"

Eyes popping open, he nearly jumped out of the bed when he saw that she had sat up and was now leaning worriedly over him.

"You groaned. Are you in pain? I had heard there could be some pain the first time."

Amaury groaned again and turned his head away. How was he to tell her—

A pounding at the door scattered his thoughts to the wind, and Amaury sat up instinctively, knocking his head with Emma's as he did.

"Sorry," he muttered as the pounding sounded again.

"Is the deed done yet?" The question was called anxiously through the door.

Emma rolled her eyes as she recognized her cousin's voice. Truly, this was going too far. "Aye!"

"Nay!"

Emma's head swiveled, her mouth dropping open at Amaury's negative answer. Why would he lie, she wondered in dismay.

"Well, get to it," Rolfe roared impatiently.

"Get you back to the celebrations and leave us be!" Amaury thundered, then turned to his wife and sighed. "My lady," he began carefully. "I fear you have misunderstood . . ." He paused to frown. "You do not seem to . . . You appear to be a bit lacking in knowledge of what consummating the marriage entails," he got out finally.

"I do?" Emma worried her lip uncertainly.

"Aye," he announced heavily. "There is more to it."

"There is?" She was definitely anxious now, and Amaury cursed her cousin, the bishop, the king, and Bertrand, along with her husband, for this situation. Especially her husband. Had Fulk attended to his duties as he should have—

A pounding at the door distracted his thoughts again and Amaury sighed. "Damn me! Can a man not have a little privacy on his wedding night?!"

"There is a party approaching!" It was the bishop this time. "We fear it may be Bertrand come from the King!"

"Damn!" Amaury cursed helplessly, seeing his dreams of owning this castle slipping away.

"Get the deed done!" Rolfe bellowed.

"My lord?" Emma clutched his bare arm anxiously. "Is there truly more?"

"Aye." He sighed miserably.

"Then we must do it," she said firmly, and Amaury turned to her in surprise.

"We must?"

"Aye, my Lord. Of course we must. I cannot allow my people to suffer under the rule of Lord Bertrand's mother. She would misuse them horribly."

"Aye, my lady, but—"

"There are no buts, my lord. If there is more, we must do it."

When he simply stared at her in an agony of uncertainty, she twitched the bedclothes away from her body and began dragging her black gown off.

"What are you doing?"

"I am naive of what is expected, my lord, but I am no fool. You came to this bed nude, so I must assume that whatever is required necessitates our both being so, else you surely would not risk a chill." The gown flew over her head as she concluded that statement, and

Amaury was left staring at quite the loveliest chest it had ever been his pleasure to view. And it was all his, he thought with greedy glee. Then he frowned. It was his if he could consummate the marriage before—

" 'Tis Bertrand!" The dismayed bellow shook the door. "He is flying like the wind. Do the deed!"

Muttering under his breath, Amaury wasted a moment glaring at the door, then turned back to his bride. "My lady. As you said, the first time is usually painful. But not for the man—"

"Prithee, my lord, do not waste our time on niceties. Simply tell me what to do."

"He be at the gate! My lady, he be *at the gate*!"

"Who the devil is that?" Amaury asked with a frown at the new voice.

"Sebert," Emma answered with a sigh, then when he looked confused, reminded him, "My . . . our steward."

"What? Have they got everyone out there?" he muttered unhappily.

"My lord," Emma said impatiently. "What do I do?"

Amaury turned back to his wife and sighed. "You do not seem to realize the pressure—"

"He be in the bailey!" This time it was Maude's voice. Even Amaury recognized the voice of the plain-faced servant who had refused to let him enter the castle on first arriving.

"They *do* have everyone out there," he muttered.

"*Do the deed!*" the bishop roared.

Emma could only think that a series of watches were keeping the people outside her bedroom door up to date.

"We are both under pressure, my lord," she pointed out grimly.

"Aye, but . . ." Muttering, he tugged the blankets aside and gestured to his—at the moment—not-too-impressive manhood. It had been quite impressive mo-

56

ments ago, while he had been thinking of his bride undressing behind the screen and imagining the night ahead. But it had shrunk and shriveled with every new shout through the door, until now, it seemed almost to be trying to hide within itself. All was lost, he thought miserably.

Emma stared at the third appendage between her new husband's legs with fascination. Never having seen a naked man before, she had not known they carried one of those around with them. She had been too embarrassed to look when Fulk had been stripped and set abed with her. She leaned forward to get a closer look at the item now. It looked to be a shrunken, deformed leg, much like the arm of the girl in the village who had been born not quite right. She didn't have any fingers or thumbs on her small stump of an arm either, just as Amaury's extra small stump of a leg seemed devoid of toes. Perhaps this was not common to all men, she realized suddenly. Perhaps her husband was displaying a deformity.

"My lord, this is not the time to be confessing your . . . er . . . oddities," she said in a strained voice. "We all have our flaws. Now, please tell me what I am to . . ." Her gaze was still fixed on the rather tiny appendage as she spoke, so when it started suddenly to grow, the words stuck in her mouth and she watched with renewed fascination. As far as she knew, the village girl's arm did not grow. What an odd ability her husband had!

"He's dismounting!" someone—Emma suspected it was Mavis—screeched.

"Have you done the deed?!" Rolfe roared, panic edging his voice.

"My lord?" Emma tore her gaze to her husband's face.

"Lie down," Amaury instructed grimly, hope rising up

57

in him again as the simple act of her eyes on his body sent it back into action.

Emma immediately dropped back on the bed, gasping in shock when he suddenly shifted to lie atop her, his sprouting third leg pressing against her inner thigh.

"Is this the consummating?" she asked anxiously, for while it was a bit more difficult breathing with him atop her, there really was no pain and she was sure he had said—

"Not yet," Amaury muttered grimly. "Open your legs."

"Open my . . . ?" Her expression was bewildered.

"He's at the castle door!" came the half-hiss, half-whisper as the castle seemed to shudder under the impact of that door slamming open. Then there came a rustling as everyone rushed back down the stairs.

"My lady . . ."

"Aye."

"I am sorry."

"Is it done?"

Amaury stared down into her anxious face, and had to wonder how just having her peer at his manhood had made it stand proud in seconds. That had been unexpected. It had also saved them, or was about to, he thought grimly as a man's bellows moved up the stairway drawing closer to the room.

"I am sorry," he repeated, once again apologizing for the pain he was about to cause and thrust forward.

Emma's cry of startled pain ended on shocked dismay as the bedroom door suddenly burst open.

Chapter Three

The population of the entire world appeared to stand in that open doorway, Emma thought faintly. At least the population of her small world. Lord Bertrand, the bishop, her cousin Rolfe, Lord Blake, Lord Amaury's men, and every single servant of the keep—including those who had been sent out on watch—appeared to be at the door to that room. Every single one of them was vying to see the couple on the bed. Eager to assure themselves that the deed had been done and they were safe from the man standing panting in the doorway, exhaustion and defeat struggling on his face as he stared at the entwined couple through the bed curtains she had thoughtlessly left wide open on crawling into bed.

There was a heartbeat of time where everyone simply froze. Then Amaury suddenly moved. Leaping from atop her, off the bed, and sweeping the blankets up to cover her in one fluid movement, he snatched his sword from where it leaned against the wall and turned to face the intruders, completely and gloriously nude.

"What is the meaning of this?"

Emma glanced sharply at him. Despite the fact that he had been more than aware of the events occurring, he was giving a most credible portrayal of a groom unexpectedly interrupted on his wedding eve. She took a moment to marvel at his ability, then glanced toward Bertrand.

Her memory had not served her well. While she had known that Fulk and his cousin had been of a similar size and were both smaller than Amaury, she had not realized by quite how much. Good Lord, the man looked like a boy before her new husband. It did not help that Blake and her cousin Rolfe crowded the doorway behind him, towering over him by a good head. He was like a dwarf amid a room of giants. A very diminutive, fair-haired dwarf. There was not a bit of bulk on his frame, and while his features were handsome, they were soft and weak next to the harsh planes and angles of her new husband. There was no doubt in Emma's mind that should there be a battle, Bertrand would not fare well against Amaury de Aneford. That being the case, she was a bit surprised when the man suddenly drew himself up to announce, "I come from the king."

When Amaury merely raised an eyebrow, the bishop pushed his way through the crowd to the front of the onlookers.

"Our apologies, my Lord Amaury," the older man said smoothly, none of his earlier panic evident in his voice. "As Lord Bertrand says, he comes with a letter from the king stating that should the wedding not already be consummated, it should be made null. However we can see—"

"We can see no such thing." There was a note of panic in Bertrand's voice now. "All we saw was them embracing. They have not consummated the marriage. 'Tis null."

Amaury allowed the tip of his sword to drop to the floor, and he leaned on it in a seemingly relaxed manner. "I beg to differ with you, my lord. Unlike your cousin, I did not dally. This marriage is well and truly consummated."

Bertrand's face twisted briefly in defeat mingled with weariness as he glanced to where Emma sat wide-eyed on the bed, the bed linens clutched to her chest. Then he smiled suddenly. "Prove it."

Emma blinked in confusion as all eyes turned to her, wondering how they were to prove it. Were they truly expected to perform that atrociously painful act again? And in front of them? Again? For they had certainly been well and truly joined when everyone had burst into the room. At least she thought they had.

Peering at the bed, Amaury knew at once the problem. The bedclothes were black . . . as was everything else in this bloody castle. Blood would show on white sheets, but doubtless would not on black.

"True, the sheets would not show," Rolfe said confidently, stepping up beside the bishop now as he too caught the drift of Bertrand's thoughts. "Howbeit, Amaury carries the proof himself."

All eyes, including Emma's, now turned to Amaury and dropped to that odd appendage she had noticed earlier. At the sudden unexpected attention, the appendage, which had remained tall and proud throughout, suddenly shriveled under the weight of so many eyes. But that was not what made Emma gasp. It was the blood that covered the member. Amaury had hurt himself. She glanced worriedly up to his face to find that, despite his injury, he was suddenly smiling.

Lifting the tip of his sword off the floor once more, Amaury took a menacing step forward. "If one and all are *quite* satisfied that I accomplished what Lord Fulk obviously neglected to do, my lady and I would enjoy some privacy," he said pointedly.

"Of course, my lord," the bishop murmured, and with the help of Sir Rolfe, managed to urge the shocked Lord Bertrand out of the room. Turning back at the door, Rolfe paused long enough to give his cousin a cheerful wink, then tugged the door closed.

Amaury sighed his relief and set his sword back to lean against the wall, then turned reluctantly to the bed, only to see that it was now empty.

Eyebrows rising, he glanced sharply around the room to find his wife standing naked by the washstand. She apparently had not wasted a moment in hopping out of the bed once the door had closed. He could hardly blame her after the painful fiasco she had just endured. No doubt she would never wish to repeat the act again, he thought glumly, and sank onto the side of the bed. Face dropping into his open hands, he propped his elbows on his knees and sighed wearily.

"My lord?" Her cool hand on his knee brought Amaury's head up swiftly. "If I might?" she said quietly, carefully avoiding looking at his manhood, even as she urged his legs apart.

"What?" Amaury asked uncertainly, his legs spreading automatically, but her next move explained all as she began to bathe his stained manhood.

"You have injured yourself," she said quietly. "It must have occurred during the . . ."

"Joining," Amaury finished for her, catching her hands in his own as he felt himself stir under her gentle touch. "My Lady—"

"Emma."

"Emma?"

"Aye, Emma," she said simply. " 'Tis my name."

"Oh, aye. Emma. Here." He urged her up off the floor

to sit on the bed beside him, smiling wryly when she suddenly noticed her nudity, blushed, and drew the bedclothes up around her shoulders to hide herself.

"We should tend to your wound," she said uncomfortably when he continued to simply smile at her, then regretted her words when that smile faltered.

"But I am not the one injured." Careless of his nudity, he stood and urged Emma's legs up on to the bed so that she was lying down again. "I fear 'tis you who has been injured," he informed her.

"Me?" She looked startled at that. "But you are the one bleeding."

"Nay." He shook his head and gently drew the sheets away to reveal her body again. " 'Tis you."

Emma glanced down when he gestured, and noticed with surprise the blood on the inside of her legs. Sitting up abruptly, she stared at herself in horror. It was not her woman's time. She should not be bleeding, and yet she was . . . from inside.

"Are you not still in pain from the joining?"

"Aye, but I have been since . . . I thought . . ." Putting her hand to her head as the room began to spin around her, she fell back on the bed with a gasp. "Am I dying?"

"Nay, my lady," he said reassuringly, then frowned at her pallor. "You've turned quite white."

"I fear I do not handle the sight of blood well," Emma confessed faintly.

Amaury's eyebrows rose at that. "You did not react so to the blood on me."

"Aye, nay. Well, but then I did not know it was mine own."

"Oh . . . aye," Amaury said wryly. Bending, he retrieved the cloth she had used on him, wrung it out, and tended to her even as she had done for him.

Face going from white to red, Emma grabbed at his hands. "Nay, I . . ." she began with embarrassment, falling silent when her new husband turned a determined look on her.

"I am your husband," was all he said, and it was enough. Emma released his hands and lay back, suffering his gentleness in silent embarrassment.

"Besides,'tis no more than you did for me," he added as he finished cleaning away the blood and tossed the cloth back into the bowl. "Rest now."

"Aye, my lord," Emma murmured in what she hoped was a suitably dutiful voice as he drew the bedclothes up to cover her. Her husband seemed satisfied with that as he stood and moved around the bed to climb in from the other side.

Emma lay silently for a moment. Afraid to move and disturb the stranger in her bed, she let her gaze move around the room. It had been her bedroom for two years. It had always looked as it did now, and yet suddenly it seemed completely different. She could not really understand how. Nothing had changed . . . And yet everything had.

Concentrating on making her breathing slow and even, she listened to the sound of revelry floating up from the Great Hall below. Her people were celebrating the marriage and its consummation as well as being saved from toiling under the hand of Lord Bertrand's mother. That thought made her wonder why the old woman had not been at the door beside her son. Emma could only assume that in his effort to get here before the marriage was consummated, Bertrand had had to leave her behind and hurry on ahead. Whatever the case, Emma was grateful for her absence. Truly the woman was formidable. Emma most likely would have shriveled under her cold fishlike eyes.

Emma's gaze slid to the window beside the bed and she sighed. It had been an unusual day. Quite taxing really, what with learning of her upcoming marriage, worrying that her husband would not arrive, awaiting him at the church, the ceremony itself, and then the exceedingly tricky business of the "joining" as Amaury had called it. She felt a bit foolish now that she realized just what consummating the marriage meant, and had to wonder what it would have been like with her first husband. As unpleasant as the chore was, she could well see why Lord Fulk had not seen fit to accomplish it. He had forever avoided anything unpleasant. Still, it was the only way to achieve children.

That thought startled Emma into laying a hand gently against her stomach. She knew enough to be aware that that was where the child would grow and be carried. Their child. Hers and Lord Amaury's. Aye, she must be carrying his child, for surely it only took one such painful joining to make a babe? Else she was sure people would have fewer babes.

Emma floated to sleep, a small smile playing about her lips as she daydreamed about the child she was probably already carrying.

"He's gone to lick his wounds."

Emma flushed and straightened from her slightly crouched position by the table in the Great Hall. She had been surveying the group of unconscious men lying about the floor, searching out Lord Bertrand. Now she turned to face her cousin as he reached her side. "Who?"

"Lord Bertrand. He departed as soon as we came back below stairs yester eve. That is who you were looking so cautiously for, is it not?"

Emma smiled wryly. "You know me too well, Rolfe."

Shrugging, he bent to press a kiss to her forehead. "Where is your husband? Still abed?"

"Aye."

"It must have been a wearing night."

Emma felt herself blush again at his teasing, and sought quickly to change the subject. "Do you wish to break fast?"

Rolfe grinned at her obvious tactics, but decided to let her off the hook. Turning, he raised one eyebrow at the Great Hall and its contents. "Aye, breaking fast would be nice. However, I doubt you shall have much luck in rousing this rabble."

"Aye." Sighing, Emma surveyed the previous night's celebrants. The Great Hall was a-clutter with people. All of them unconscious. Men and women alike were strewn across the floor like dropped chess pieces. It would be difficult to cross the hall, let alone make room at the table to dine. Turning abruptly, she strode toward the double front doors. "Come."

Eyebrows rising, Rolfe followed at once, the promise of food a strong lure. "Where are we going?"

"Around to the back door of the kitchen to find something to eat," Emma announced, tugging the door open and leading him out into the crisp morning air.

Rolfe grimaced at that. "I do not much care for the idea of eating in the kitchens, Em. Cook will have our ears."

"Cook is unconscious by the table beside his wife. 'Sides, I was thinking we might go on a picnic."

"A picnic?"

"Aye." Emma threw a grin at him over her shoulder as she led him around the building. "We have not had one for ages. And I have missed our little excursions." Emma smiled softly as she thought of those brief escapes from the castle when they had been children. They had collected bits of food while the cook wasn't looking, and then crept out into the woods surrounding her father's castle to feast on their stolen fare before playing hide and seek in the trees. "There is a lovely clearing just ten minutes away on horseback. It has a little brook running through it."

"Sounds charming." Rolfe smiled slightly, caught up in remembrances of his own. Emmalene had not been a proper lady then. She had been a hooligan of the highest order. And she had always insisted on being the dashing Lord Darion when they had played "Catch-me-if-ye-can," rather than the fair maiden as he had been sure she should. She had been as daring as any boy as she had flown through the woods, scrambling up trees and swinging from branches. Her skirts had never slowed her down, for she had hooked them at her waist to keep them out of the way. Or simply borrowed a pair of Rolfe's braies. If her father, his own uncle, had ever caught them at it, he would most likely have tanned them both.

Ah, who was he fooling, Rolfe thought wryly. Uncle Cedric had indulged them in all things, especially Emma. He most likely would have turned a blind eye. In fact, he more than likely *had* been aware of their games and *had* turned a blind eye.

"Here we are," Emma announced. Pushing through a door into the kitchen, she collected a basket from the corner and began filling it.

Shaking his mind free of thoughts of the past, Rolfe peered down at the food Emma was packing away. "Whoa, cousin, you do not need that much. There are only the two of us."

"I thought mayhap the bishop might like to join us. I saw him crossing the bailey as we came around the building."

Rolfe felt a brief shaft of jealousy at the thought of sharing their childhood ritual with the bishop, then shrugged and nodded. They were no longer children. And this was not his uncle's castle. In fact his uncle's castle was now his own.

"As you wish," he said easily, taking the basket from her and offering her an arm.

Amaury was not a morning person. He never had been, but this morning of all mornings he was feeling particularly black. He had passed the night fitfully, kept awake by the throbbing of his own poor manhood. It seemed that, while his mind was chivalrous enough to be determined not to put upon his poor young bride any further on her first night as his wife, his manhood was not nearly so sympathetic. It had not helped that he had found himself constantly sitting abed, lighting the candle beside it, and staring at her beautiful face in repose. Truly, his wife was a delicate flower in her loveliness. Even her snoring had been dainty.

Amaury had finally drifted off into unconsciousness as the sun began its journey across the sky. One short hour later he had awakened in his new home, his new castle, his new bed, to find his new bride conspicuous in her absence from that bed. Now, after a thorough search of the castle and bailey, he had yet to discover her whereabouts. The bailey was nearly as dead as a tomb. There were only two men guarding the wall. The rest of the castle population, along with a good number of the inhabitants of the attendant village, appeared to be in his Great Hall, snoring loudly enough to raise the roof. It seemed everyone had fully enjoyed his wedding celebrations. Except him, of course. Which only managed to irritate him more. They had probably gone through a lake of ale to drink themselves into the stupors they were all enjoying on the Great Hall floor. His ale and his Great Hall floor.

Anger rising with each thought crossing his mind, Amaury strode back into the cluttered hall, perched his hands on his hips, spread his feet, and bellowed, *"Where is my wife?!"*

The only response he got for his trouble was the stirring of one or two of the drunken louts at his feet. Furious now, Amaury marched straight out of the castle again. Gathering a pail along the way, he strode to the stables and filled it with water from the trough for the horses, then returned to the Great Hall.

While his first bellow had not garnered much attention, his second one, accompanied by a wash of water from the pail that he splashed across the floor's occupants in a wide arc, certainly reaped more attention.

The women woke up with squeals of protest and shock, the men with curses as they grabbed for their swords. Amaury waited until the hall had fallen back into near silence as everyone realized who had so rudely awakened them. Then he spoke in a deadly quiet voice. "Now, if yer all ready to listen. I would know where my wife has got to!"

The silence that met his words was emphasized by blinks of surprise that told him what he should have already known by their unconscious conditions. None of these people knew where his wife had gone.

Sighing, he frowned slightly. "Well, know any of you of something she does, or a place she goes every morning?"

"Mass."

It was the plain-faced Maude who spoke the word, and Amaury turned to her gratefully as he recalled that she was his wife's maid. He had opened his mouth to respond to that when a man to the side commented, "Aye, but Father Gumpter is away just now. There will be no Mass."

Maude shrugged. "The Bishop could hold one."

"Nay." Amaury shook his head before they could carry the conversation further. "I checked the church. She is not there. Neither is the bishop," he added with a frown, his gaze now moving over the sea of faces in search of that good man's visage. He wasn't there, of course. It seemed no one he sought was apt to be present this morning. For instance, Blake was missing as well. Amaury had noted that while searching for his wife, more than aware that the man was inordinately attractive to women. Though he refused to admit to himself the suspicions that that knowledge raised.

He was grateful he never voiced the suspicions in his head, even to himself, when Blake suddenly crawled out from beneath the long table they had all been seated at the night before, a buxom blonde at his heels.

Getting to his feet, his friend straightened his clothes with a show of great dignity, then aided his companion to her feet before turning to face Amaury. "Ah, awake I see, friend," he called cheerfully, crossing the room as if nothing at all were amiss and Lord Amaury came bellowing into rooms every morning splashing water everywhere.

"My wife is missing."

Blake raised his eyes at that announcement, and glanced about the room as if expecting an answer there before suggesting, "Mayhap she is at—"

"She is not at the chapel. I checked there."

"Ah, well . . ." He thought quickly. "Where is her cousin?"

Amaury's eyes widened at that, for he had not thought to look for her cousin. Now he scanned the crowd quickly. "Where is Rolfe?"

He frowned at the congregated people so hard that it took a moment for a pretty young serving girl to find the courage to step forward and murmur her answer.

"I cannot hear ye!" Amaury roared irritably, making the poor girl jump.

Swallowing, she took another hesitant step forward and cleared her voice before speaking a bit louder. "He slept near me last night, yer lordship, yet he is not here now."

Her blush told him that his wife's cousin had done a lot more than merely sleep by the woman. Probably a lot more even than *he* had managed with his own young bride in the rush the night before. That only managed to annoy him more, and he frowned at the girl darkly before Blake distracted him from the hapless female.

"There, you see! She is probably safe with her cousin. Mayhap they went for a ride. Did you check the stables?"

"I did, but there was no one in the stables and no way for me to tell if any horses are missing. The stable master was absent."

"Ah . . ." An older gentleman cleared his throat and began to sidle around him, careful to keep a distance between himself and his new lord. "That would be me, yer lordship. I'll . . . er . . . see to it right now."

Amaury opened his mouth to flay the man for neglecting his duties, but as he did, a tinkling of laughter flowed into the room behind him. Whirling on his heel, he stared at the front door as it finished opening, allowing his wife to enter the castle, followed by the bishop and her cousin. All three of them were smiling at some private joke, totally unaware of the storm that had been raging in his chest since awakening to find her missing that morning. "Where have ye been?" he roared.

All three appeared surprised by the anger in his voice and face as he confronted them, but it was Emma who spoke first. "Is aught amiss, my lord?" She glanced anxiously around the room full of disgruntled-looking people and frowned.

"Where have ye been?" Amaury repeated grimly.

"Why . . . on a picnic."

"A picnic?" He looked nonplussed at that. Then his

frown returned. "Beyond the walls?" His stomach clenched at the thought.

"Aye." She looked surprised at his tone, then pointed out, "Well, my lord, there was nowhere in here to break fast."

Amaury was about to argue that point when he realized that she was, of course, right. Frowning instead, he simply ordered, "You shall not leave the grounds again unprotected. Is that understood, wife?"

Emma's eyes narrowed slowly on the man standing before her.

Recognizing the temper coming to the fore in his cousin's eyes and deciding it did not bode well, Rolfe stepped forward to smooth the way. "You are right, de Aneford. 'Tis not safe to leave the castle unattended. However, myself and the lord bishop were there to protect her."

"He's right, Amaury. Lord Rolfe could guard her well. 'Sides, all is well, she is found." Blake stepped to his side, then sent Lady Emma a charming smile. "Do not mind his temper this morn, my lady. No doubt his lordship is hard put to believe his luck in gaining such a lovely bride—as well as this home—and is simply nervous of losing you to the same fickle hand of fate that gave you."

Amaury opened his mouth to refute Blake's words, then snapped his mouth shut again, his expression revealing sudden surprise. Good God, Blake was right, he realized with dismay. While lack of sleep had made him surly, his fury on not being able to find his bride *had* been raised by the possibility of losing her. With his guilt over having botched the wedding night, he had feared she might have decided him a great clumsy oaf and fled to the king to petition an annulment. For someone who had worked and striven all his life to gain even the sparest crumb, being handed so much so easily was terrifying. Had Lady Emmalene been a hag, it would have been one thing, for in Amaury's experience, nothing was gained without pain or unpleasant duty, but his wife was no hag. Surely so much good fortune must have a price?

"My husband is lucky to have such a faithful and charming friend, Sir Blake," Emma murmured, moving forward to take Blake's arm and lead him toward the table he had so recently crawled out from under. "I hope he appreciates you."

Amaury did not hear his friend's no doubt charming response; his wife was seating Blake at the table across the room, well out of his hearing. As he watched in amazement, a few soft words from her had the entire hall moving as people set about their business. Those who should have been on guard returned to their posts. Those who worked the kitchens headed there. The rest seated themselves quietly at the table to break fast. All of them gave Amaury a wide berth as they did. Another moment, and then servants were bringing food and ale from the kitchen.

Amaury simply stood, feeling slightly forlorn as he watched his wife set their castle to rights. He hardly noticed when Rolfe and the bishop passed him, throwing him odd looks, before moving to a table for a tankard of ale. His thoughts were wholly focused on his feelings of being an outsider once more. It was a feeling he had experienced often as a child. Being the bastard of a high-ranking noble, he had been excluded from his father's family's ranks, and yet also had been set apart from the other children in the village he had been born into.

When his father's wife had tired of seeing him in the village—a live reminder of her husband's infidelity—and had insisted he be sent away, his father had sent him to squire with another lord. A kindness that. His father could have simply banished him. And yet he had still been an outsider in his new home. A bastard son squiring among so many legitimate ones. He had become a strong, skilled fighter through necessity, defending himself from the attacks of these other squires who delighted in taunting him. Blake had been one of those squires at first, but they had only fought once. They were an equal match, and had fought until they both collapsed from weariness. On regaining themselves, they had awakened side by side to become fast friends. That friendship had gone a long way toward his being accepted by the other squires they trained with, so that the scuffles had ceased there. But there was always someone ready to call him bastard and battle him; squires of other lords they met at tournaments, or simply on travels. Even later, once they were both knighted, there had been other knights who had been happy to remind him that he did not belong.

Amaury had always thought that if he had a home of his own, this sense of being an outsider would leave. He would finally belong somewhere. Yet instead, he stood in the center of his own Great Hall experiencing those very same feelings again as his wife—very deliberately he suspected—ignored him as punishment for his temper and arrogance and set about making his friend more at home than Amaury had ever felt anywhere.

For one moment his temper rose, and he nearly began bellowing again, but then he reigned his temper in. Perhaps this was little more than he deserved. He *was* a bastard. The son of a duke and a village girl. And last night he had treated his wife most sorely. True, it had been out of necessity and from lack of time. Still, realizing that Bertrand was following, he should have insisted they take care of the bedding directly after the ceremony was over so that he might give his new bride the attention and tenderness she had deserved. Besides, had he not dallied on his journey here, they would have been wed and bedded an entire day earlier, and there would have been time for him to treat her with the care she had deserved, he thought.

Sighing, Amaury turned away from the pleasant scene of his wife talking and laughing with Blake as he broke his fast, and walked out of the castle. Ignoring his own hunger pangs, he stalked to the stables to retrieve his horse. He intended on riding through the woods surrounding the castle. Hopefully it would improve his temper somewhat . . . and allow his wife's irritation with him to ease a bit. Mayhap then he could start again. He always believed one should start out as they meant go on, but this morning was not one he wished to repeat.

Emma's smile faded as soon as her new husband had left the castle, a regretful sadness taking its place at once, if only briefly. She was not used to being ordered about, and had been taken aback by her husband's attitude on returning to the castle. She had also been mightily angered by his possessive behavior. Neither growing up under her father's gentle hand nor marriage to the absent Lord Fulk had prepared her for a husband who barked orders and demanded obeisance. Her temper at his attempt to order her about had led her to deliberately ignore him and fawn over his man, but the expression on Amaury's face as he had left the castle had been so forlorn. . . .

"He is a good man."

Emma turned her eyes sharply to Blake's face as he spoke those words. His expression was serious now as well. "Why did he act as he did?"

Blake was silent for a moment, his gaze thoughtful and considering as he peered at the tankard in his hand.

Emma knew instinctively that he was considering what he should tell her, or what he *could* tell her without betraying his friend.

"What do you know of your husband?" he asked at last.

Emma's eyes widened slightly as she tried to recall what her cousin had told her the day before. It was very little really. "He is a hero. He saved our lord king from assassins while at war in Ireland."

Blake's eyebrows rose at that. "Is that all?"

"Aye."

Blake sighed and shook his head. "I know not if I should tell you, but you will hear soon enough," he muttered to himself. Then he took a gulp of ale and announced, "Your husband, my lady, is a bastard."

Emma gasped at his words; then anger entered her eyes again and she stood abruptly. "You should not speak of my husband so, sir! His behavior may have been surly this morn, but that does not give you leave to call him—"

"Nay, my lady," Blake's eyes filled with laughter as he realized that his friend's little wife thought he was slandering her husband. Taking her hand, he urged her back to her seat. "Nay, my lady, I do not mean in temperament. Though truthfully, when angered, he can be so," he added with amusement.

Emma frowned at him grimly, and he sighed. "His father was the Duke of Stamford and his mother the village blacksmith's daughter," he explained dryly.

Emma's eyes widened at that, her mouth making a perfect O.

Blake nodded slightly as he saw that she understood. "His father's wife was a noblewoman who never bore fruit and resented the fact that someone else had with her husband. She made Amaury's mother miserable until she bore the child and died, then made it her task in life to make Amaury even more miserable. When he was about six, she tired of her torture and demanded he be sent away. His father sent him to foster."

Emma was silent, her gaze fixed on her hands as they twisted in her lap. She knew about bastardy, of course. She might have been foolishly naive when it came to what a husband and wife did in the marriage bed, but she knew the ways of the world. Many men had bastards. In her opinion, it was not the fault of the child, and the child should not be punished for it.

"As a child he never quite fit in anywhere," Blake continued now. "He was half nobleman, half serf, but belonged to neither, if you see what I mean."

Emma nodded silently, still avoiding meeting his gaze, and Blake sighed.

"At any rate, he has never really had a home, and I fear he simply cannot believe his good fortune in gaining this one. I suspect it was fear that made him behave so this morning. Fear that he would lose you and all of this before he could even really enjoy it."

Emma stood abruptly and crossed the Great Hall. Blake hurried to follow, grabbing her arm to stop her as she reached the door. "He is a good man. His parentage is not his fault," he said urgently, and Emma turned to him in surprise.

"Nay, of course not."

Blake blinked, then released her arm and took a step back. "You are not offended to know of your husband's parentage?" he asked uncertainly.

"Fie, sir, you wound me by your thoughts."

"Oh." He looked discomfited. "My apologies, my lady." He cleared his throat. "I thought . . . your silence . . . Then you started to leave. . . ."

Emma smiled slightly and patted his shoulder as if reassuring a child. "I thought only to find my husband

and see if he will not break fast."

"Ah." He straightened a bit and nodded with a slight smile. "Of course. Well, then, I shall return to mine own."

Chapter Four

The bailey was a beehive of activity when Emma passed through it. It was hardly recognizable as the same place she had walked through with her cousin and the bishop only moments before. Still, with all these people around, she had to ask four of them before she found out where her husband was, and then it was only to learn that he had left the bailey on horseback.

Thanking the stable master, the source of this information, Emma turned away and walked slowly back toward the castle as she debated what she should do, then picked up speed as she came to a decision.

Blake was the only one to notice her return as she crossed the Great Hall. Emma gave him a small smile, but did not pause to answer the question in his eyes. Continuing on in to the kitchen, she quickly packed a second basket full of food and a flask of ale for her husband. It was a peace offering of sorts, she supposed, and a small gift of welcome. Perhaps even a symbol of her

Lynsay Sands

gratitude for his gentleness the night before, for she was aware that he had been as kind and thoughtful as the circumstances had allowed. He had had no need to be. Husbands were not required to treat their wives with kindness. Her life had not been so sheltered that she had not heard the stories of the women who had been given in marriage to extraordinarily cruel men who beat them, or treated them poorly.

Emma was more than aware of her good fortune in the two husbands she had had to date. Her father had chosen her first husband very carefully. She had originally been betrothed at the age of nine. Unfortunately, her betrothed and his family had all been in London the year before the wedding was to take place, and had been struck down by the plague, much as her aunt and uncle, Rolfe's own parents, had been several years before.

Emma's father had dallied about arranging another betrothal after that until she was almost nineteen. Then he had set about it very carefully. Lord Kenwick had hired two rather rough-looking fellows to investigate all the possible candidates. Lord Fulk had appeared to be the best of the bunch. Castle Eberhart had been near enough for her to be able to visit her father as often as she wished, and there was absolutely no hint of Lord Fulk ever having shown signs of being abusive to women. Instead, he had appeared to be a studious man who spent a great deal of time in intellectual pursuits, which kept him away from home for great lengths of time.

That had most likely been the clincher for her father, Emma thought with a bit of insight now. He had probably thought that fact most advantageous to his daughter, who was not used to being under another's rule, for while she had ever obeyed her father—well, most of the time—his rule had not been overly firm.

80

In truth, he had chosen well, for except for the fact that her husband had never been able to bring himself to the marriage bed, Emma had been relatively happy during the two years of her marriage. In fact, her life had continued much as it had run in her childhood home. Now, she had a second husband, and no doubt she had her cousin to thank for the choice in this one. For Emma was sure that Rolfe would have seen it as his duty to counsel the king on a choice now that her father was dead.

Aye, she was very lucky to have had two such men in her life as her father and her cousin, she thought as she detoured upstairs to collect her bow and arrow from her room. And now she was lucky enough to have a third one. For surely her husband had already proven that he was a kind and gentle lamb of a man by his tenderness the night before. In truth, the picture she was beginning to get of him was of a strong and fierce-looking man who was really just a small injured boy inside. A homeless waif, looking for somewhere to call home and the arms of a good woman to support him. Emma was just the woman for the job.

"Damn and blast ye!" Amaury roared, gutting the villain who had been brave enough to come closer with his slashing sword and take a slice out of his arm.

The man's eyes widened in shock as the fire of the sword pressed through him. Then he stared down in horror briefly at the lifeblood squirting from his stomach before he collapsed to the ground. His comrades immediately backed off a step or two from the warrior they had circled, watching for an opportunity to have at him.

Aware of their intentions, Amaury was grateful for the tree at his back, as well as his forethought in putting it there when the bandits had jumped out of the woods

81

Lynsay Sands

and trees around him, startling his horse into dumping him at their mercy.

Once again he cursed the sour mood that had made him so distracted that these knaves had been able to take him so by surprise. Had he been paying attention, mayhap he would have been forewarned of the attack. Or at least have managed to keep his seat rather than having to scrabble through the weeds to the nearest tree to protect his back as he squared off against half a dozen men . . . alone . . . with only his sword and a dagger in hand. He could only be grateful that only three of them had swords, while two of the others held clubs, and one waved a dagger menacingly. Well, there were only two with swords now, he thought with satisfaction, cursing then as one of the five remaining men grabbed up their dead comrade's sword and dropped his club.

A muscle ticking in his temple, Amaury glared at his adversaries, watching for the first sign that one of them was going to charge him. So long as they were foolish enough to continue attacking him one at a time, he would walk away from this day. But should they all charge at once, he would most likely be done for, though he would take at least two, perhaps even three, with him. He should have known, of course, that his good fortune would be short-lived. He had learned quite young that fortune was a fickle thing. It was just his luck to gain a lovely wife and rich estate one day, then be killed the next.

A flicker of movement recalled his attention to the men surrounding him, and Amaury did not even have the time to curse his inattention as he found himself set upon from all sides. It seemed none of his attackers wished to suffer the same fate as their friend had by attacking him alone. They were coming at him all at once.

82

* * *

"Er . . . my lady, perhaps ye should not . . ." Eldrin's raspy old voice faded into uncertainty as Emma turned to him questioningly. Sighing, the stable master straightened his shoulders and reminded her, "His lordship said ye were not to leave the castle unguarded," he reminded her now.

Emma frowned slightly, then smiled unconcerned. "Aye, Eldrin, but I go in search of him. Surely this time does not count?"

Anxiety clear on his face, the elderly man hurried forward to catch her mare's reins as she mounted her. "But my lady . . ."

"He can well guard me once I find him," she said reassuringly, taking the reins from his hands and into her own.

"Aye, but ye will be unguarded until ye find him and . . ." He let his argument die without truly attempting it again. There was no use; Lady Emma had already sent her mount striding across the bailey away from him. Muttering to himself, Eldrin shook his head and walked back into the stables. The new lord did not look to be someone one disobeyed. No doubt her ladyship would learn as much soon enough.

Emma rode out in the direction her husband had been said to take, fully expecting to run into him quite quickly. Unfortunately, it appeared her husband had ridden further than she had anticipated, and had gone deep into the woods where the danger of being beset by bandits was high. Emma stopped her horse and was debating returning to the castle when a horse suddenly flew out of the woods before her and charged past.

Shifting in the saddle, she watched the frightened animal run toward the castle, then bit her lip and glanced back at the deep woods before her. There was no doubt in her mind that that had been her husband's stallion.

Who else could it belong to? But now she was left to wonder what had happened to Amaury.

The skin was beginning to prickle on the back of her neck with premonition when the sound of clashing steel suddenly came from some distance in front of her.

Muttering an unladylike curse for her husband's stupidity in riding so far alone, Emma pulled her bow from her back and urged her horse into a run.

Amaury truly thought this to be the last day of his life. With three swords, a dagger, and a club coming at him, it seemed to him that his only choice was to be which of his attackers to take to Hell with him. It was possible he could take two . . . or three if he struck hard enough, he thought grimly. With that in mind, he threw his dagger into the neck of the man with the sword on his left, even as he swung his own sword at the man on the far right of him. His hope was to hit with enough force that he took down the one with the sword on his right, and that it then continued on into the neck of the man next to him who held the dagger. That, of course, left the man in front of him with the sword to kill him, or the one with the club to bludgeon him to death. But at least he would have the pleasure of knowing he had not gone down alone.

His aim was true and his anger such that his hopes were realized. He managed to take out both men on his right with the one swing. Though the second man received the sword in his shoulder rather than the neck, the wound was enough to disarm him. But the killing blow he had expected from the bandit coming from straight ahead never struck. Turning to face that danger, Amaury found his opponent staring back at him with wide-open, shocked eyes, his sword raised to hack at him even as he sank to his knees and fell to his face, an arrow out of his back. Amaury was so taken aback by this turn of events, he forgot entirely the man with the club . . . until it struck.

A step ahead of his friend and unaware of the attack from the unseen archer, the last bandit brought his club down on Lord Amaury's head with decided vigor, but his victory was short lived. Even as his victim fell before him, he felt the bite of an arrow in his own back.

Emma didn't even wait to see her second victim fall before urging her horse forward. As soon as the arrow had left the bow, she grabbed up the reigns in her free hand and urged her horse to run the fifty or so feet to the spot where her husband and his attackers lay.

The battle site was a gruesome mess. Emma did her best to ignore the gore all around her as she hooked her bow over the saddlehorn and slid from her horse's back to kneel at her husband's side. Amaury was lying flat on his face. Grabbing his far arm, she tugged him toward her, scooting backward out of the way so that he lay flat on the ground on his back, then looked him over. There was a wound on his arm, but it appeared to be only superficial. In fact it had almost stopped bleeding. The wound on his head was another matter, however. Raising his head gently in her hands, she turned him slightly to get a better look. He had taken quite a blow there before she had managed to fell his attacker, and the wound was bleeding quite freely.

Biting her lip, Emma glanced back the way she had come, but there was no sign of help yet, though no doubt there would be soon. Once Amaury's horse reached the castle, the guard would immediately send men to search for him.

She had just decided that it would be better to wait until they were back at the castle where she had the items she needed to tend her husband's wounds properly when a rustle of sound drew her attention.

The first thing Emma had seen on arriving on the site had been the bloodied man beside Amaury. That had been enough to assure her that she truly did not wish to see more, so she had avoided looking at anything but her husband after that. Now she realized her mistake, for not all the bandits were dead, it seemed. One, a weasel-faced fellow with a serious but not deadly shoulder wound, even now was on his feet inching toward a sword that lay nearby.

Cursing her stupidity, Emma dropped her husband's poor head to the forest floor and lunged for his sword. She was on her feet almost at once, sword at the ready to defend him. Still a few inches from the sword he had sought, the bandit stopped, licking his lips as he took measure of the situation. To cover the small distance needed for him to reach the nearest sword, he had to come in range of Emma and the sword she held. For a moment she feared he would go for the sword anyway, but apparently thinking better of it, the bandit spun suddenly on his heels and disappeared into the woods.

Emma stared at the spot where the man had disappeared for a few precious moments, aware that her heart was pounding so hard it seemed to be trying to break out of her chest, then dropped the sword and turned frantically to her husband.

The only thing that kept going through her mind was that she was useless with a sword. That was the one thing her father had been firm on. No daughter of his was going to train with a sword. In his mind it was bad enough that he had allowed a Welsh retainer he'd had for a while to train her with the bow. Under no circumstances was he going to allow her to train with the sword. Emma had tried everything she could think of to get him to relent: begging, sulking, temper tantrums even, but he had stood firm on this one thing. There was no need for her to learn to deal with a sword; she was well guarded, and the sword was definitely too un-ladylike a weapon for her to be trained in, he had insisted. Even Rolfe had thought her mad for wanting to learn how to use one, and had refused to help her in that endeavor.

Bending down, Emma grabbed both of her husband's hands and tugged at him ineffectually. There was no longer any question of tending his wounds here, nor of waiting for help to arrive. It was too dangerous. The woods were full of bandits, certainly more than the six who had attacked her husband here. If the fellow who had just fled into the woods came across his comrades, they could return at any moment. She could not defend them in this position.

"Emma!" Rolfe crashed into the clearing on horseback, alarm on his face.

"Thank goodness," Emma said with a sigh as he drew his mount to a halt.

Leaping to the ground, he hurried across the clearing to her side. "Are you all right?"

"Aye, but Amaury is not."

"What happened?"

"He was attacked by bandits," Emma answered. Turning quickly back to her husband, she frowned over the blood still pouring from his head.

"Were you with him?" Rolfe's concern obviously was more for her than her husband. Could he not see how hurt the man was?

"Nay, I came at the end of the battle. Help me get him up. We must get him back to the castle. He is bleeding badly."

Nodding, Rolfe lifted the other man quickly into his arms with a grunt, then turned with him toward Emma's mare.

"Nay, Rolfe, not like that," she protested at once as he slung the unconscious man over the saddle so that his head hung down one side and his legs the other. "Sit him up. He will be sore uncomfortable that way."

"He is not even conscious," her cousin pointed out dryly, mounting his own horse and leaning down to catch her about the waist.

"But—"

"Hush." Rolfe settled her before him, then caught up his reigns in one hand and reached for the reigns of her mare with the other. "We'll get him back quickly and make him more comfortable," he muttered as he turned his mount to start back the way he had come. He paused, however, as he caught sight of the bows still quivering in the backs of two of the attackers. "Your work?" he asked quietly.

Emma glanced down, then quickly away with a shudder. "Take us home, Rolfe," was all she said.

Seeing the pale tinge to her skin, he nodded and urged his horse forward, leaving her the time she needed to regain her composure as he negotiated the path through the trees. He knew she was rallying when she sighed and glanced over her shoulder to ask, "Did no one else come with you?"

"The stable master told me you had followed your husband alone, despite his order that you not leave the castle unguarded. I had him saddle up my horse. I thought to catch up to you before you caught up with him."

Emma smiled slightly. "To spare me from his temper?"

"A temper you rightly deserve. You should not have ridden out alone."

"Neither should he," Emma countered with annoyance. It was very rare that her cousin chastised her so, and she didn't like it when he did—usually because he was right.

"Nay," Rolfe agreed, and Emma relaxed somewhat.

One thing about Rolfe, he was always fair. "It appears the bandits are becoming brave," Rolfe added. "Fulk should have seen to that."

"There was much my husband should have seen to," she muttered dryly.

"Hmm." Rolfe grunted.

"Did you see my lord's horse?" Emma asked now to change the subject.

"Aye. No doubt help will arrive shortly." As soon as the words left his mouth, help broke from the trees ahead of them. There were at least twenty men, some of them from the castle, some men that had arrived with her husband, and all of them led by a grim-faced Blake.

"Lady Emma." Blake looked her over quickly as he reined in beside them. Once assured that she was fine, he turned his attention to Amaury's inert form, frowning over the blood still dripping from his head.

"He has an injury to his arm as well," Emma announced. "We must get him back to the castle quickly and tend his wounds."

" 'Twas bandits." Rolfe gave the information Emma had neglected. "You will find five of them in a clearing back there a bit."

"Be that all of them?"

"One was injured but got away," Emma told them.

Nodding, Blake assigned two men to accompany them back to the castle, then took the others and rode off in the direction Rolfe had indicated. No doubt they would collect the injured—if there were any still alive—and search out the one who had escaped.

Amaury did not stir as he was brought down off the horse and carted above stairs to the bedchamber by two of the larger men. Emma followed quickly on their heels, shouting orders to Maude to bring boiled water and clean cloths.

Moments later, her husband was lying sprawled on the bed and Emma was bathing his wounds. She tended to his head first. The arm wound was insignificant really, not much more than a scratch. The head wound was a worry, however. Such wounds always were. Injuries to the head could be the trickiest of wounds. A small one with hardly a bump could be enough to kill a man, while a great gaping one, like her husband's, could heal quickly with but a few headaches to show for its trouble. On the other hand, it could go the other way as well.

Sighing, Emma set the bloodied cloth back in the bowl Amaury's squire had been holding for her, then accepted the needle Maude had threaded. She had just set to work on closing Amaury's head wound when Blake entered to join the half dozen people standing about the bed.

"Did you catch the one that got away?" Rolfe asked quietly, a wince in his voice as he watched his cousin push the first stitch through her husband's skin.

"Nay. I left the men still looking and came back with the dead. There were five of them as you said." The gruff tone to his voice when he spoke told Emma that he had been distracted by watching what she was doing as well. It was odd how squeamish men could be about closing a wound. They weren't nearly so shy about causing one.

Rolfe grunted acknowledgment. Then there was silence for a moment before Blake went on. "Two of the men had arrows in their backs."

Emma stopped midway through a stitch, her gaze shooting a warning to her cousin. His eyebrows rose at the silent message, and he appeared uncertain for a moment. Then he sighed and muttered, "Aye, I saw that."

"The battle was over when you and Lady Emma arrived?" Blake's words startled Emma. It had not occurred to her that her husband's men would assume that her cousin and she had left the castle together, but then she supposed he just assumed that she had asked her cousin to accompany her for protection until she met up with Amaury. Giving one last silencing look to her cousin, she turned her attention back to her husband's wounds.

"Aye," Rolfe said finally. " 'Twas well over by the time I arrived."

She could almost hear Blake frown as he digested that. "Then who is it that shot the two men?"

Emma held her breath. She did not want it known that the bandits' blood lay on her hands, and neither did she wish her skill with the bow to become common knowledge. Rolfe was the only one aside from the Welshman who had taught her who knew of her skill. Her father had known, of course, but he was dead. As was her first husband.

Emma sighed as she recalled telling him of it. It had been the day after the wedding. She had thought to impress him with the knowledge of her skill. She had been desperate to impress him somehow. He had seemed hardly to notice her presence either at the wedding feast, during the breaking of fast on the following morn, or throughout the day.

Unfortunately, rather than being impressed, Fulk had appeared quite horrified by this knowledge of her unladylike skill. She still wondered if that were not part of the reason he had turned away from her. He had left for his house in London shortly afterward without a word to her. Perhaps he had not found her womanly enough. Whatever the case, that possibility was enough to make her shudder at the very idea of her second husband finding out about it. She did not wish to see him turn from her as well.

"Perhaps it was Lord Darion," Rolfe said at last, and Emma sagged with relief.

"Lord Darion?" Blake stared at him in confusion. "I have not heard of him. Does he have a keep around here?"

Emma glanced over her shoulder to see her cousin shake his head. There was a sparkle of mischief in his eyes as he met hers. "Nay. Darion is a spirit of the woods. And a defender of the weak. He has been known to protect unwary travelers who are set upon . . . always with a bow and arrow."

"Have you seen this Darion?"

"Oh, aye. Lord Darion saved my life a time or two. The first time I was a mere boy."

Emma grimaced as she recalled the occasion her cousin was speaking of. It had been a year after Rolfe's arrival at the castle and perhaps a month or two into their training with the bow. They had been running through the woods like ragamuffins, playing at being grown-ups. As usual, she had insisted on being the dashing Lord Darion, leaving her cousin little choice but to be a dastardly evil villain. They had been pretending that she had come upon the villain in the process of being very mean to a small helpless child. Then, of course, the chase had begun with the two of them running wild through the woods. Her cousin had been in the lead, with her following a goodly pace back, hampered by her skirts, which she so rarely wore, her bow slung over her shoulder. Emma had carried that bow with her everywhere as a child, she had been so pleased at being allowed to learn to use it.

A sudden cry from ahead had warned of trouble. Slowing at once, Emma had crept quietly forward, following the sounds of a small scuffle. A small and very short scuffle. She had ended perched behind a tree, staring wide-eyed at a pair of large, rather mean-looking *real* villains who had accosted her cousin. One of them had been holding him none too gently by the arm as they had debated what to do with him. Ransom had been an option, but they had decided by his dress that he must not be very rich. Emma and Rolfe had always been admonished to wear their most common clothes when playing in the woods lest they ruin perfectly good ones.

Deciding that he was just a village brat, they had determined between them that it would be best simply to kill him so that he could not tell of having seen them. Then they had begun discussing how they should accomplish the task. That was when Emma had realized that she had to save her cousin. She had been the only one capable of it at the moment. With very little thought, she had notched her bow with an arrow, aimed carefully at the nearest of the two villains, and let her arrow fly. The second arrow had been quivering against her bow before the first had hit its mark and had then quickly been released as well. A mere second later Rolfe had found himself standing between two dead men. He had known at once who his savior was and had called her name, but Emma had been too busy throwing up in the bushes to answer.

"And you never saw your savior?"

Emma heard Blake's question, and realized that even as she had been remembering the incident, her cousin had told of it, obviously leaving out mention of her. As she listened, he continued to do so. "Oh, aye, I have seen Lord Darion. On that day and many others."

"What did he say to ye?" one of the men who had helped to carry Lord Amaury to his room asked now, all of the men had listened with deep interest to the story.

"Ah, well, he was a bit too busy at the time to say much, as I recall."

Emma rolled her eyes at the laughter in his voice. He had teased her endlessly ever since over her losing her stomach that day.

"Too busy?" Blake frowned slightly.

"Aye, and then he was gone and Emma was there."

"Ah," another man said. "He didn't have time to even hear yer thanks. He fled afore anyone else should see him." His gaze turned to Emma, who was now busily stitching up her husband again. "Have ye ever seen him, my lady?"

"Oh, aye, Lord Darion saved her life once too," Rolfe answered for her.

"Really?" Blake glanced at Emma curiously.

"Would you tell us the story, my lady?" Alden asked shyly.

Emma glanced at the boy. He had been silent and resolved throughout this endeavor, ready and willing to do whatever was necessary to help. There was not a sign of squeamishness on his face now as she pushed needle through flesh, just curiosity and interest. She wondered briefly if she might have a budding healer on her hands as she shook her head. "Mayhap another time. However, I think my cousin can tell the story better. Perhaps down in the Great Hall," she added pointedly.

"Oh, aye. 'Tis best to let her tend his lordship. No doubt we are just in the way here." Rolfe moved toward the doorway and waited for the others to follow.

Alden hesitated, then stayed where he was as the rest of the males in the room immediately filed out.

Pausing at the door, Blake peered back. "Will he be all right?"

Emma stopped after pushing another stitch through the unconscious man's skin, then sat back to peer at Blake's pale face unhappily. "I do not know. He took a hard knock."

Blake was silent as he accepted that, then sighed

94

wearily and turned away. "Call me if he wakes, if you would, my lady."

"Aye," Emma murmured as he closed the door. Then she turned to finish stitching up the wound on her husband's head. "Alden? Mayhap you could fetch Lord Amaury's bedclothes. We will change him into them after I finish here."

"His lordship has no bedclothes, my lady."

Emma paused, her head raising at that. "No bedclothes?"

"Nay. He only has the two tunics as well. He says that a warrior has no need for more than the two. One to wear while the other is laundered." His young brow furrowed. "Is that true, my lady?"

"Well . . ." Emma had no idea how to answer the boy. She had never known anyone in her class to have only two tunics before, but then she had never known a warrior before. "I am not sure, Alden, but if my husband says 'tis so, then it must be."

"Aye." Alden bit his lip unhappily. "But my father is a warrior and he has many tunics. Fine ones. Some with jewels bedecking them *and* his crest."

Emma's eyebrows rose at that. "And who is your father, Alden?"

"Lord Edmund Northwood, he is the Earl of—"

"Aye. I know," Emma interrupted. Pursing her lips, she shook her head. "If your father is an earl, why do you train with Amaury?"

"He is the best." He said it with such pride, one would think he were responsible for Amaury's reputation and abilities. "My father said so. Lord Amaury turns out the best-trained knights. Father said, should I be trained by him, I would live to a ripe old age and garner many titles and fine tales along the way. Father said he would trust me to no one else."

"I see." Emma glanced at her husband with new respect. Not only was he a savior of kings, he was considered first among trainers of knights. Even by earls.

"Truly my father is a good warrior as well," Alden told her now.

"I am sure he is," Emma agreed soothingly.

"Yet he has many tunics as well," Alden pointed out fretfully, and Emma smiled gently at his obvious distress.

"Your father is an earl as well as a warrior. He must dress accordingly."

Alden nodded with relief. "Aye. 'Tis so." Then he perked up. "Now that Lord Amaury is a duke, he shall have to gain more vestments too."

"Aye, I suppose he will," Emma agreed with a frown. "Dress is very important."

Her eyebrows rose at his serious tone. "Is that so?"

"Aye. I heard the king say so."

"Ah." Emma sighed over that. 'Twas true. Even Rolfe told her their king was most concerned with fashion. No doubt she had been a great disappointment to the king with her plain clothes. Probably to her previous husband as well. Easing back in her seat, she peered at her present husband closely for the first time since they had been wed the day before.

She had managed a peek or two, first at the church, then at the reception, and once or twice after, but this was her first real chance to look her fill and allow her eyes to run over his strong features slowly.

He was a handsome man, she supposed. Not handsome as Fulk had been. Fulk had been almost pretty in his attractiveness, like a deer perched on slender legs. This man was a more rugged sort. Stronger and dark, he made her think of wolves and bears.

Leaning forward, she brushed a strand of hair off his face. Even in sleep he held on to his strength, a fearsome scowl on his face. Her father had had a strong face too, as did Rolfe, but on the few occasions when she had caught them in slumber, it was to find their features softened and almost boyish. There was nothing boyish about her husband. That told her more than Blake's words could have that his childhood had been full of hurt and sorrow. Even in repose he was afraid to let down his guard.

She would change that, Emma determined without even really knowing why she wished to. She would give him a good home that he could be proud of, and a wife he could be proud of as well. If he lived long enough to allow it, she thought suddenly with a frown.

Chapter Five

"Is he awake?"

Emma took in her cousin's hopeful expression as she joined the table at dinnertime, then sighed as she shook her head. She had been sitting with Amaury throughout the day, watching him until her eyes blurred with the effort, but he had not even turned in his sleep. His silent stillness was beginning to worry her greatly. "Nay, he hasn't stirred a bit," she admitted reluctantly. "Alden is watching him. He will call if there is any change."

Rolfe frowned, his gaze meeting that of the bishop, who sat on his other side.

Catching the exchange, Emma raised her eyebrows. "What?"

Both men turned to her then, their expressions pitying.

"What are you thinking?" Emma asked warily. "You look at me as though I were doomed."

"I believe your cousin and the bishop are fretting over

98

what will become of you should your new husband die," Blake told her quietly, and Emma turned to the man on her left sharply.

"My husband will not die," she said more harshly than she had intended. " 'Sides, nothing would happen to me."

"Do you not think that should your second husband die so soon after the wedding, Bertrand would not be knocking once more at the door?"

Emma stiffened at the suggestion. "Nay. I . . ."

"You would be a widow again, just as you were yesterday. Still in control of the land Bertrand wants."

Emma paled sickly at his words, her gaze flying worriedly to the servants moving about the room. The thought of how these people she had grown so fond of would suffer under the hand of Lady Ascot made her stomach turn. Perchance she herself might even be at risk under her rule. Then too, there was the matter of the king and the danger Lord Bertrand represented to him should he gain more power. And she did not even have the hope of an heir to hold that possibility off with. Her woman's time had made its arrival that very afternoon.

He could not die. It was that simple. He could not die . . . Because she would not marry Lord Bertrand.

Reaching out, Rolfe covered her hand with one of his own to comfort her, but Emma shook it away and stood quickly. "I must see to my husband," she murmured, slipping away from the table.

Amaury remained asleep for more than three days, three days during which Emma stayed steadfast by his bedside waiting and watching. No amount of worry or arguing from Rolfe, Blake, or her servants would move her from that spot. Even the bishop had a go at her, but gave up when he saw it was hopeless.

Despite her constant worry and hope that he would awaken, Emma was not immediately aware of her husband's finally rousing when he suddenly opened his eyes as if he had just been napping. Emma saw it, but it took a moment for her brain to register what her blurred gaze had witnessed. When it finally made it through to her muddled mind, she leapt from her seat with a start and dropped to her knees beside the bed, whispering his name.

Wincing at the shaft of pain that went through his head as he turned it, Amaury stared at her through squinted eyes.

"Your head is paining you," she murmured, stating the obvious, then stood and moved quickly to the door. Pulling it open, she called for Maude and Alden, then paused and glanced at the bishop, who was passing just then. "My lord, bishop!"

"Aye, my lady, is there something I can do for you?" He shuffled to a stop before her, craning his neck slightly in an attempt to see into the room beyond.

"Aye, sir. If you would? Fetch Maude for me and have her bring up the tea I had her make this morning for his lordship's head. He is awake."

"He is?" The older man didn't bother hiding his relief over this news.

"Aye."

"I will fetch her straightaway," the bishop promised, turning on his heels, only to turn quickly back. "You had her prepare it this morning?"

"Aye, I feared his head would be aching when he came around."

"But . . . how did you know it would be today?"

"I did not. I have had her prepare a fresh batch every day," Emma informed him, then closed the door on his surprised face and moved back to the bed.

Her husband's eyes were closed again. She was not

sure if he was sleeping or not, but decided not to disturb him until Maude arrived with the tea. It was a noxious brew. No doubt he would balk at having to drink it, but it would ease his paining greatly.

Biting her lip, she looked him over carefully as she regained her seat. There appeared to be just a tinge of color now to his pallid skin, but that was the only difference in his appearance.

The door opened following a light tap and Maude hurried in, Alden on her heels. Both of them looked eagerly over the man they had helped tend as Emma took the mug of tepid tea.

"Is it true, my lady?" the squire asked eagerly. "He awoke?"

"Aye."

"Oh, sweet Saint Vitus, thank you," Maude murmured fervently.

Bending to her husband, Emma touched his face gently, then smiled when his eyes opened. "Maude has brought you a drink to aid with your head," she murmured quietly. "If I help you, think you you could sit up to drink it?"

"Aye." Amaury frowned as he heard his own answer. He had meant to speak in his normally robust voice, yet it had come out as barely more than a husky whisper of sound. He then tried to sit up, only to find that he didn't seem to have the strength to do so.

Seeing the difficulty he was having, Emma ignored the scowl on his face and set the mug down on the table beside the bed, then moved to help him even as Alden hurried around to the other side of the bed to add his assistance. Both of them ignored the way he grumbled and muttered vexedly as they aided him into a sitting position, then lifted the mug to his lips.

Amaury took one sip of the brew before spitting it out across the bed in disgust.

"You live."

Emma turned the scowl she had produced at her husband's behavior to the door at the sound of that cheerful voice. Blake and her cousin were entering, the bishop directly behind.

"Not for long," Amaury gasped in a thin voice, not much stronger than it had been the last time he had spoken. "My wife is trying to poison me."

Emma turned her scowl back to her husband. " 'Tis not poison, 'tis—" Her words died in mid-sentence when a large hand suddenly seized her own much smaller one as she tried to press the mug back to her husband's lips. Head jerking up, she gaped at the man towering over her like death. He was at least a hand taller than her giant of a husband and easily twice as wide. He was also as ugly as sin, with a face that looked as if at birth God had covered it with a hand and pressed down, squishing his features almost flat for all time.

" 'Tis just tea," she whispered, intimidated by his size despite herself. "Made from white willow bark. 'Twill ease the pain."

Eyes so bright a blue they rivaled the beauty of the sky turned on her, and Emma found herself catching a breath. God's truth, it was a bit of a shock to find two such jewels in such a homely visage. Emma was still trying to get over her surprise, when the man suddenly nodded and leaned past her to tip the cup to her husband's lips.

"Plug your nose, 'twill help," Emma murmured when Amaury looked about to refuse the drink. "Ale will help kill the taste afterward," she added, grabbing up the mug of ale that had sat by the bed all morning in case he should awake and be thirsty. Muttering something under his breath, her husband allowed the stranger to feed him the liquid, then grimaced and reached immediately for the mug she held. Knowing he was really too weak to hold the drink, Emma moved it to his lips for him and tipped it up, helping him drink until he gestured that he had had enough.

Setting the mug back on the table, she watched him anxiously, doing her best to ignore the man who still loomed at her side like an avenging angel.

After much muttering and shuddering to show his distaste of the medicine Emma had given him, Amaury sighed and glanced at the man. " 'Tis glad I am to see you, Little George." His voice was raspy from disuse, but stronger at least than it had first been, he noted with satisfaction as his friend smiled at him. "I take it your task was successful?"

Turning to the newcomer, Emma saw him nod one brief nod.

"Good." Amaury turned his attention to Blake and Rolfe, who had moved around the bed to stand where Maude had been but a moment ago. "What happened?"

"You were attacked by bandits," Blake informed him.

Amaury nodded as memory returned. "Six of them," he muttered grimly.

"Aye."

"I was taken unawares. They startled my horse. He unseated me," he admitted testily.

Blake raised his eyebrows at this news, for it was a rare occurrence indeed for Amaury to be taken unawares, let alone unseated.

"I killed four . . . nay, three. The fourth I only wounded, I think."

Blake nodded. "He got away."

"And the other two?"

"Dead."

"The arrow," Amaury murmured, as he recalled his own brief surprise at the sight of the shaft sticking out of the one man's back. That distraction had cost him dearly, he realized now, raising a hand to prod gently at the bandage Emma had used to bind his head.

Remembering the pain that had seemed to explode through his skull as he had gaped at the man, he grimaced. It had only been then that he had remembered the last man and his club. No doubt his assailant had fallen under an arrow as well, probably mere seconds after landing his blow with the club. Were that not the case, Amaury had no doubt he would be dead now.

"Two were struck down by arrow," Rolfe said, verifying his thoughts now.

"Whose arrow?" Amaury asked, frowning.

"Lord Darion," Alden told him excitedly.

He blinked at that. "Who?"

"Lord Darion. Lord Rolfe says he's a spirit of the woods."

Blake grinned slightly at the boy's excited face. "It seems, aside from a serious problem with bandits, you also have a mysterious lord of the forest on your hands. And lucky you are that you do, else you most likely would have died." Blake's smile faded as he added, "You have been unconscious these last three days."

"What?" Amaury was stunned to hear this.

"Aye, my lord," the bishop announced, stepping up behind Emma now to join the conversation. "Three days. We have been sore worried about you."

Amaury finally allowed his gaze to drop to his wife. He had avoided looking at her since first finding her bent over him smiling. That smile had been so bright it had almost hurt his head. He had been hard pressed to see why she would smile at him so. So far in their illustrious marriage he had given her little reason to do so. Unfortunately, now that he wished to see her expression, her head was bowed, her thoughts hidden from him.

"You should rest, my lord," she murmured now, still

peering at the hands she was so busily wringing in her lap.

"I have slept for three days," Amaury responded irritably, peeved that he could not see her expression.

"Aye, but Lady Emma is right," the bishop murmured now, a hand dropping to her shoulder. "You needs must rest to continue healing, and so must you, my lady," the bishop added sternly, giving her shoulder a gentle squeeze as he spoke. "You have not slept these two nights and three days."

"He is right, my lady." Alden peered at her across the bed. "Ye've not left his Lordship's bedside since he was injured. You will make yourself sick do you not rest soon."

Amaury perked up slightly at that news, then frowned over it. "Aye, wife. You will rest. I will not have you sick."

Emma glanced up at that, but her expression was not what he had hoped for. Rather than being pleased by his recovery or his concern, she looked vastly annoyed. "Why is it that everyone is always ordering me to bed?"

Rolfe grinned at her disgruntlement. "Because, sweet cousin, you appear ne'er to have the sense to go there on your own."

"Why is he called Little George?" Emma asked the following morning as she joined her husband's friend at the table in the Great Hall.

Blake glanced up from the bread and cheese he had been breaking fast with to follow Emma's gaze as she took a seat beside him at the table. He smiled slightly when he saw the way the servants were giving the huge man a wide berth and nervous looks where he sat at the table with the other men. "Because he is so large."

Emma frowned at that. "That makes very little sense, my lord."

"Life makes very little sense, my lady."

Emma raised her eyebrows at that.

Blake shrugged. "Explain to me why your first husband did not see to his duty by you." He had meant the question as proof of little sense, for truly, anyone would wonder at a husband who did not find this woman attractive enough to bed. He realized the moment that her face flushed in shame, then paled, that he had made a mistake.

"Perhaps he found me ugly," she whispered unhappily, and Blake fairly goggled at her. Not for the words so much, for many was the time that women had said similar things to him in an effort to elicit compliments. His shock was due to the fact that this lady truly seemed to believe the words.

"My lady, has no one ever told you you are pretty?" he asked now.

Emma sighed again. "My father . . . and my cousin, of course," she murmured quietly. "But then they loved me and would say it because they thought it would please me." She obviously did not believe it was true.

"No one else?"

Emma shook her head, her eyes trained on the trencher before her as she played with a piece of cheese in it.

"Well." Blake straightened in his seat and gave her his most brilliant smile, despite the fact that she wasn't even looking. "Allow me to tell you, Lady Emma. You are quite a lovely creature. Your hair is the color of spun gold. Your lips as sweet as the petals of a newly bloomed rose. Your eyes as large and dewy as a deer's. Truly you are . . ." He paused uncertainly when she suddenly turned to him and patted his arm soothingly.

" 'Tis very kind of you, my lord, but you need not lower yourself to lie."

" 'Tis no lie," he returned quickly.

"Then why did Fulk not bed me?" she asked simply. Before he could answer that, she got to her feet and quit the table.

Emma was halfway across the room when her cousin met her. Smiling, he bent slightly to kiss her forehead in greeting.

"Good morrow, sweet cousin. I trust you slept well?"

"Aye," Emma sighed. "And you?"

"Like a babe."

" 'Tis good," Emma murmured, moving past him and toward the door to the kitchens.

"Where go you?"

"To get Lord Amaury some tea. His head is most like still paining him. The tea will ease the ache and help him sleep."

"He is already sleeping," Rolfe told her at once, falling into step beside her. "I have just left from seeing him. I stopped to tell him that the Lord Bishop and I intend to leave today."

"Today?!" Emma paused abruptly and turned back at this news, her expression dismayed. "But you have only just arrived."

"I have been here four days," he reminded her gently.

"Aye, but we have not yet had a chance to visit."

"Aye." Rolfe smiled wryly. "I had hoped we might have a chance to do so on the way back to court. However, with your husband being injured, it does not appear you will be able to travel back with us."

Emma blinked at that. "Why would Amaury and I have traveled to court with you?"

"He must pledge his fealty to the king as the new Duke of Eberhart."

"Oh, aye." She peered at the floor unhappily, then perked up. "Could you not delay your return until my husband is well enough to travel? We could—"

"Nay." Rolfe shook his head gently. "The king is no

doubt already fretting over the delay. He most likely thinks that Bertrand succeeded in arriving before the wedding and disrupted his plans."

"Send a messenger."

"Nay. None but those involved must ever be trusted with this information, Emma. Bertrand must never find out that the king planned it this way. He would make much trouble." Smiling at her woebegone expression, he gave her a brief hug. "I shall give the king your greetings and your gratitude and tell him to expect you and your husband to follow us in . . ." He raised one eyebrow. "Two weeks?"

Biting her lip, Emma peered down at her hands uncertainly. She had only been to court the once, when she had gone to have her audience with the king. Her father had not cared for court life, calling it promiscuous and corrupt. He had refused to take her there as a child. On her first visit as an adult, Emma had found him to be right. She had arrived the day before her audience and planned to stay for two or three days after, but had changed her mind the first night. Truly, she had never thought to see so many peacocks in one room, and such spiteful birds they had been too. They had taken great delight in trying to humiliate Emma her first night at dinner, tittering loudly behind their hands about how dowdy and unsophisticated she was.

It was the truth. Next to them she had probably appeared a dull little wren in her plain unfashionable clothes. But then she spent most of her time in the country, and who had she to impress? Still, it had not been their comments and insults that had upset her and changed her mind on staying over. It had been Rolfe's furious reaction. He had been offended on her behalf by just one of the comments of a less cautious lady. Had Emma not stopped him, she suspected he would have replied scathingly to the unfortunate creature, but she *had* stopped him and soothed his temper with a slightly amused smile.

Emma probably had more wealth than all of them put together. That was what made the ordeal almost amusing. She could surely afford raiments ten times more fine than their own, or at least equal to them. Emma had not brought land or livestock to her husband as dower; those had remained behind for Rolfe. Emma had brought riches, all those she had inherited from her mother, plus more added by her father. She now suspected that that was the only reason Fulk had married her. Eberhart Castle had been in sore need of an influx of monies when she had arrived. It had not been far from crumbling down around the ears of its lord and his people. Some of that money had been put to good use on her arrival, rebuilding and refurbishing the estate until it once again resembled its former glory, but the amount of funds it had taken to do so had been a mere fraction of her dower. Which was no doubt why Lord Bertrand had been so eager to claim her along with the estate. Such riches were not easily turned away.

Sighing, Emma peered at her cousin, recalling the anger he had displayed at the slight at court. She had decided then that it was not worth it for her to remain after the audience. She'd had no wish to shame her cousin, or see him upset by such petty behavior. Now she had to consider her husband as well. She had no wish to shame him . . . Or to see him belittled and shamed as well, she thought suddenly as she recalled Alden informing her that his lord had only the two tunics: the one he had worn to his wedding and the one he had been wearing the day he was attacked, a worn old tunic that was even more worn now with its new rip at the arm.

Amaury was a duke now, and the Duke of Eberhart

should not be so poorly garbed, she decided grimly. Aside from that, there was the worry that he would surely die of a chill if he slept unclothed every night.

"Make it a month," Emma told her cousin now. "And pray, do me a small favor when you reach London?"

Rolfe raised his eyebrows questioningly.

"Find the finest tailor in the city and send him out here. Tell him I will make it worth his while and tell him to bring his finest fabrics."

" 'Twas Fulk's doing, Amaury. The poor girl has absolutely no confidence thanks to his neglect. She thinks herself ugly. Did you know? I talked to Rolfe, her cousin, about it. I like him by the by, he seems a fine fellow. At any rate, he claims her life was much sheltered. There were few visitors to Kenwick. His uncle, her father, had little heart for company after the death of his wife, it seems. He lived his whole life from then on for Lady Emma and her cousin."

Amaury frowned as he watched Blake pace back and forth beside the bed. It was very rare that he saw Blake this worked up. Amaury had half a mind to tell him to shut up and sit down. He didn't like to see the man he had heard many a woman call as beautiful as an angel this worked up over his wife, even out of indignation for her hurt feelings.

Shifting against his pillows with disgruntlement, he tugged a wrinkle out of the bedclothes with a peevish flick. His wife had insisted he stay abed today to rest. He had blustered and fretted over it at the time, but given in in the end because he was frightfully tired. He had spent another restless night last night, tossing and turning as he avoided touching the woman in the bed beside him. She had intended on taking a guest room for the night when she had finally given in to his and everyone else's wish that she sleep, but he had forbidden that, ordering her to sleep in the bed with him. She had complied with the order most dutifully, waiting until everyone had emptied the room before quickly changing into that god-awful black nightgown again behind the screen and slipping into bed.

His lady wife had fallen asleep almost before she had fully laid her head on her pillow, proving to him that she had been exhausted. He, however, had not been so fortunate. Despite the exhaustion that had claimed him quickly after her delicate snores had filled the room, Amaury had been unable to turn off his mind and fall into the deep sleep that had been waiting to claim him. It was his thoughts, of course. Had he been able to control their lecherous meanderings, he might have gained some rest. Instead, he had lain there staring at her sleeping form and imagining what it would be like to make love to her . . . properly . . . without two or three dozen people outside the door cheering them on as if they ran a race.

He had finally drifted into a restless sleep just before the dawn, only to awake shortly afterward when the sound of the chamber door closing quietly announced his wife's leaving their room. She had returned moments later to catch him up, swaying on his feet as he tried to reach his own clothes. She had, of course, immediately ordered him back to bed. Amaury would have balked at her ordering him about . . . had he not been about to fall down anyway. As it was, he had barely managed to arrange his collapse so that he fell across the bed. Emma had helped him lie down properly in the bed, flushing and turning her face away from his nakedness, then had informed him she would fetch him some tea.

Despite his arguments that he was not tired and need not stay abed, he had found himself dozing off shortly after she had left him, only to be awakened moments later by Lord Rolfe. Emma's cousin had stopped in to inform him of his and the bishop's leave-taking. Amaury had listened to that information with a distinct lack of interest, but managed a somewhat sincere "God's speed and safe journey" before Rolfe had then turned the conversation to his cousin. Amaury had quickly deduced the real reason behind the man's visit as Rolfe set about lecturing him on how to treat her, adding dire threats of the consequences should he abuse her in any way.

He had been mightily angered at first by Rolfe's belief he had the right to interfere, but then Amaury had reined in his temper enough to admit to himself that had the positions been reversed, he most likely would have done the same thing. That being the case, rather than grab up the sword beside the bed and hack the man down where he had stood wagging his finger at him, Amaury had merely closed his eyes and feigned sleep halfway into the lecture. It had taken a few moments and a couple of snorts and snores before Lord Rolfe had noted his feigned sleep; then he had muttered a few disgruntled words and left him to it. But it was a mere moment later when his friend Blake had then burst into the room.

At first, Amaury had been glad of his friend's arrival, thinking to ask him to have Little George take some men out and see to the removal of his problem of bandits in the woods, being careful, of course, not to harm anyone carrying a bow. He had no wish to repay the man who had saved his life with death as a gift. But before he could even utter a greeting, Blake had blurted out the conversation he had had at the table with Emma and begun ranting and raving about the "sad state of her esteem" and how he felt Amaury should "handle it." Which he was still doing, Amaury noted with some disgust as he resumed listening to his friend's words.

Truly, it was most insulting the way everyone thought he needed guidance in dealing with his wife. Did they all really think him such a bumbling fool?

"You must help her rebuild her confidence, Amaury. She is in sore need of flattery. You must—"

"*You* must stop telling me how to take care of *my* wife and mind your own business!" Amaury finally snapped.

Blake stiffened at that. "I was only—"

"Butting in where you are not needed. Find your own wife to take care of."

Blake's disgruntlement disappeared as quickly as it had appeared, amusement taking its place. "My apologies, Amaury. I did not mean to make you jealous. I knew not that you were so fond of her already."

Amaury's eyes narrowed at once. "I am not jealous."

"Aye, you are."

"Nay, I am not."

"Aye, you are."

"*I am n*—oooh!" Amaury grabbed his head and groaned as a shaft of pain shot through it when he began to roar.

"I knew you were." Blake laughed, then turned and quickly left the room.

Muttering, Amaury lay back in the bed and closed his eyes. Perhaps now he could get some sleep, he thought grimly. Truly it was impossible to do so with his sweet little wife lying beside him. He wondered briefly what his wedding night might have been like had Fulk actually seen to the consummating, then realized with a bit of a start that there very well might not have been a wedding had that been the case. Lady Emma most likely would have had a couple of bairns and the freedom to marry or not as she wished. Lord Bertrand would have been no threat to her.

That thought was a bit dismaying. But for Lord Fulk's peculiarity in not bedding his wife, Amaury would not be lying here . . . in this bed . . . in this castle . . . with a sweet little wife who disturbed his sleep.

Sighing, he turned his head to peer out the window beside the bed, only realizing then that it wasn't an open window at all as he had thought the first night. It was glass. Damn! His castle had glass windows, he realized with a smile. It was an expensive item and not all that common. He had seen glass in but one other castle to date, the king's.

He had glass windows, he thought with pleasure, then shook his head once again. It was amazing to him that Fulk had not wished to stay here. Imagine . . . A beautiful wife, glass windows . . . What else could a man ask for?

Recalling his stalling on the trip here and the assumptions he had made as to her looks, he grimaced, but did not feel too foolish at his assumption that she would be a hag. What else was he to think? By all accounts, they had been married some two years and Fulk had not only not bothered to bed his wife, but had kept her a veritable secret from all of London. Perhaps all of England.

Which was probably how his wife had reasoned that she must be ugly, Amaury realized now. After all, Blake had said Rolfe had told him that there had been few visitors to her home as a child. That her time had been spent mostly with her father and cousin. There would have been no one to court her or to tell her of her beauty but the two men she knew loved her. When her husband had neglected her so, there would have been very little else for her to think but that she was unattractive.

It was the truth, Amaury thought on a sigh. Her confidence would be sorely lacking. She was in powerful need of flattering and building up her esteem, and as her husband it was his duty to recognize and fulfill her needs. That being the case, he had a great deal of work before him, he thought with a frown. Aye, he would have to tell her of her beauty.

Drumming his fingers impatiently on the bed, he glared around the room. It was vastly annoying that Blake had seen this need of his wife's before he had. After all, it was *his* chore. Even more annoying, suddenly, was the fact that she was not at his side now. She was somewhere in the castle, doing whatever it was women did to fill their time, while Blake—the man Amaury had witnessed women coo and faint over—was also somewhere in the keep.

Cursing, Amaury tossed the bedclothes aside and turned to sit up on the edge of the bed. He was damned if his friend was going to tend to his wife's tender feelings. That was his job, dammit! He was her husband!

"My Lord! Lady Emma! Lady Emma! He is trying to get up!"

He turned to glare at the door as the maid Maude hurried away, eager to tattle on him. Muttering under his breath, Amaury shook his head and turned his attention back to struggling to his feet.

This was his castle, blast it! He could get up if he wished. He was lord here, after all, and he would tell his wife that too, he decided grimly, gaining his feet.

"My husband!"

All of Amaury's bluster fled to be replaced by a guilty grimace at her dismayed voice as his wife reached the room and saw what he was about.

Chapter Six

"What do you? Are you mad?" Emma berated her husband as she rushed into the room. "You must rest to regain your strength, not waste what little you have left."

Amaury scowled at her, then sighed and decided to ignore her bossiness. It was difficult to argue that he need not stay abed when he was swaying weakly on his feet. It appeared he had used up most of what little strength his anger had given him. Aside from being a bit dizzy, he also was feeling rather weary all of a sudden.

Reaching his side, Emma grabbed quickly at his arm to steady him, then urged him to sit on the bed once more. His legs already collapsing beneath him, Amaury gave a grunt as he slipped back to sit on the bed, then sighed resignedly as his wife fussed and fretted around him, helping him to return to a lying position beneath the bedclothes and tucking him in. Some of his strength returned, however, to send him surging up in bed when she then moved to leave the room.

"Where go you?"

Emma turned back, her surprise at the sharp tinge to his tone obvious. "I thought to go to the kitchen to see about dinner."

"Nay, your place is here."

Emma's eyebrows rose at that pronouncement. "Aye, but you must rest, my lord, and I have duties to—"

"As your husband, am I not your first duty?"

She frowned over that. "Aye, my lord, but you needs must rest."

Amaury grimaced over that, but did not argue the point. "You should rest also, wife."

"Me? But I am not the one injured," she protested at once.

"Aye, but you have two nights of no sleep to make up for."

"But . . . I am not tired."

"Aye, you are."

"Nay, I—"

"Do not argue, wife. Do I say that you are tired, then you are."

"But—"

"Am I not your lord?" he asked with an impatient sigh.

"Aye, but—"

"Then your place is at my side. To bed."

Emma stared at him blankly for a moment, then let her shoulders drop with a sigh and moved behind the screen to change. It seemed best to humor him just then. He had suffered a head injury after all and those were known to addle the brain some. She hoped the affliction would pass with a bit of time.

Grunting his satisfaction, Amaury sank back against the pillows and relaxed. He was terribly satisfied with himself. It was true, he seemed too weak yet to be able to leave his bed. However, no one would have the chance to compliment his wife and repair the damage done to her esteem but himself this way. Besides, his wife had shown a distressing tendency toward bossiness since his injury. Exerting his authority as he had, had been enough to remind her of her place. It was not good to let a woman get above herself, he was sure.

Amaury remained thoroughly satisfied with the way he had maneuvered things right up until his wife walked out from behind the screen in her black gown and climbed into bed beside him. Then some of his satisfaction slipped as he watched her plump her pillow and pull the sheet up before lying on her side facing him and he realized what he had done.

Damn, but he had put her right back in bed beside him again. He would never get any rest now. Frowning, he peered at her still form, then forced himself to look away and peer at the sunshine pouring in through the window.

"Husband?"

Amaury turned quickly to glance at his wife at her timid murmur. "Aye?"

"You should rest," she reminded him gently.

"Hmm." Shifting against the pillows, he frowned slightly and turned back to the window, wondering what the men were doing right then. No doubt they were lazing about, growing fat and sloppy. He would have to see to correcting that once he was up and about. He would also have to tend to the bandits, he thought grimly.

"Husband?"

"Aye." Amaury growled the word, then tried not to look so fierce when he saw his wife's uncertainty. Truly, she appeared an odd mixture of bossy and timid.

"Can you not rest?"

He was about to deny that, then sighed and shrugged.

"Would you like to talk, perchance?" she asked then, and Amaury turned to her with some surprise.

"Talk? To who, wife? There is none other here but you."

Emma's gaze narrowed at that. "Aye, husband. 'Tis true I am all that is available. So mayhap you would care to talk to me?"

Amaury hardly noticed the snap to her words, he was too caught up by the question. Amaury had never "talked" to any woman. His mother had died at his birth, and he had been raised for the first few years of his life by his grandfather, a surly old man to be sure. Then he had been sent off to foster. The lord he had fostered with had had a wife, of course, but had rarely seemed to address her except to give her orders. He certainly had never seemed to see a necessity to "talk" to her of anything of interest or import, so Amaury had followed suit and done little more than nod her way in passing as a show of respect.

The only other women who had been in his life were camp followers. He had spent a great many years fighting this battle or that, trying to earn the money needed to purchase a home of his own. During those various battles, he had hardly had the time to make proper use of the services of those women, let alone waste time "talking" to them. Truth to tell, it had never occurred to him to bother. What would he have said?

"My lord?"

Catching the impatience in his wife's voice, Amaury turned his eyes back to her, brows rising slightly at her expression. His little wife looked quite fraught with anger at the moment. Clearing his throat, he considered what he might say to her, then remembered his intention to rebuild her confidence. "You are pretty."

Emma blinked at his words. They sounded more like

an accusation than a compliment. Truly her husband was odd, she decided. That thought brought her mind around to the other oddity he had displayed for her on their wedding night, and her eyes dropped surreptitiously to his lap. Of course, she had realized by now that it wasn't truly an oddity, not after what he had done with it. If that was the consummation, then all men must surely have such an extra limb. A disquieting thought that. Had Fulk had one? And if so, had his been quite so large when grown? She doubted it, for Fulk had been small and well formed everywhere from what she had actually seen of him.

"Wife?"

"Aye?" Emma flushed guiltily as she raised her eyes quickly back to his.

"I said you were pretty," He reminded her now. "Have you nothing to say?"

"Nay, I do not believe I am."

Amaury stiffened at that. "If I say you are pretty, then you are."

"Aye, husband," Emma murmured dutifully.

Amaury grunted, but continued to frown. He suspected she was simply agreeing because it was her place to do so, not because she had realized the truth of his words. "I said you were pretty," he repeated once more.

"Aye, husband. 'Tis kind of you to say so."

" 'Tis not kind. 'Tis the truth."

"If you say so husband. Tell me of how you saved the king." When he merely scowled at her, she prodded, "Rolfe told me you saved the king from assassins in Ireland?"

Amaury nodded reluctantly. "Aye."

Emma waited for him to expound on the subject, but he simply sat there pursing his lips with displeasure.

"Who were they?" she asked finally.

"Irish."

She rolled her eyes at that. "Aye, surely they were Irish, but—"

"Wife, 'tis not fitting for a man to discuss war with a lady."

Emma peered at him suspiciously at that announcement. Rolfe discussed war with her. So had her father before him. They saw nothing wrong with it. Surely he was jesting? Unfortunately, she had seen little evidence so far that her husband ever jested. "Why?" she asked finally.

"Why what?"

"Why is it not fitting for a man to discuss war with a woman?"

Amaury scowled over that, trying to recall what he had heard on the subject of war and women. The truth was he had never heard anyone discuss the merit, or lack thereof, of discussing war with women. He had simply assumed it was unacceptable. After all, by all accounts, women were delicate creatures, swooning and weeping at the least provocation. He had even heard that they suffered occasionally from heart palpitations.

"You would most likely swoon and palpitate," he informed her now, then nodded to emphasize his words when she peered at him doubtfully.

"Swoon and palpitate?"

"Aye. 'Tis well known women are weak of disposition, wife," he informed her knowledgeably. " 'Tis why you are resting now."

" 'Tis?"

"Aye. Women are the weaker gender. They are weaker physically, weaker willed, and even weaker in the mind. 'Tis why they must be taken care of, first by their fathers and then by their husbands."

Emma's eyes were mere slits as she glared at him. Never before had she heard such rot. Certainly her father and cousin had never said such things to her. They had treated her as an equal, except when it came to the issue of practice with the sword. Still, she knew what he said was a common belief, so tried to remain reasonable. "I grant you that men are generally stronger physically than women," Emma said.

"And mentally," Amaury insisted quickly.

"Nay."

"Aye, and in character, wife. Women, if not guided with care, are the most treacherous of creatures."

"Nay. Surely you cannot believe that!" She stared at him aghast.

Amaury shrugged. "Consider Eve."

"Consider the Virgin Mary!" Emma snapped back quickly.

He paused over that. " 'Tis true that the Virgin Mary was an exceptional woman; however—"

"And look at Judas or King Herod as examples of men!"

"You cannot count them for they were evil men," he protested at once.

"Just so, then we cannot count Eve or her flawed decisions."

Amaury looked briefly confused, then he regained some of his arrogance. "My lady, according to Thomas Aquinas—"

"Oh, aye. By all means let us hear what he has to say. A celibate who most likely detested women. Aye, his judgment would be untarnished."

Amaury's frown darkened. "You—"

"He is also dead," Emma added dryly.

"I think 'twould be a good idea to change the subject, wife."

"Why?"

"You are beginning to palpitate."

Emma opened her mouth to argue, then thought better of it. She was not getting palpitations, but she was becoming very angry. She did not wish to argue with her husband, however, so she decided a change of subject might be the best of all possible options. "Who is Little George?"

"My first in command."

"I thought Sir Blake was your first?"

"*Sir* Blake?" He grinned suddenly. "Nay, he is *Lord* Blake. My friend and partner."

"Partner?"

"Aye." He perked up slightly, pride entering his face. "We are warriors. We lead two hundred of the finest fighting men in England. We are much in demand. We can ask nearly any fee we wish. We . . ." His voice faded, a frown slowly sliding across his face as he realized he couldn't lay claim to that anymore. He was a duke now with a large estate and servants at his disposal. Unfortunately, it was all due, not to his own hard work, but to a marriage to the petite woman beside him. In truth she was the master here. He had been made witness to that on the morning of his attack. The servants followed her softly spoken directives with respect and alacrity, all eager to please her. He had yet to see if they would listen to him, and if they did, he feared it would be out of fear, not due to respect he had gained, for they knew him not.

It was an odd position for Amaury to find himself in. He had been well respected and followed for his skill in battle, his fairness, and his sharp tactics. As soon as he had finished his training and earned his knight's spurs, he had begun to hire himself out to those in need of a strong sword arm. It hadn't been very long before he had found himself being followed from job to job by several other men. Without a word being said, he had somehow ended up being their leader, arranging jobs, paying their fees, and storing away as much as possible of what was left over to one day purchase his own home. Over the years, the size of his men had grown so that when he had met up with Blake again some years back, the size of his band had reached well over a hundred and fifty.

At that time, Amaury had been considering letting some of the men go, and had been agonizing over the decision. Their size had grown to such an extent that while they were the first to be considered for large contracts, they were too large for many of the smaller but more plentiful jobs. That had resulted in their finding themselves with little to do but drink and wench on far too many occasions.

Blake had been the solution to his problem. With him for a partner, they could separate the men for smaller contracts, yet be available for larger ones when needed. The arrangement had been very successful.

"Why was he lorded?"

Amaury took his mind away from his thoughts and glanced at his wife with a small frown. "What say you?"

"Lord Blake. How did he gain the title of lord? Did he save someone important too?"

Amaury grinned slightly and shook his head. "Nay. He was born a lord. He is *Lord* Blake Sherwell."

When she simply stared at him blankly, Amaury said, "His father is Lord Rollo Sherwell, the Earl of Hampshire."

Emma gaped at that, her face flushing with embarrassment. It was bad enough that she had called him sir when he was a lord, but she could have been forgiven for that were he newly titled. Calling him sir when he was an earl's son was unforgivable. And it was all her husband's fault of course. He should have explained things to her.

Amaury burst out laughing at her expression, and Emma frowned at him.

" 'Tis not funny, husband. I might have insulted him somehow."

"Nay," Amaury said now, sobering at once. "You are my wife, you did nothing to insult him."

Emma sighed at that proclamation. It seemed her husband thought he simply had to order something to make it so. There was no sense arguing with him on that fact, so she turned her attention to her curiosity instead. "Why would the Earl of Hampshire's son become a mercenary?"

Amaury shrugged. "He was tired of sitting about waiting for his father to die, I s'pose."

Emma gaped at him. "He said that?"

"Nay. But why else would a man leave his very own home?" It seemed nonsensical to him. He had wished for a home of his own for so long, he simply could not fathom why another man would leave his. Of course, now that he had one, he was beginning to be uncomfortable at how he had gained it. It was one thing to work hard and earn it, or even to marry a mean old hag who would make his life miserable. Then he would feel he had earned it as well. But to have it gained by marriage through the sweet woman sitting beside him seemed just short of thievery to him somehow.

Emma caught the expression of displeasure on her husband's face, and decided discussing his friend was upsetting him. And that was the last thing he needed just now while recovering from his injuries, so she changed the topic yet again.

"Where is Little George from? I heard him speak this morn and he has an odd accent."

"He comes from the north."

"How did he become your first?"

Amaury shrugged. "I have known him near as long as Blake. We squired together. He is the fourth son of a baron with a small demesne just south of Scotland."

"What was the task he was accomplishing that delayed his arrival here?"

"He was getting wed."

"He was?" Her eyes widened at that. "I should like to meet his wife."

"You cannot. Not yet anyway. She stopped off to visit relatives on the way here. Little George said she shall follow in a week or two."

"Oh," Emma murmured with disappointment. She really would like to meet the woman. Her husband's first was such a large man, surely his wife must be an Amazon to accommodate him? Emma flushed at the indecency of her own thoughts and endeavored to turn her mind to other topics. "Tell me more about the assassins who tried to kill King Richard. How did—"

"This *talking* business is very wearing," Amaury said suddenly, lying back on the pillows. "Sleep."

Emma glared at his closed eyes, then sighed and lay back on the bed. She wasn't fooled by her husband's claim of weariness. It seemed he didn't wish to discuss his brave act. A frustrating attitude for him to take. And selfish too, she decided. Especially when her curiosity was so high. Ah, well, she decided, closing her eyes. She would find out eventually. She'd pester her cousin until he revealed the whole story. In the meantime, she would apologize to Lord Blake for her mistake in calling him sir, explain that it was all her husband's fault, and ask him his opinion on her husband's health. She had considered it carefully while they had spoken, and she thought mayhap Amaury's odd beliefs about women and their wickedness might simply be due to the injury to his head. As was his insistence that she rest when she was not tired. Surely it could not be otherwise? She simply refused to give credence to the idea that he believed the things he had said.

* * *

Amaury opened his eyes and peered at the empty bed beside him, then cursed and sat up. His wife had slipped away while he slept again. She was sadly lacking in obedience, it seemed.

Muttering under his breath, he stood up, relieved that for once the room did not spin. It seemed the rest had helped him some. He was struggling into his clothes, when Blake came into the room.

"Your wife will not be pleased when she hears you are up," he commented with amusement.

Amaury grunted and tugged his tunic over his head.

"She is quite worried about you, know you?" Blake commented now, mischief sparkling in his eyes. "She fears the injury to your head may have . . . er . . . tetched you somewhat, and wished me to speak to you and see if I do not notice anything . . . er . . . amiss."

Amaury stilled at that, his head coming up in surprised horror. "What?"

"There is no need to roar, Amaury. I am standing right here."

His eyes narrowed. "You are jesting," he accused grimly.

Blake shrugged. "Disbelieve if you will."

"Aye." Amaury nodded. "I disbelieve you," he muttered, turning his attention back to straightening his tunic. "Where is she?"

"Down in the kitchen, no doubt, talking to the cook. Or off in a corner sewing. Is that not how most women spend their time?"

"How the devil would I know?" Amaury muttered, peering about for his sword. "Where is my squire?"

"Most likely with your wife. Alden has rarely left her side since your injury. 'Tis building his confidence, I might add. He does not stutter, stumble, or trip about around her."

Amaury merely shrugged at this news about his

clumsy squire, and got quickly to his feet, cursing when the room wobbled around him.

"Steady on, friend." Blake caught his arm. "Mayhap you should stay abed. You've grown suddenly pale."

" 'Tis just that I stood too quickly." Amaury swallowed the bile at the back of his throat, then turned to move slowly and cautiously toward the door.

"Emma truly will not be pleased at this, Amaury. She will fret."

"She is my wife. 'Tis her duty to fret for me."

"Oh, aye." Blake didn't bother to hide his amusement as he hurried forward to open the door for him, then followed him down the hall to the stairs leading to the Great Hall.

Amaury managed the stairs on his own, though he was as pale as death with a fine sheen of sweat on his brow by the time he reached the last step.

"My lord husband!" Emma paused in the doorway of the castle, consternation on her face as she spotted him at the foot of the stairs. Handing Alden the basket of willow bark they had been out collecting, she left him standing at the door with Maude and hurried to Amaury's side. "You should not be up, my lord. 'Tis too soon."

"I told you she would fret," Blake muttered before she reached them. "Good day, my lady. You look positively blooming with the kiss of the sun on your cheeks."

Emma hardly heard the compliment, her attention focused on her husband, who was busy scowling at his friend. "Please sit down, my lord. You look frightfully pale."

Amaury stopped scowling at his friend to say accusingly, "You left the bed."

Emma sighed at his expression. "Aye, my lord. I could not sleep, so I thought to—"

" 'Tis not your place to think, wife," he snapped irritably. " 'Tis your place to do as you are told."

Emma went quite stiff at that announcement. Blake was rolling his eyes and wondering how to save the situation when the little serving woman, Maude, rushed forward to save the day.

" 'Ere, my lady, if you would take this a moment? I'll fetch his lordship a chair so he might rest." She thrust the basket into her mistress's hand, giving her little choice but to unclench her fists to take it, then ran to the corner of the room, returning a moment later with the heavy chair that generally sat before the fire. " 'Ere you are, my lordship. Rest 'ere a heartbeat or two."

Amaury looked about to argue, then gave in to the demands of his body and dropped onto the chair with a sigh.

"I told him he should not be about," Blake announced, trying to distract his friend's wife.

Not aware of what he was up to, Amaury glared at him for his tattling.

"But he would not listen," Blake added. "I fear he may be getting bedsores from his time abed."

Amaury's jaw dropped at the rude lie. Then he flushed slightly when his wife's gaze immediately went to his derriere, now resting in the chair. " 'Tis not true," he began, but paused, coloring furiously when Blake leaned closer to his wife to murmur.

"A delicate subject to a man, my lady. Makes them cranky too. Especially so when his head is no doubt paining him as well. Leave him in my care and I'll see him safely to the table. I am sure you had something you wished to do with the contents of that basket?"

"Oh, aye," Emma gasped, worrying about her husband anew. "The tea. I shall have some ready in just a moment, husband." She hurried off toward the kitchen, Alden and Maude rushing behind.

"Bedsores?"

Blake turned his attention away from watching Emma's voluptuous little behind sway across the hall to glance at his friend. "You may thank me later."

"Thank ye!" Amaury choked on his own anger, and Blake gave his back a sturdy slap before nodding.

"Aye. Since you seem to be sorely lacking in knowledge of this sort, my friend, allow me to inform you that you never tell a woman 'tis not her place to *think*."

"Well, 'tisn't. 'Tis my . . ." He paused as Blake rolled his eyes and began to shake his head.

"You know that, and I know that, but a smart man never lets his wife know that," Blake told him.

Amaury frowned. "Why?"

" 'Tis their feelings."

"Their feelings?"

"Aye, it hurts them. Women are tender creatures."

"Oh." Amaury scratched his head. " 'Tis the truth I don't understand her. When I ordered her to bed this morning, she asked me if I wished to *'talk'*."

Blake shrugged. "Some women like to talk before—"

"Nay. My head was pounding too loud to bother with that. I wanted her to rest, but when she saw I was not asleep, she asked if I might wish to *talk* to her. I ask you, what would I talk to a woman about?"

Blake considered that briefly, then shrugged. "I usually give them compliments. That generally works."

"I did, but she was not much impressed," he confessed with disgruntlement.

"Perhaps they were not the right compliments. What did you say?"

"I told her she was pretty."

Blake waited a moment, but when Amaury simply peered at him, he sighed. "You cannot just tell a woman she is *pretty*."

"You cannot? Why?"

130

"Women like flowery words when you give them a compliment."

"Flowery words," Amaury muttered, scratching his head again.

"Aye. Say things like . . . your hair is the color of spun gold, your lips as sweet as a rose, your eyes like those of a deer's. But say them in your own words."

Amaury wrinkled his nose in distaste and grunted over that, then glanced away from his friend to see his wife crossing the room toward them.

"Here you are, husband. This should help your head."

Amaury stared at the mug she was pressing toward him, and nearly groaned aloud. By God's sweet knees! He swore that rot tasted like horse piss. It was bad enough to have to take it when his head did hurt, but he was blessedly free of pain just now and she was still pressing the rot on him. Thanks to Blake, he thought, throwing his friend a nasty look.

"I will see that he drinks it," Blake assured Emma suavely, taking the mug. "I am sure you have much more pressing matters?"

"Thank you, my Lord. I did wish to fetch some salve for his Lordship's . . . er . . . complaint." She whispered the last word, then hurried away.

Blake stared after her in befuddlement. "I wonder what she meant by—"

"My blasted nonexistent bedsores," Amaury reminded him grimly.

"Oh, aye." Blake smiled slightly as he dumped the mug of tea into the fireplace. "I wonder what she'll think when she sees that there are none."

"What do you mean sees that there are none?"

"Well, I presume she means to apply the salve since she's gone to fetch it."

"Right here?" Amaury stared aghast at the thought, imagining her coming back and ordering him to disrobe right there in the middle of the busy Great Hall. He wouldn't put it past her. She had shown a distressing tendency to order him about now that she thought he was not well. He had thought he had taken care of that by enforcing his order for her to retire earlier, but the fact that she had snuck off as soon as he slept had corrected him on that issue. He would definitely have to put a stop to that tendency of hers.

"When she comes back with the salve, I will delay her until after dinner; then you can offer to help me apply it," he decided firmly.

"Me?"

"Aye, *you*," Amaury said dryly. "You would not wish her to know that you had lied, would you? It might hurt her *tender* feelings."

"Your hair is the color of gold, your lips as . . . er . . . red as a rose, and your eyes like a deer's." Amaury recited the words quickly as they sat at the table for dinner, then nodded his satisfaction as he awaited his wife's response.

Lady Emma stilled in the midst of raising her tankard to her mouth, gave her head a slight shake, then continued eating.

Amaury frowned. "Wife, I said your hair is the color of—"

"Gold. Aye, I know, husband. Lord Blake told me that earlier."

Slamming his ale back on the table, Amaury turned to his friend and glared.

"I told you to use your own words," Blake said at once, having heard the exchange. "Those were just examples."

Muttering under his breath, Amaury turned back to his meal and began stabbing at food with his dirk.

"Is aught wrong, husband?" Emma asked, a hint of

laughter marring her concern. "Is your head paining you? Shall I make more—"

"Nay!" Amaury reigned his temper in and sighed. "Thank you, but nay, I need no more tea." He shuddered just to think of it, then sighed and sat back slightly, having lost his appetite. He was also beginning to grow a bit tired after his short excursion. It probably had something to do with all the arguing and fretting he had done since coming below stairs. It had been quite a battle to get his little wife to leave off applying the salve until bedtime. She could be a stubborn little cuss when it came to his health. He wasn't sure whether he should be pleased by that or not. Perhaps he would be if Blake hadn't explained that she was probably worried so about him because she feared having to marry Bertrand if Amaury himself died on her. It wasn't much of a compliment to be preferred over Bertrand.

"I fear I grow weary from all this excitement. Mayhap I shall just retire to bed and have a sleep," he announced with an expectant glance at his friend.

Nodding, Blake continued to eat. It was Emma who stood up at once to offer her assistance. "Of course. I shall see you up and apply the salve."

Amaury glared at Blake at that, but when his friend merely continued to eat, he waved her back to the table. "Nay, wife. I can manage on my own."

"You cannot put the salve on on your own, husband," Emma argued sensibly.

"Blake will see to it," Amaury announced, elbowing him as he spoke.

"Oh, aye." Wiping his blade off, Blake stuck his own dirk back in its sheath and rose quickly, offering her a smile. "I shall look after him, my lady. You must eat to keep up your strength."

"But you have not finished your meal," she protested.

"Nay, but then I have stuffed myself well these past

133

several days, while you have touched next to nothing as you fretted over your poor fallen husband," he pointed out.

Amaury frowned at his wife with displeasure on hearing this. "You have not been eating?"

Emma closed her mouth on the protest she had been about to give Lord Blake, and glared at him instead before turning to her husband. "Aye, my lord, I have." When he frowned even harder at the obvious lie, she added with a reluctant sigh, "Just not overly much. Worry upsets my appetite."

"Eat," was all he said before turning and heading for the stairs.

Giving her an apologetic look, Blake grabbed a mutton leg off the table and saluted her with it. "I will just take this to tide me over as I see to my duties as friend."

Chapter Seven

"There is some blessed thistle, my lady."

Emma glanced to where Maude was gesturing. "Oh, good! Blessed thistle improves the appetite. I noticed last night at sup that my husband did not eat much. Mayhap that will help."

Nodding, Maude moved to gather some of the plant.

"If you see any burdock, pick some of that as well, Maude. 'Tis a good blood purifier. Butcher's broom and red clover too if you chance across some."

"Aye, my lady."

Emma grimaced at the woman's tone of voice, more than aware that the servant thought she was going too far in her desire to insure her husband's health.

Emma had been dosing her husband with a combination of medicaments said to increase general health and strength, ever since he had awakened from his injury. And there was absolutely nothing wrong with her doing that, she thought defensively, but she knew it was

Lynsay Sands

not so much what she was giving him, as how she was giving them to him that had Maude upset. Amaury had shown a distressing aversion to taking medicaments, so she had thought it better to simply sneak them into his drink at meals. Unfortunately the potions had filled nearly half his tankard and had changed the taste of his ale somewhat. When he had complained of it, Emma had just told him it was the aftereffects of his head wound. It might be a sin to lie, but Emma felt sure God would understand. Her husband had to remain healthy and give her a child. It was the only way to protect her from having to marry Bertrand.

She was honest enough to admit to herself that mayhap she *was* taking her precautions a bit far, but truly, until an heir was born, it did seem better to be safe than sorry. Her gaze dropped to her flat stomach and she sighed. The wedding night had not produced the hoped for results. That fact meant that they had to consummate some more. Unfortunately, her husband had shown no inclination to do so.

Emma had not been too worried at first; after all, he had still been recovering from his injury. But Amaury had been up and about for several days now. He had spent the last three days out in the bailey overseeing the men. Surely he was recovered enough to see to his husbandly duty? She had even mentioned to him—with much blushing—that her woman's time had come and gone, but that hint had had little effect. She was beginning to fear he could not bring himself to do it.

Sighing, Emma bent to the damiana plants by her feet again. It said in the books she had on medicinal cures that damiana was a powerful aphrodisiac. If so, then her husband must have a resistance to the plant, for she had added it to the list of other herbs she'd been dosing his ale with as soon as her woman's time had ended, yet he had shown no signs of increased ardor.

136

Damiana was also said to be able to cure impotence in men. She wasn't sure if that problem afflicted her husband, but was worried by the fact that their first conjugal experience had not resulted in a child. Surely it could not take more than the one time to conceive? She was positive most women would not forbear and have so many children if it took more than one or two tries. Of course, now she understood why women were said not to enjoy the act.

Those women who had had ten or more children must have been clever with herbs and known what to take to ease the discomfort, she thought as she bent to pluck another plant. As she dropped it into the basket, her gaze slipped briefly to the willow bark she had already collected. Amaury had not needed it for several days. This was for herself. Since her husband showed absolutely no inclination to bed her, she had every intention of approaching him herself. Which was what the bark was for. This time, she intended to be prepared for the pain and discomfort of the joining. She would prepare a drink of hops and white willow bark to ease the pain she knew to expect. She also intended to drink the unwatered ale she had had her alewife put aside. Between the two concoctions she hoped that the event would not be nearly so painful. It had felt as if her husband was trying to rend her apart with the consummation on their wedding night.

If there *was* an event. Sighing, she bent to pluck another plant. She had little idea of how to approach the issue. That was distressing. How did other wives ask their husbands to commit the joining?

Mayhap they didn't have to ask. That was what she feared most.

"My lady, I've found some blessed thistle, burdock, and red clover. I could not find any butcher's broom, though."

" 'Tis all right," Emma murmured, straightening. She placed her hand at her back as she arched it, her eyes moved over the sky.

" 'Tis getting late," Maude said, following her gaze.

"Aye. We should head back. Everyone will be sitting down to sup by the time we get there."

Nodding, the maid hefted her basket and began to follow Emma toward the horses and the guards that waited with them.

Amaury was fair impatient by the time his wife came riding into the bailey. He had not been pleased at her announcement that she must go look for more of her roots and barks. Had she not added that she had used up all of hers on him, he would have refused to allow her to go. He had sent four men with her, only to decide as soon as she was gone that he should have sent six. That worry had distracted him all afternoon as he supervised the men training in the bailey.

Despite his not being conscious to give instructions for so long, Blake and Little George had seen to everything he would have wanted them to. They had kept the men practicing daily, including Fulk's men, who had proven to be better fighters than expected. They had also sent troops of men out every day to see to the problem of the bandits. Unfortunately, the bandits had apparently expected as much, and had not appeared since the attack. So far they had eluded capture.

Knowing that was what had made him so uncomfortable with his wife being out in the woods. It was also why he had spent the better part of the afternoon fretting over her. He was quite surly by the time the call rang out that her ladyship was returning.

" 'Tis about time," he muttered, sheathing the sword he had been waving irritably at his men as he roared his criticisms and orders at them. He realized he had taken his temper out on them. He spared a moment to feel guilty about that, then caught sight of his wife riding into the bailey, headed for the stables. Amaury immediately headed that way himself.

"My lord husband."

Amaury swallowed down some of his temper at her smiling greeting and forced what he thought was a smile to his face. To Emma it looked like a pained grimace, and anxiety covered her face at once.

"Are you in pain, my lord?" she asked, slipping quickly off her horse.

"Nay."

"Feeling dizzy . . . or weak?" Reaching up, she felt his forehead, relieved to find it cool and dry.

"Nay, wife. I am fine."

"You are not tired, are you? You have not overdone it today and—"

" 'Tis more than a week now since my injury," he pointed out with exasperation. "And nay, I have not overdone. I merely supervised my men. Stop fussing, wife."

"Oh. Good." Lowering her head, she hid her relief at that news. He was not in pain, not tired. Tonight she would approach him about reconsummation. If he didn't approach her himself. He might very well do so yet. Mayhap it merely took several days for damiana to work. She would give him a double dose in his ale at sup. It could not hurt, she thought. Then she realized that her husband had been talking to her for several minutes and she had not heard a word of it.

Dragging her attention away from her own thoughts, she listened to the end of his lecture, which was actually a poorly disguised order that she not leave the castle grounds again without at least six men. It was dangerous. The bandits were still about.

Emma nodded solemnly as he finished, then turned

and made her way to the castle, her precious herbs nestled in the basket she held. It was not as late as she had feared. She had just enough time to boil down this latest batch of damiana before dinner.

"Do you feel all right, wife?" Amaury frowned as he caught her arm to keep her from falling backward off the bench. She was terribly unsteady in her seat.

"Aye." The word slipped out on a hiccup, and Emma quickly covered her mouth as a giggle followed, then took the hand away to fan herself. "Oh, my, 'tis hot in here. Is it not, husband?"

"Nay. 'Tis not," Amaury muttered. Bewildered by her odd behavior, he reached out to press his hand to her forehead as she had done to him repeatedly over the last week. She did not feel feverish. "Wife—"

"Oh, damn me, 'tis *so* hot!" Weaving in her seat slightly, she tugged fretfully at the top of her gown, trying to get the material away from her skin.

Amaury gaped at her, then glowered over her choice of words and turned to a wide eyed Blake with an expression that said, "What does a husband do in this situation, my lord?"

"She appears almost to be sotted," Blake said helplessly after regaining his composure enough to respond to his friend's look.

"My lord, ladies do not become sotted," Emma lectured, leaning across her husband to wag her finger in his friend's face as she caught his comment.

"Mayhap a bath is in order, my lady," Maude murmured, appearing at her mistress's side now.

"A bath?" Emma swung back to peer at her woman, nearly losing her balance as she did. "Oh, aye. I would like that. Anything to cool me from this damnable heat."

Amaury's gaze narrowed as he watched Maude patiently help his wife to her feet and walk her to the stairs.

"Think you she is a tippler?" Blake asked quietly.

Amaury scowled at the thought, but remained silent. His gaze returned to the stairs his wife and her maid had ascended, and stayed there until Maude came below stairs once more and hurried into the kitchen. When she came back out a moment later, a basket over her arm, Amaury stood and called her over.

Maude hesitated briefly, then walked reluctantly to his side. "Aye, my lord?"

"What is that?" he asked, gesturing toward the covered basket in her hand.

Maude pulled the small linen covering back. " 'Tis to scent her ladyship's bath."

Amaury peered at the contents, eyebrows rising slightly at the mixture of dried flowers. Then he noted a small bowl filled with a greenish yellow muck. "What is that?" He gestured toward the bowl.

"A mixture of chamomile and lemon . . . for her ladyship's hair."

"Hmm." Amaury picked up the bowl and sniffed. It wasn't unpleasant. He glanced at the nervous woman now. "Has her ladyship tippled?"

"Tippled?" Maude's voice came out on a slight squeak as her eyes widened. "N-nay, my lord."

"She appears sotted."

"A-aye," Maude agreed.

"She is?!" He looked ready to explode at that.

"N-nay, my lord!"

"Then what the devil is ailing her?!"

"I—it must be the hops, my lord," Maude blurted out.

"The hops?"

"Aye . . . and the white willow bark."

His bewilderment showed. "What about hops and willow bark?"

"H-her ladyship dosed herself with both before sitting down to sup," Maude confessed. "Mayhap they reacted with the ale from dinner."

"Is white willow bark not what she was giving Lord Amaury for his head?" Blake asked now, getting up from his seat to question the servant as well.

"A-aye, my lord." Maude nodded at the second man. "What is hops?"

" 'Tis for pain too . . . or to ease belly problems. Some take it to calm their nerves."

"Is my wife ailing?" Amaury was furious at the very thought.

Seeing that, Maude immediately began shaking her head, then sighed and admitted, "I do not know, my lord. She has not said so. Mayhap she is just suffering from the gas." She shifted uncomfortably before him. "By yer leave, my lord. Might I not take this up to her ladyship? She will be sore disappointed should her bath grow cold ere I get these to her."

Expression grim, Amaury gave a sharp nod, then watched the woman flee the Great Hall before dropping back to his place at the table.

" 'Tis most likely she has gas," Blake told him reassuringly, catching Amaury's expression as he retook his own seat. "Surely she would have told her woman were she ailing."

"Aye," Amaury agreed, but he was worried.

"My lady?"

Emma opened her eyes at Maude's tentative voice. The servant had helped her with her bath, then wrapped her in a linen and sat her before the fire to brush her hair. Emma had almost been wooed into sleep by the warmth from the fire and the soothing stroke of the brush through her hair.

Reaching up, she felt her tresses, surprised to note

that they were almost fully dry already. Mayhap she *had* dozed off a bit. It was probably due to the ale. She had double dosed herself with her herbs, then drunk every drop of ale the cook had put aside for her. It had taken her emptying and refilling her tankard three times to empty that pail, but it had had an amazing effect. Truly, she had never felt so. . . . free. So unaffected, unconcerned, relaxed. It was a wonderful tonic for the night ahead. That thought made her sigh as she recalled her first experience as wife. It would have gone much easier for her had she thought to prepare herself like this, she decided. But then, she had not realized what all it entailed.

"My lady?" Maude repeated.

"Aye?"

"Yer not ailing, are ye?"

Emma turned her head to the woman in surprise, then giggled. "Nay, Maude. Why would you think so?"

The servant was silent for a moment, then continued to brush her hair as she confessed, "I saw ye taking the hops and white willow earlier. I thought mayhap ye were ailing?"

"Nay." Emma stared into the fire and bit her lip, then sighed and admitted, "I drank some unwatered ale too. I thought mayhap 'twould help with the joining."

"Help with the . . ." The brush stilled in her hair.

"Aye," Emma murmured, flushing bright red. "My woman's time came. We did not conceive, so we needs must reconsummate."

Maude's brows drew together in worry briefly, then she sat back to brush Emma's hair again before murmuring, " 'Tis true the first time is a mite painful—"

Emma snorted inelegantly at that and Maude stilled the brush again.

"Well," Maude sighed. "His lordship was a bit rushed on yer wedding night. There was some need for speed.

143

He most like didn't have the opportunity to prepare ye for it."

"Prepare me? Well, he did warn me and apologize afore he did it." Turning, she caught Maude rolling her eyes in dismay.

"That is not preparing, my lady."

" 'Tisn't?"

"Nay," she said heavily. "My lady, did no one teach ye about the bedding before ye wed Lord Fulk?"

"Aye—nay." Emma laughed as she recalled her naive thoughts. "My father told me my husband would share my bed."

"And that is all?"

Emma nodded.

"Oh, my lady!" Maude looked dismayed. "Ye should have told me. Mayhap I could have prepared ye for what was to come."

" 'Tis all right," Emma assured her with a wry smile. "I am prepared now. 'Tis why I took the hops and willow. All will be well tonight. I will forbear. 'Tis the truth I hardly think I will even notice the discomfort. I am fair sotted."

"Nay! My lady," Maude started urgently, only to snap her mouth shut when the chamber door opened and Lord Amaury stepped in. Spying them by the fire, he frowned over the fact that the maid was still there. He wished to speak to his wife alone.

"Leave us," he said.

Maude hesitated briefly, then rose and reluctantly left the room.

Amaury watched her go, then turned to survey his wife. She looked fair lovely before the fire. Her hair shone as it tumbled over her shoulders and down her back. It was more than obvious to him that she wore nothing beneath the black linen wrapped around her either. It was damp and clung to her body.

Amaury felt his throat closing up as his gaze wandered over that body. He very distinctly recalled it lying beneath his. He also distinctly recalled the agony he had suffered afterward when he had been denied release. He suspected that denial was the reason he was so easily aroused by his little wife now. It seemed to him he had spent almost every minute since their marriage, at least the conscious moments, in a state of arousal. Damned if he hadn't. And it appeared that he would not be gaining satisfaction anytime soon. Not if his wife was ailing.

"You are ill," he said.

Emma's eyebrows rose at that accusation; then she shook her head.

"Aye. You are, and I wish to know what is ailing you, wife."

"Nothing, husband."

"You will tell me what is ailing you. 'Tis your duty as my wife."

Emma frowned at him. She had no idea why he would think her ill, unless he had also somehow learned of her taking the white willow bark and hops. If that were the case, she definitely did not wish to explain her reasons to him. It would be fair embarrassing to discuss. Deciding that distraction was needed, she managed to gain her feet without losing her balance, then dropped the linen to the floor. "Do I look ill, husband?"

Amaury stood rooted to the spot. He could not believe she had done that. He had spent the time ever since his wedding night battling with himself over pestering her for his privileges, his body nearly ordering him to do so and his mind arguing that he mustn't rush her. He had suffered an agony of guilt over the pain he had unfortunately caused on his wedding night. Now, here she was, as much as offering herself to him. At least he hoped to God she was offering herself. He thought he'd

145

die if he was misunderstanding her and she suddenly crawled into bed and went to sleep. Terrified that that was exactly what she intended to do, he stood where he was, counting out the passing seconds in his head. He would give her to the count of twenty—nay, ten—to get into the bed, else . . .

Dropping the linen had been one of the hardest things Emma had ever done in her life. Still and all, as a distraction it was mightily effective. Her husband looked as though he had not only lost his train of thought, he had lost thought altogether. He simply stood there gaping at her for the longest time, then suddenly strode across the room, swept her up into his arms and carried her to the bed. Dropping her there, he immediately began tearing at his clothes.

Emma watched him with something akin to amazement. It was not quite the reaction she had expected. She had hoped it might give him ideas, but had fully expected she would have to at least ask him before he would relent and agree to the joining. To see him ripping so impatiently at his clothes instead made her wonder if perhaps the joining were not much more enjoyable for the man, for truly it did seem he was eager. He already had his tunic off and was now hopping about the room on one foot, tugging at the boot on his other. The boot came off at last and he tossed it over his shoulder, then turned his attention to the second boot. A moment later that went flying over his shoulder as well. He then wasted little time in untying the stays of his hose and shoving them down.

Emma's eyes widened when his oddity was revealed. It seemed even bigger than it had been the last time she had seen it. She was suddenly extremely grateful for the foresight that had led her to dose herself.

Realizing that he had suddenly gone still, she raised her eyes to his face. The hunger was still there, but now his face showed an expression resembling pain. Frowning, Emma licked her lips. "Husband?"

Amaury groaned and closed his eyes at the sight of her little tongue darting swiftly across her lips. Hell, didn't she realize he was trying to contain himself? Did she not know the restraint needed to keep from pouncing on her? For that had been his full intention as he had torn at his clothes. Then, of course, he had managed to overcome his baser instincts long enough to remember that she was still new to this business of marital bliss. And that he had sworn to himself that the next time he forced himself on her, he would take the time to make it as pleasurable for her as he could. Or at least as painless as possible, for it was a fact ladies did not enjoy the act.

"Husband?"

Sighing, Amaury opened his eyes and forced a smile, then eased himself onto the bed beside her.

Emma gave him a slightly tense smile in return, and rolled onto her back. It was what he had ordered her to do the night of their wedding. She fully expected that he would move over top of her again and commence the joining. Instead, he merely raised his eyebrows slightly, then allowed his gaze to run down over her body. When his eyes reached the apex of her legs, Emma suddenly remembered his other instruction of that night and opened her legs.

Amaury's gaze shot immediately back to her face at the action, trying to escape the thoughts it brought immediately to his mind. Her face seemed the safest place for him to look while he regained his self-control . . . until he saw her tongue dart out again.

Groaning, he dropped his face into the pillow.

"Husband?"

"I can do this," he muttered through gritted teeth into the pillow.

"Do what, husband?"

" 'Tis not your place to ask questions, wife. Just lie there quiet."

"Aye, husband," Emma answered worriedly, her insecurities running riot. He hated her. Couldn't stand to look at her. Couldn't bear the thought of joining with her. Even now he was trying to convince himself he could manage the deed. Hell, she wished she were beautiful. Just for this night. It was shaming to be found so ugly that your husband couldn't bear the idea of getting you with child.

Amaury pressed his face deeper into the pillow and held his breath, counting to ten repeatedly as he imagined the most unpleasant things he could think of in an to attempt to control his desires.

The pock-faced old hag who made the ale.

Bathing.

His wife's tree tea. Nay. That was no good. It made him remember his wife, who at the moment was lying naked beside him.

The painful headaches he'd suffered after his head injury. Nay. That was no good either. It simply brought to mind images of her bent over him, feeling his forehead for fever.

Talking to his wife. Damn! Could she not stay out of his mind?

Emma stared helplessly at her husband's back, suffering an agony of uncertainty. Then her temper began to rouse as she watched him burrow his face deeper and deeper into the pillow. Was he trying to smother himself? Was mating with her truly a fate worse than death? Good God, this was damned insulting!

"Husband!" she snapped summarily. "I have not asked you to kill yourself, simply to close your eyes,

pretend I am more attractive to you, and do that . . .
thing . . . you did the other time. We need an heir, and
it seems you failed last time to produce one."

Amaury stilled at that, then turned his head to peer
at his wife blankly. "What said you?"

Emma sighed impatiently. "The joining, my lord."

"Nay. What mean you when you say that I *failed* to
produce an heir the last time?"

Realizing his manly pride had been wounded, she
sighed and tried to soothe him. " 'Tis sure I am, that
'twasn't your fault, my lord. Mayhap 'twas the pressure
of the consummating that was at fault for our lack of
success at getting me with child. Mayhap it weakened
your fertility, but—"

" 'Twas my *kindness* that prevented getting you with
child!" Amaury snapped. When Emma merely blinked
at him, he explained, "I did not spill my seed."

Her confused expression did not clear much at that,
and Amaury sighed impatiently. "A man must spill his
seed, planting the babe in the woman's belly. But there
was no time on our wedding night. We were interrupted
and after the pain I caused you, I thought not to force
myself on you further that night."

"Seed?" Emma murmured, glancing down at her
stomach.

"Aye."

She raised suspicious eyes to him again. "Where is
this seed you are supposed to plant?" she asked skep-
tically.

Amaury opened his mouth, closed it again, then
flushed quite red, almost purple, in fact. For a moment
Emma feared he might have a fit. Then he leapt off the
bed and strode to the door, tugging it wide open.
Framed naked in the doorway, he bellowed for his
squire.

Emma quickly covered herself with the bedclothes

before the boy raced up from the Great Hall at the summons.

"Fetch me some ale!" Amaury snapped when his squire slid to a halt at a safe distance from him. Nodding, Alden turned eagerly to flee, then froze and whirled when Amaury called out to him again. "Make it wine! Lots of it!"

Closing the door on the boy's fleeing back, he turned to survey his wife. She was an alabaster statue amidst the ebony linen of the bed. Whirling back to the door, he opened it once more. 'Twas safer to stand in the door watching for Alden's return than to face his wife and risk more questions. Damned if he was going to explain the facts of life to her. Damned if he would.

Emma stared at her husband's back in an agony of despair. Things had seemed so hopeful just moments ago when he had disrobed so quickly, but she was beginning to think his speed had had more to do with a determination to get the deed done quickly than with any eagerness on his part. Now it seemed he needed spirits to help him find the courage to perform the duty.

Her thoughts were distracted by Amaury's grunt as Alden returned. It seemed the boy had accomplished his task at lightning speed. He must have run both ways.

"What of my tankard?"

"Y-yer tankard, my lord?" Alden stuttered under his Lord's frown.

"Never mind," Amaury snapped impatiently, and slammed the door in his squire's face. Glancing at his wife, he muttered something under his breath, then tipped the bottle to his lips and emptied nearly half its contents in one long gulp.

"Prey, do not overindulge, my lord!" Emma exclaimed, slipping off the bed and hurrying to his side in an attempt to snatch the bottle away. "I have heard overindulgence can affect a man's potency."

"There is nothing wrong with my potency, wife!" Amaury snapped, pulling the bottle away from his lips and holding it out of her reach, then freezing.

Emma had left the bedclothes on the bed when she fled it. She now stood before him in all her glory. Her body stretched catlike as she hopped before him, grabbing for the bottle he held above their heads. For a moment, his eyes simply would not turn from the sight of her bouncing breasts; then he cursed and forced himself to look away. Just when he was reminding himself that he was angry with the little wench and her assumption that it was some lack in him to blame for her not being with child, she lost her balance and stumbled against him. Perhaps it was only the wine he had just consumed, but her breasts seemed as hot as the embers of a fire as they grazed across his chest.

Sucking in his breath, Amaury forgot the bottle in his hand, and unknowingly allowed it to lower to within her reach, but his little wife had quite suddenly lost interest in it as well. Instead, her gaze had now turned to her own chest, a look of astonishment on her face as she peered at her raised nipples and the way they poked out pertly toward him like buds reaching for the sun.

Swallowing, Emma raised her hands uncertainly toward herself, then paused and glanced at her husband in confusion. Her nipples were as hard as pebbles, their color a dark rose. 'Twas a situation that usually only occurred when she was cold or damp, or both, but the sensation that had raced through her just now as she had brushed against her husband's chest had not been coldness, but heat. A warm tingly sensation had flashed through her, seeming to shoot from each of her breasts to somewhere in her lower stomach.

She was still puzzling over this condition, when her husband suddenly reached out to brush the thumb of his free hand across one of the affected buds. Emma would not have believed it possible for her nipples to distend any further, but they did. . . . And the shivery feeling returned as well, shuddering through her like a small bolt of lightning that seemed to leave a trail of molten heat. She couldn't repress the small moan of mingled pleasure and fear that slipped from her lips.

Amaury was somewhat startled by that moan, for it had seemed to be one of pleasure. Yet wives were not supposed to enjoy the marriage act. Still, the sound itself started a smoldering in him that reached all the way down to his toes, and he decided quite suddenly that he wanted more of those sounds. Many more. Dropping the bottle carelessly to the floor, he caught his wife under her arms and lifted her before him until her breasts were level with his face. He then leaned forward and closed his lips around the nipple he had just touched.

"Oh." Emma's eyes widened briefly, then squinted closed. Her husband was feasting off her like the veriest baby, seeming to be almost trying to make a meal of her as he suckled, nipped, and tugged at first one nipple, then the other. 'Twas the oddest thing Emma had ever heard of a body doing . . . and she liked it. What had been a tingly sensation that zipped through her like a firefly before, now became a swell of torrid flame that licked at her insides, scorching her throughout and curling her toes.

Head dropping backward, she cried out and clutched at his shoulders for purchase as wave after wave of sensation surged through her. Emma hardly noticed when he walked to the raised bed and set her on it on her knees so that he no longer needed to hold her. Her mind was full of new demands and desires she did not understand. She gave up all attempt to unravel those thoughts, however, when his newly freed hands began traveling, for the senses they awoke would not be ignored.

She shuddered as his warm palms rose to cup her breasts, holding them and teasing them by turn as he feasted from first one, then the other. She moaned when he drew one hand away to skim it across her trembling belly before sliding it around to her behind and pulling her forward to cuddle his member. A whole new fire began then, and Emma cried out in response. Her hands moved instinctively to tangle in his hair. Clutching his head closer to the breast he attended, she trembled as his other hand suddenly dropped, grazing across her hip before feathering down her outer leg. But she jerked in his arms slightly, a gasp of startled protest on her lips, when that hand started up her inner thigh.

Catching the objection with his own lips, Amaury startled her again by sliding his tongue into her open mouth. For a moment, Emma wasn't sure what was occurring. She had never been kissed like this before. But then the fire that had been numbed by her surprise burst back to life with a vengeance, threatening to consume her as he lured her own tongue into an oddly intimate dance. She was suddenly filled with a hunger she had no idea how to sate. Clenching her fingers in his hair, she moaned wildly against his mouth, her tongue quickly becoming as demanding as his own as she pressed her body closer. Some part of her seemed determined to meld her body into his.

She was pushing herself so close and pulling him so tight, it almost hurt where their bodies were pressed together, and still she felt hollow inside. An emptiness she did not understand and could not explain seemed to cry out from the very depths of her belly, aching in places she had not known could ache. It was almost a relief when his hand finished moving upward and cupped her womanhood . . . almost. Emma sobbed and ripped her mouth away, a wail of confusion, despair, joy, and pleading torn from her lips as he slid his fingers between the curls to touch her core, his own lips slipping to her neck to suckle and nip the sensitive flesh there as he caressed her.

Emma whimpered as the fever built within her. Her body was trembling like the quiver of her bow from tension as she strained toward something she both feared and needed. She felt as if she was about to explode, as though she very well might die if she did not reach what she was clutching at. She dug her nails into her husband's back in frustration as her goal hovered stubbornly just outside reach of her terrified grasp, and Amaury nipped at her ear lightly in revenge, even as he increased the speed of his hand against her slick skin.

Just when Emma felt sure she would shatter into pieces in his arms, the control Amaury had been clutching at so desperately snapped and he withdrew his hands to push her back. She felt the bed embracing her. Then her husband came down on top of her as he had on their wedding night, his mouth taking hers savagely once more as he plunged into her.

Emma's eyes flew open in shock at this intrusion. She recognized it at once as the same that had occurred on her wedding night. Only this time there was no pain, just unbearable pleasure as he moved against her. His body enclosed in hers and wrapped around her, he drove her back to the pinnacle she had stood on before he had pushed her back on the bed. Then, with one last forceful plunge and a shout of success as he reached his own heights, Amaury shoved her off the world to float in the stars as she burst into a thousand sparks of light.

Chapter Eight

Emma opened her eyes slowly. Amaury had covered her while she slept. Partially. The bedclothes reached just past her waist, leaving her upper body bare and revealing the small marks left behind by his ardor. A flush covered her cheeks as she recalled just how she had gained those marks and she smiled wryly as she thought of the ale and potions she had taken to ease the pain of joining.

"What do you smile at wife?"

Glancing to the side quickly, Emma blushed anew as she saw her husband lying on his side watching her. She wondered briefly how long he had lain there staring at her as she slept, then shrugged as she admitted, "I was thinking I now understand why some women have so many children."

A purely male smile curving his lips, Amaury chuckled deep in his chest, his hand moving to cup the breast nearest him. Emma's body responded at once, her nip-

155

ple growing hard and alert before he covered it with his mouth, nipping at it teasingly, then suckling it by turn. He didn't bother to hide the chuckle of satisfaction that whispered across her skin when she shifted restlessly beneath his attention and arched into his caress.

"You like my touch."

Emma's ardor cooled slightly at the arrogance in his tone, her pride prickling. "Aye," she said calmly after a moment's thought, then added silkily, " 'Tis sorry I am that my first husband could not bring himself to the marriage bed. Think of all the pleasure I have missed."

Amaury stilled at once, his head lifting to spear her with a look before she could hide the satisfaction in her face. Eyes slitting slightly, he watched her closely as he continued to palm her breast, then as quick as a hawk, his hand dipped down between her legs and he plunged a finger into her tight opening.

Emma gasped and squeezed her legs closed, her hands moving to push his away, but he would not be denied. With cool deliberation, he pushed his finger in and out, his thumb rubbing the nubbin where all sensation seemed to be centered. Closing her eyes, she tried to fight the feelings swelling up inside her, but it was impossible. Giving in, she cried out and arched into his touch.

"Think you Fulk would have made you feel like this?"

"N-noooo. Oh, please," Emma begged, reaching to clutch at his arm, groaning and arching higher when his thumb began to massage her faster.

Amaury watched his wife with satisfaction for a moment, taking in the fire in her eyes and passion's flush on her cheek as she made little gasping sounds and writhed beneath his touch, but then a thought raised some discontent in him.

Ladies were not supposed to enjoy the bedding.

Plunging his finger deeper, Amaury watched her buck

against the action and began to frown. God's truth, she
wasn't behaving like a lady at all, let alone a Duchess,
he thought with disgruntlement. Her head was twisting
frantically, her legs spread on the bed, knees drawn up
slightly and heels digging deep as she pushed her hips
upward seeking the release he offered.

His frown turned to a scowl when she began moaning
and whimpering. Then he stopped touching her altogether and lay back on the bed to scowl at the drapings
above them.

Emma stiffened, her eyes shooting open at his with-
drawal. Her body was heavy and achy with need as she
took in his grim expression. For a moment she did not
know what to do, then her gaze dropped to his oddity.
He was as stiff as a Maypole. Deciding he was teasing
her for her taunt about her first husband, Emma caught
him unawares by rolling on top of him. It made perfect
sense to her. After all, if the horse would not come to
the rider, the rider must go mount the horse, she
thought with determination, pushing herself to sit
astride his hips.

Amaury no longer looked so grim. Instead, he quite
suddenly looked dismayed. Emma took a moment to
ponder that, then rubbed herself instinctively against
his member.

"What do you?" he asked, looking almost scandal-
ized. His hands came up to clasp her waist to lift her
away, but Emma rubbed against him again and he
stilled, clasping her, but not moving her away as his
expression tightened.

Grunting her satisfaction, Emma moved against him
again, her hands braced on his chest as she pleasured
herself against the base of his staff. Amaury lay as still
as death for a while, struggling to control his desires
enough to order her off of him, but it seemed an impossible feat. He simply could not manage it. Instead

of easing, his ardor was mounting by the moment. Still, he held out until he was so roused it hurt, then lifted and shifted his little wife so that she came down hard on his manhood before rolling her onto her back once more and taking over again.

Emma was relieved to leave him to it, for she found it hard to keep to a rhythm as he did and found that rather than increase her own pleasure she had dampened it somewhat. She was just beginning to think she had ruined everything with her inept fumblings, when he suddenly reached a hand down between them to stimulate her again.

Amaury grunted as his wife began moaning and crying again. For a few moments there she had gone still and silent, her expression showing uncertainty and disappointment. Oddly enough, rather than please him, that had seemed to affect his own pleasure, reducing it a great deal. Against his own better instincts, he had then begun to stimulate her again. Now she was bucking and sobbing his name like he was God. It made him feel damn good. . . . and it was just the trick for his flagging desires. At this rate, he could ride her all night, he thought and silently thanked a fool named Fulk.

"Good morning, my lords. You both look fit on this fine day."

Blake couldn't help but return Emma's bright smile as she breezed by on her way to the kitchens. "She appears in good cheer this morn."

"Aye," Amaury muttered glumly.

Blake's eyebrows rose as he watched him slam his tankard down on the table. "Is aught amiss?"

"Nay." He raised his tankard, slammed it down again, then suddenly turned to his friend. "Our wedding night was rushed and painful for her."

Blake's eyebrows rose, but he nodded solemnly.

"There was much pressure."

"Aye," Amaury growled, swilling some more ale before punishing the table with his mug once more. "I left off approaching her after that because of it. I thought to give her time to adjust and to allow the memory of the ordeal to fade."

"Hmm." Blake was almost afraid to speak and inadvertently bring an end to this conversation. It was becoming most interesting.

"Then last night . . ." Amaury hesitated and frowned.

"Ah," Blake murmured delicately with a nod, allowing a moment to pass before glancing again at his friend. "I take it by her demeanor today that it could be considered a success?"

Amaury grimaced. "She has been smiling ever since. 'Tis indecent."

Blake burst out laughing at the rancor in his friend's voice, then slapped him on the back. "Truly, friend, I wish I had your problems. This fine estate. No parents or in-laws to interfere . . . well, except for Lord Rolfe, of course. And a wife who enjoys bedding you. 'Tis a sin for any man to be so lucky."

Amaury gave a disgruntled shrug. "But ladies are not supposed to enjoy the bedding," he complained, and Blake sighed.

"Do you not enjoy her?"

Amaury peered at him as though he thought he were mad.

"And does her pleasure take away from yours?" Blake asked patiently, smiling slightly at the gleam that suddenly entered his friend's eyes.

"Nay. In truth it fires me up."

"Then there is naught to worry about," he said simply.

Amaury glowered again. "But ladies are not supposed to enjoy—"

"Aye, aye," Blake said impatiently. "I have heard the priests' claims that ladies forbear and all that. But priests are just men, and men have been wrong afore. Are you going to sit about complaining about this, or enjoy your good fortune?"

"Both, I think," he admitted honestly, and Blake rolled his eyes.

"Then complain to someone else. I do not have the time to listen to the whining of someone too dull-headed to count his blessings," he said dryly, turning back to his meal.

Amaury glared at him for a moment, then turned irritably back to his own meal.

"My lady?"

"Aye, Sebert?" Emma continued stirring the pot of steaming liquid she had set over the fire. She was making some more of the damiana concoction for her husband. It seemed to her to be in everyone's best interests to keep his ardor hot until they conceived. The king was counting on her to protect him from Bertrand and his grasping mother. Besides, after last night and learning what the joining was truly all about, Emma found she did not mind it a bit.

"My lady?"

Emma glanced at her steward, concern covering her face. He looked vexed. Sebert very rarely looked vexed. He was usually as placid as a cow.

"There is a . . . *man* . . . in the hall," he told her grimly, injecting the word "man" with an odd distaste.

Emma straightened slowly, wiping her hands on a cloth. "A man?"

Sebert's mouth worked briefly, then he blurted out, "A pompous little peacock named Monsieur de Lascey. He's sashaying about the Great Hall as though he owned the place. He says Lord Rolfe sent him."

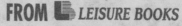
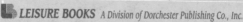

Get Four Books Totally
FREE — A $21.96 Value

▼ Tear Here and Mail Your FREE Book Card Today! ▼

PLEASE RUSH
MY FOUR FREE
BOOKS TO ME
RIGHT AWAY!

Leisure Romance Book Club
P.O. Box 6613
Edison, NJ 08818-6613

"The tailor!" Emma's hand flew to her chest in dismay. She had quite forgotten all about asking her cousin to send her a tailor to have clothes made for the trip to court.

Lifting her pot off the fire until she could return to it, she led the way out into the Great Hall, eyebrows rising when she spotted the little man posed in front of the fireplace. Posed was the only word for it. She suspected he was trying for a decidedly superior look as he leaned an elbow on the stone wall around the fireplace, looking down his nose at the Great Hall, its contents, and the two serving women clearing away breakfast in their black garb.

Emma tried not to wince at her servants' clothing. It was evidence of her distress at the time, but blacking everything in the castle seemed foolish even to her now that she had gotten past her temporary madness. She could only wonder that her servants had been good enough to go along with her actions without a single word of protest.

Perhaps they had believed her mad and decided to humor her, she thought with a sigh as de Lascey turned his emaciated face to her and peered down his sliver-thin nose in distaste at her own black gown.

"Monsieur de Lascey. How good of you to come." Despite her irritation with his attitude, Emma managed to force some welcome into her voice.

His disdain did not slip a bit as he accepted her hand in a limp grip of his own. "*De rien.* Your coosin said zat you would make eet worth my while," he drawled in an odd French accent.

"Why, of course," Emma said stiltedly. "I realize 'tis an imposition to make you travel all this way, and I shall reward you accordingly."

Managing a nod and a snooty sniff at the same moment, de Lascey returned to his pose, gazing into the

161

fire as he announced, "I shall need zee three rooms. One for zee fittings. One for zee *fabrique* and one *pour moi*. My servants will sleep in zee ozer *deux* rooms."

"Servants?" Emma raised an eyebrow, then turned as the Great Hall door burst open and at least half-a-dozen women came clamoring in, arms loaded with rolls of fabric. It seemed Rolfe had made it clear that she would be needing a great deal of clothes made in a rather short time. "Sebert?"

"Aye, my lady?"

"See Monsieur de Lascey and his workers to Lord Rolfe's room, the room Lord Fulk used when he was here, and the room in between," she instructed, then excused herself and retreated to the kitchen once more.

Ten minutes later, Sebert was at her side again. "My lady?"

One glance at his face was enough to make her set the pot of damiana aside and give her full attention to him. Emma did not think she had ever seen him quite so put out.

"The peacock is demanding your presence," Sebert informed her grimly.

She felt herself stiffen at those words. "Demanding?"

"Aye." He nodded slowly, then added through gritted teeth, "At once."

Muttering under her breath, Emma started for the door, but paused to step out of the way as it swung open to allow four of de Lascey's female workers to enter.

"Apologies, my lady." The women hurried out of the way at once when they saw her about to leave. "Mister de Lascey said we might come fetch a drink. 'Twas a long trip and—"

"Aye, of course," Emma interrupted with a smile, then glanced at Sebert.

"I will see to it, my lady," he assured her at once, not

even bothering to glance away from the woman who
had spoken.

Emma's eyebrows rose slightly at his expression. It
seemed he was quite taken with the seamstress, Emma
realized suddenly, noting for the first time that her
steward was actually a quite attractive man for his age.
He was always so grave and diligent about his duties
that she had never really paid attention to his looks before. Now, seeing the shy smile on the seamstress's face,
she realized that he actually cut quite a dashing figure
in his solemn clothes.

Shaking her head slightly, she stepped past the
women and crossed the Great Hall toward the stairs.
No doubt the pompous little popinjay wanted to start
fittings right away. She really could not blame him for
that. There were a lot of clothes to be made in a very
short time. However, she suspected his attitude would
not have improved in the short time since his arrival
and she would have a trying few hours ahead of her.

Emma was not mistaken.

In the two hours she spent cooped up in the small
bedchamber designated as the fitting room, she found
herself driven to the point of contemplating the benefits
of murder several times. None of the fabrics she favored
were "quite right" according to de Lascey, nor were the
styles she chose. As for her figure, while he had no complaint with her waist and hips, he fretted endlessly over
her chest. It was not the fashion to be so buxom, he
kept saying. Her "boosums" would ruin any design he
chose to grace her with. "Zey would have to be bound."

By the time the nooning hour rolled around and she
was able to escape, Emma had been clenching her teeth
so hard for so long that she had a pounding headache.
The noise and clamor in the Great Hall when she entered to join the midday meal simply aggravated the
ailment. Emma briefly considered putting off returning

Lynsay Sands

to the fitting room and retiring for a nap after lunch until the ache had gone, but then decided there was little use in that. The ache would no doubt return the moment she returned to de Lascey's presence, and she would have to do that eventually if she wished new clothes for court. It was best to simply get it over with.

The scrape of something heavy being pushed along the stone floor drew Emma's gaze from her lunch to the room around her. Her eyebrows knitted in bewildered surprise as she saw that the men had finished their meal and were on their feet, pushing the long trestle tables against the walls.

"Husband? What happens here?" she asked, frowning over the activity.

Amaury stilled, his tankard halfway to his mouth as he realized guiltily that he had not informed his wife of his plans for the day. He had intended to tell her last night that he planned to hold court. But then she had behaved so oddly and the worry of her being ill had come up, and then the surprising occurrence of her baring herself to his sight had transpired, followed by the torrid interlude when he had finally made love to her. . . .

Frowning at Amaury for his silence, Blake leaned forward to speak around him. " 'Tis for court, Lady Emma."

"For court?"

"Aye." His forehead furrowed at her expression. "Did you not know he was to hold court today?"

"Nay," Emma said heavily.

Amaury frowned at the censure in her voice.

"Why are they clearing the room so?" she asked, unable to keep the anger out of her voice.

Blake glanced at his friend's surly expression, then answered the petite woman himself. "Amaury thought 'twould be better to make more room. The people have

164

been neglected for so long that he is sure there will be many complaints."

"Neglected?" she repeated carefully.

"Aye. Well. We are aware that Fulk was much absent. Doubtless he had not bothered with a court day for quite awhile before his death."

"Nay, he did not. He did not hold court once in the two years after our marriage," Emma admitted grimly, then added, "I did."

Amaury was startled into speech at that. "You?"

"Aye. I ruled in my husband's absence," she pointed out with a distinct chill to her tone. "I saw to the running of the castle, the training of the men, and presiding over court."

Blake raised his eyebrows. "*You* saw to the training of the men?"

"Well, I saw that they had a proper trainer," she said quickly.

"Hmm." Amaury eyed her silently for a moment, his mind considering that. He had been quite surprised at how well trained her men had been. He had expected them to be lazy and inept. Instead they had been skilled and hardworking. Not as skilled as his own men, of course, but then his men were warriors. The best in the kingdom. Still, they were skilled. She had done well in seeing to their training.

He briefly considered commending her on her efforts, then decided against it. He would most likely embarrass her with such improper praise. Women preferred compliments on their looks and the running of the household to praise of their abilities in such manly matters as training for battle.

Emma peered silently at the transformation of her Great Hall. It was the custom for the lord to hold court once a month for his people, to hear their complaints and resolve any differences between them. It was a chore Emma had aided her father with before marrying and then taken over completely after moving here. As they had thought, Fulk had shown as little concern for his people and their problems as he had for his wife.

She supposed that, had she thought about it, she would have expected her new husband to take over the duty. Amaury was not as unconcerned with his people as Fulk had been. Still, she would not have expected him to simply take over the task in such a summary way, and she certainly would not have expected to hear about it like this. It seemed she was the very last to know. Even the servants had been aware of it before her. She found she wasn't just angry, she was hurt. After last night . . .

Sighing, she drew her eyes away from the men before her and peered at her hands as they twisted in her lap. Last night had been exciting and even beautiful. Emma had thought that they had shared something . . . special. She had felt that they were closer now. She had hoped that they would talk more, get to know each other better, discuss things. It seemed her husband did not feel the same way, she realized disheartenedly. She glanced toward him now, only to find that he no longer sat there. He and Blake had moved to stand by the fire while she was caught in her thoughts.

Rising, she moved to join them. "My lord?" She paused in surprise at the anger on his face as he turned to her, then took a breath and forced herself to continue. "I thought that since I am already apprised of the problems and past complaints of the villagers and servants, mayhap you would like my assistance."

"I need no interference, wife," Amaury snapped irritably. " 'Tis insulting for you to think that I might."

"I merely thought—"

"Have you so little faith in my abilities as lord?"

166

"Nay," Emma said quickly, trying to soothe his hurt pride. "But—"

"But nothing, wife. You see to your business and I shall tend to mine." Amaury turned to walk away, but got only halfway to the head table before stopping. He had not meant to be so short with her. In truth he knew he should have told her himself, and the fact that he had forgotten to had made him angry with himself. It had not helped that Blake had dragged him off into the corner to lecture him for not telling her and hurting her tender feelings. Again. Amaury was heartily sick of being told how to take care of his own wife. He turned back now with the intention of apologizing to her, but she was no longer by the fireplace where he had left her. She was mounting the stairs to return to her fittings.

He started to follow her to apologize, but just then the first of the villagers and servants with complaints to present before him began to file into the room. Sighing, he decided to leave it until later, and turned to begin court.

"Finalement!" Hands propped on his hips, de Lascey glared as he sashayed across the fitting room to confront her when she stepped through the door. "How do *vous* expect *moi* to get anyzing done when you are not available for zee measuring?"

For zee torturing, more like, Emma thought grimly, but pasted a penitent expression on her face and offered her apology. "My apologies, Monsieur de Lascey. I was delayed."

"Hmm." Pursing his lips, he eyed her doubtfully, then gave a dramatic sigh and turned to strut across the room. "Gytha, bring me zee gold cloth!"

Two hours later, Emma was standing on a stool in the center of the room, her gown discarded and her

Lynsay Sands

shift hidden beneath yards of a gold cloth that was draped and pinned about her body. Her back was to the door of the room. She did not see her husband enter, so when he called her name from behind, she nearly fell off the stool in her surprise.

Smiling gratefully at Gytha, the seamstress who had grabbed her arm quickly to steady her, Emma turned carefully on the stool to face her husband.

"I . . ." He paused, his eyes widening incredulously at the sight of her swathed in gold. It was the first time Amaury had seen his wife in anything other than black. Even when she'd been naked, it was in the bedroom with a backdrop of black linens on the bed. Damn, but she looked lovely, he thought admiringly. Like an angel. Beautiful . . . Ethereal . . . Glowing . . . Flat . . .

Flat? Blinking, he focused his gaze directly on her chest, or where her chest used to be. "God's wounds, where be they?!"

Emma frowned in confusion. "Where be what, my lord?"

"Your . . . Your . . ." Lifting his hands, he held them before his own chest as if cupping two invisible melons to his plate mail.

"My lord!" Flushing deep red, Emma glanced askance at the others in the room. The women were rather wide-eyed, but the tailor looked as if he were about to burst out laughing. That expression was replaced by one of dismay when Amaury suddenly crossed the room and lifted him up by the front of his collar.

"What did you with my wife's b—"

"Bound!" the man squawked at once.

Frowning, Amaury cocked his head. "Bound?"

"They are still there, my lord. I simply bound them up. Gytha did it," he added quickly when Amaury's expression darkened. His accent was noticeably absent. "I, of course, would ne'er lay a finger to her—"

168

"Well, have her unbind them!" Amaury roared, interrupting him.

"Of course, right away."

"Nay, husband," Emma protested. "They will simply have to bind them again after you leave." Though she would have been grateful for the chance to be able to really breathe again, her breasts had just finally gone numb. It was painful to have your chest squished so flat. She did not wish to go through that again.

Still holding the tailor off the floor, Amaury turned to frown at her. "Why do they bind them at all?"

"For the fittings."

"But then your dresses will not fit."

"They will when I bind my chest." When his expression began to darken as understanding set in, Emma repeated what she had been told over and over again all morning. " 'Tis not fashionable to be so generously endowed."

"So you intend to tie them up?! Like Lady Gresham does with her dogs when company comes?!" He looked nonplussed by the very idea. "They are not dogs, wife! I like them! They'll not be bound!" Turning to the tailor, he gave him a sharp shake. "Is that understood!"

"Aye, my lord. Certainly. No binding of your wife's breasts. I'll remove the dress so Gytha can unbind her at once."

"Aye, ye will!" he roared into his face, then shook him again, his expression darkening. "Nay, ye'll not. Ye'll not be undressing my wife!" Dropping the little man, he strode to Emma and swung her off the stool into his arms, then strode toward the door.

Clasping her arms around Amaury's neck, Emma repressed a smile and shrugged at the tailor as her husband saved her from several hours of being poked, criticized, primped, and pinned.

He carried her directly to their room, set her down

beside the bed, and began tugging at the material draped around her. Emma was silent until the pinned-up gown was a pool of gold on the floor. Amaury then started on the binding.

As soon as the last of the cloth that had bound her slipped away, Emma's breasts came screaming back to life. When her husband then reached to touch the aching orbs, she immediately distracted him. "Did you want something, my lord?"

Amaury paused and stared at her blankly. There were a great many things he wanted at that moment. To get his wife naked and in bed was not least among them. It was something he had wanted quite frequently since their wedding, but seeing her bedecked in gold had raised that want to a fever pitch.

"You did come to the fitting room for a reason, did you not?" she prodded when he was silent for so long.

"The fitting room? Oh, aye. Aye." Sighing, he let his hands fall back to his sides and took a step back. Now that he had been reminded of the reason for approaching her, it seemed more important to discuss it . . . first. " 'Tis sorry I am I did not speak to you about holding court. 'Twas wrong for you to have to hear about it as you did."

He peered over her expression closely and sighed once more. "I also regret having called your offer of assistance an interference. In future you shall stand beside me at court and have a say in any decisions made. 'Tis your place."

When Emma suddenly smiled widely at him, Amaury paused and swallowed. Damn, but it was like the sun coming out after months of winter. Feeling like a drowning man reaching for help, Amaury reached for his wife. His hands tried to touch her everywhere at once as his mouth descended on hers. He settled for grasping her chemise and tugging it upward to remove the cloth that hampered his hands from caressing her skin.

Emma tugged her mouth away at once as she felt cool air graze across the hips he was baring. She had intended to ask him how court had gone, but the moment she stepped away, Amaury took advantage of their separation to tug her gown over her head. Then he pulled her back into his arms and drove the question from her mind with his passion.

Chapter Nine

"Nay."

"But, husband."

"I said nay!" Amaury slammed the bedroom door and strode down the hall toward the stairs.

"Do not tell me you have allowed your annoyance with your wife's pleasure in her duty to persuade you to refuse her that duty all together?"

Pausing at the top of the stairs, Amaury glanced back to see Blake a step behind him. Grimacing, he shook his head. Had it been merely the joining his wife had wanted, he would have happily complied. Amaury had quite gotten over the problem of her enjoying the act. Twice he had tried to refrain from enflaming her passions with his touch before mounting her, and both times he had found the endeavor trying and sadly disappointing. It seemed he enjoyed her enjoyment. Therefore, he had decided—quite magnanimously, in his opinion—to take the blame for his little wife's flaw himself. After all, he was the one who made her enjoy it. Without his touch or kisses, she was as limp as a wet tunic in the bed and forbore his attentions silently, just as other lady wives were said to do. So, her unladylike behavior was obviously his fault.

It was perfect logic to Amaury, and it soothed his worries about how ladies should or shouldn't behave, allowing him to enjoy her at every opportunity. Which he had proceeded to do these last three days since seeking her out in the tailor's room. Which was also what he had been in the process of doing when she had announced that that French jackanapes required his presence for fittings today.

Amaury's passion had shriveled up like a grape in the sun at her announcement, as had his manhood, which had simply added to his irritation, causing him to snap his refusal to his wife before pushing away from her to dress himself. He found the loathsome little tailor's pomposity unbearable enough at mealtimes; putting up with it between meals was unthinkable. Besides, he didn't need any more clothes. He already had two tunics. That was enough. It always left him with one to wear while the other was being laundered.

Still, he thought with a sigh now, he should not have been so short with her. He had probably hurt her feelings, and she did seem to be very sensitive. He had come to that conclusion after three days when he had subjected himself to the difficulty of actually "talking" to her. He had been serious when he had said that she would stand beside him at court and have a say in all decisions. These were her people too. She had ruled them quite well on her own without his interference. That being the case, he owed it to her to include her in decisions he made now.

But talking to a wife was a difficult task. At least it had been at first. It was not like talking to your comrades at all. If his wife represented all women, then it would seem they were a sensitive lot. He made decisions based on practicality and justice. Emma seemed to think one should include such considerations as feelings and intentions. She was most thoughtful, thinking of the things that he did not. It had distressed him at first, but eventually he had come to understand her softer nature and find it a fine compliment to his own harder, more pragmatic one. Things were not always black or white; his little wife seemed able to see the gray as well. Finally, after three days of stumbling awkwardly through conversations with her, he'd found it much easier and more rewarding. He was proud to say it. His wife had a fine mind.

"Nay," he said in answer to Blake's question now. " 'Twas not the joining she wanted. She was trying to persuade me to spend the day locked up in a room with that French peacock, being measured. She seems to think I need more clothes."

"Ah." Blake shrugged. "Well, you do only have the two tunics. Mayhaps she is afraid you will be embarrassed at court."

Amaury rolled his eyes at that. "I have been to court afore. The people who clutter its halls are vain and foolish. I do not care for their opinions."

"Mayhap she does."

Amaury frowned at that suggestion. "What mean you?"

"Just what I said, mayhap she cares what they think."

Amaury shifted uncomfortably, worry crossing his features. "Think you she will be embarrassed to be at court with me?"

Shrugging, Blake moved past him and started down the stairs. "She is a duchess, Amaury. And you are now a duke. The title brings certain expectations."

"Damn!"

Pausing, Blake turned back. Amaury still stood at the top of the stairs, a stunned expression on his face. Before he could comment, a door opened down the hall. Glancing that way, he saw Lady Emma come out of the bedroom Amaury had exited moments ago.

Seeing her annoyed expression before she turned her head away to ignore him and moved toward the room the peacock inhabited, Amaury sighed and hurried down the stairs past his friend. He would go to the blasted fittings then if it meant so much to her, he thought irritably, but he was damned if he would tell her so now. He did not even wish to think about the sorry chore until he had put something in his belly.

Emma was crossing the bailey after the nooning meal, headed for the stables, when she spotted her husband surveying his men as they practiced. Frowning, she turned her stride and headed in his direction. She had been most surprised when he had announced his change of mind this morning after breaking fast. He had made his dislike for the tailor very clear before storming out of their room at dawn, and yet had agreed with obvious reluctance to attend the fittings de Lascey had ordered.

Emma had spent the morning busy in the Great Hall, seeing to all those things she had neglected during the three torturous days of her own fittings. God's truth, de Lascey's attitude was a trial to bear. She had been fully understanding as she had heard her husband repeatedly roaring from above stairs. That had not prevented her from laughing over it, however. Now, though, it seemed her husband had changed his mind again, and she was determined to find out exactly why he had not returned to the fitting room after lunch.

Amaury sighed as he saw his wife approaching. She had that determined set about her that he was beginning to recognize. No doubt he had angered her again somehow. It did seem his wife got a bee in her cap quite regularly. At least since the French turnip had arrived, he thought grimly. After having spent a morning in the repugnant little bedbug's presence, he fully understood why.

"Good afternoon, Lady Emma." Blake gave her a smile that had melted many a woman's heart, managing to irritate his friend no end. Amaury graced him with a glare, then greeted his wife as well.

"Wife."

Emma got right to the point. "Why are you not at your fittings, husband?"

"My fittings are done," Amaury announced dryly. When she looked skeptical, he shrugged. "You may ask him if you wish, but the French turnip said he would not need me back this afternoon."

"But *my* fittings took three days," she complained.

Amaury leaned forward to murmur by her ear, "Mayhap there is more of you to measure." A wicked grin curving his lips, he let his eyes drop to her chest.

Blushing as memories of the night before flashed into her mind, Emma shook her head at her husband, then turned to continue on toward the stables.

"Wife?"

Pausing, she turned to peer back. "Aye?"

Amaury gave her a stern look, then scowled when that had no effect and pointed at the ground directly in front of him.

Sighing, she moved back to stand before him.

"Where go you?"

"I need to collect more herbs."

"In the woods?"

"Aye."

"You will take six men."

Emma grimaced, but nodded and turned to move away once more.

"Wife."

Pausing again, she peered back, only to mutter under her breath and return to stand in front of him once more when he raised one eyebrow grimly. "Husband, I do not have time for this. The day grows late."

Amaury merely peered at her thoughtfully for a moment, his head tilted to the side, before asking, "What do you with all these weeds, wife?"

"I—they are for medicines," she mumbled, flushing guiltily.

"Hmm." Amaury's head tilted to the other side. "Are you ill?"

"Nay, of course not."

"Then who is? You seem to use a great deal of them. You have gone out to collect them at least—"

"There are a lot of people within the castle, my lord," Emma blurted out quickly. "O'er a hundred and eighty including the servants and your men. Someone is always ill." Pausing, she took a breath, then asked nervously, "Was that all, husband?"

"Aye. Nay," he denied as he recalled why he had called her back. He had decided that now was as good a time as any to inform her he did not wish her to have the popinjay make a single dress in black. "About your gowns the French mouse is making . . ."

"Aye, my lord?"

Amaury hesitated. "I do not wish to see you in . . . You will refrain from having de Lascey make any in black. All your gowns are to be of bright colors."

When she raised her eyebrows at that, he reached out to rub a silky tress of her hair between his fingers, his expression softening and his voice deepening as he said, "Several gowns in that gold you wore the other day would be nice. 'Twas as radiant as the color of your hair."

"My hair?" Emma blinked at that, finding a slow curl of heat unfurling in her belly at the deep tone to his voice. It was the same one he used in their bed when he was murmuring what he wanted, either from her, or to do to her.

"Aye. And one or two in a shade of green like your eyes. As rich as the woods after a rain." His hand moved to feather across her brow by one of those eyes that was as wide as an apple right then, then slid to run gently across her bottom lip.

Emma breathed in deeply, then swallowed, feeling the touch on her lips as if it had been on her breasts. The Good Lord's liver, she thought dreamily. It seemed her husband need not even touch her there to touch her there.

"And at least a dozen in red."

"Red?" Her eyes widened.

"Aye, a red as luscious as your lips when I kiss them."

"Ohhh," Emma breathed, swaying toward him. The sounds of mock battle and men's yells faded in her head as she watched Amaury's face drift closer. When his lips finally found hers, she sighed dreamily. Only to gasp and pull quickly away at Blake's startled shout. A glance in his direction showed that he had stumbled over a pair of playing children, no doubt as he had tried to back discreetly away.

Emma shook her head as she watched him regain his feet. He looked quite embarrassed. Smiling, she walked to his side and patted his shoulder. "Thank you."

Blake's eyebrows rose at that. "For what, my lady?"

"For the lovely compliments you gave my husband to use."

He flushed bright red at that, his eyes shooting to Amaury, who was looking quite upset. They had practiced for hours exactly how to phrase the words, the tone of voice to use, and even the caresses to accompany them with. All to no avail, it seemed.

After searing his hapless friend with a fierce glare, Amaury straightened his shoulders and turned back to her.

"Blake may have aided me in phrasing them, but the words were true," he told her grumpily. "I do not wish to see you in black. You should only wear colors such as gold. You were. . . ." He frowned, searching for words of his own. "You fired my blood in the gold, and 'tis sure I am that you will please me in red or green as well."

Emma's eyes widened at that, and a slow smile started on her lips, but her husband was not finished. It seemed he thought a lecture was in order.

"As your husband, 'tis my place to recognize your needs and fulfill them. I have noticed that you are in sore need of esteem. The only way to build that up is to give you compliments."

" 'Tis?" Surprise was evident on her face.

"Aye. So . . . there you are. You are lovely, wife," he told her stiffly. "In fact, I have never set eyes upon as lovely a woman as you are. Fulk was a fool not to have recognized his good fortune in finding you. You are fair lovely."

Emma merely stared at him. Some part of her mind was daring to tell her that he must have some affection for her to be so concerned with issues such as her esteem. Another part was telling her not to be so foolish.

"Well?"

Emma blinked. "Well, what, my lord?"

"Have you nothing to say? I said you were lovely. You *are* lovely."

"If you say so, my lord," Emma murmured dutifully, then headed away again, her mind taken up with the possibility that her husband might have some real feeling for her. Not the dutiful love a husband must have for a wife, but one born of liking and respect. A husband need not see to a wife's feelings, yet Amaury concerned himself often with hers. That must mean something, she thought hopefully.

Amaury glared after her in vexation. "She agreed only to placate me."

"That would be my guess," Blake agreed. "Mayhap you should go convince her."

"What?"

Blake shrugged. "Everything is in hand here. We thought you would be in fittings all day. Why not join her on this trip to the woods and give her a tumble? That should let her know you find her desirable."

Amaury scowled at him. "I do not tumble my wife. She is a lady. 'Sides," he added grimly, "none of my other tumblings seem to have raised her confidence in her looks." But even as he offered the protest, his mind had been caught by the image of making love to his wee wife in the woods. Emma, naked and natural with naught but grass for a bed, the sky for a roof, and trees as the walls of the room . . . And not a stitch of black anywhere to be seen. He would have to get her completely naked, he determined. He did not even wish to see a bit of black hose.

"Then compliment her while you tumble her."

Amaury's imaginings faded slightly at that. "Compliment her while . . . ?"

"Aye. Tell her what you like about her while you're loving her."

He considered that briefly, his gaze running down the length of her body as she paused to talk to the stable master just outside the stable doors. "She has a fine mind. The finest mind I have ever found in a woman."

Blake rolled his eyes at that. "I think you can leave that compliment out. Stay with things you find attractive about her looks. Tell her what you like and why."

His mind filling with all sorts of things he liked about her, Amaury murmured thoughtfully, "Aye, mayhap that will work." His eyes began to sparkle with something other than good humor as he inventoried each individual part of her anatomy, the reasons he liked them, and things he would like to do to them. "Aye, I will." Ignoring his friend's laughter, he headed off after his wife.

Amaury peered at his wife in repose and smiled. He had loved her well and thoroughly, revealing each inch of her body and explaining what he liked about it as he went. It had been most satisfactory. He was now positive he had gone a long way toward mending her esteem problem.

The snapping of a twig nearby drew his narrowed eyes to the surrounding woods, but there was nothing to see. Still, the memory of the attacking bandits was now brought to mind and Amaury frowned, wondering if he truly should have dismissed the guards that had prepared to accompany Emma on this trip. He had only been thinking of loving her in the woods, not of any danger there might be.

A second sound, a rustling, this time nearer, made him stiffen further as he realized how vulnerable they were at the moment.

"Wife."

Emma's eyes popped open, a shy smile coming to her lips as she met his gentle, if concerned gaze.

"Come. 'Tis growing late," he murmured in a normal voice, not wishing to worry her.

Sitting up slowly, Emma peered toward her half full basket, recalling that she had yet to collect the burdock she had wanted. Her husband had quite distracted her from her task after only fifteen minutes of watching her poke through the woods. "I needs must collect some more—"

"Nay. Dress," he ordered softly, handing her her clothes.

Emma frowned, her eyebrows rising, but did as she was told even as he stood to dress as well. Amaury was much quicker than she, his clothes on and sword in hand before she had managed to re-don her tunic. By the time she had her gown on, he had brought the horses over and was soothing their nervous movements as he peered at the trees surrounding them.

It was then Emma realized there was a problem. The horses were nervous and so was Amaury.

"Is something amiss?" she whispered, stepping to his side.

He did not answer, did not even look at her. Expression grim, he merely lifted her silently onto her mount, then moved toward his own. It was then that the first man stepped out of the surrounding woods. He was followed by three more.

"To the castle!" Amaury roared. Slapping the rump of her horse, he sent it lurching off into the woods carrying her to safety, then turned to face the men now closing in upon him. Each one carried a sword and two of them had full mail on. It was hard to make love in armor so Amaury had forsaken his for this short jaunt. A mistake.

His gaze swept over the attackers again, taking their measure. Mercenaries. Not very successful ones either, he decided, noting the poorer quality of the armor they sported. Successful or not, he feared he might very well be returning to his little wife draped across his mount's back. Their numbers and what little skill they possessed were more than enough to bring down a lone man.

Even a warrior as proficient as himself, Amaury thought, putting his back to a tree with resignation.

Amaury had slapped her horse so hard, it took Emma a bit of time to regain control and slow her down. Bringing the nervous animal to a complete halt, she urged her back around toward the clearing. She knew she should probably obey her husband and return to the castle to await his return. He did dislike being disobeyed. Besides, he could well take care of himself. But then, so could her cousin, yet she had saved his sorry hide a time or two.

She would just check on him, Emma told herself as she urged her horse into a gallop. If all seemed well, she would leave him to it and follow his instructions. If not . . . She wished suddenly that she had brought her bow.

All thoughts of her bow flew from her mind when her mare jumped a bush and crashed down unexpectedly into the clearing. It seemed they had not ridden as far away as she had thought. Amaury was going to be furious.

Emma had little time to worry over that, however. Even as she began to slow her mare, she recognized the unfair odds her husband faced. Cursing, she used the only weapon she had to aid him, her horse. Urging the mount to speed up again, Emma tugged her reins hard to the left, toward the nearest of the villains. The mare responded at once, bearing down on the man in her path.

Warned by the sound of pounding hooves, that unfortunate man was already turning. Catching a glimpse of the horse and rider, he immediately tried to throw himself to the side, but Emma turned her mare to follow, wincing inwardly as he fell beneath the hooves.

The second man was a surprising bonus. Emma had merely been following the first man, but he had led her horse into the path of the second one who now drew up his sword to deflect the mare. Seeing the action, Emma realized her mount would rear and immediately set about leaping from the beast. She hadn't intended on knocking into the third man, but when she saw him to the side of her it seemed too good an opportunity to miss and she launched herself toward him from her mare's back.

Amaury stared at the chaos about him with amazement. He hadn't been able to believe it when the tense silence that had cloaked the clearing had suddenly been broken by his wife crashing into the center of the glen on her mount. His shock had been replaced by fear when a glance had shown that the mare appeared to have gone a bit berserk. The beast's eyes had rolled backward in her head even as she had moved to trample one of the men beneath her hooves. Then she had reared, throwing Emma from her back as she pawed at the air in front of a second villain.

Amaury's heart had lodged itself in his throat as Emma had flown through the air. When she had slammed into another of his would-be assassins, he had immediately made a move to see that she was all right, then remembered his attackers and brought himself back to face them. Or what was left of them. The first man the horse had trampled was most definitely dead. At the moment, the second one was still trying to get out of the way of Emma's mad horse, and the third man—the one Emma herself had landed on—appeared to have been knocked senseless as he fell by the base of the tree. That left the fourth man for Amaury to deal with.

He put up a paltry fight at best. While Amaury had regained his concentration quickly, his opponent was still gawking over the chaos about them as Amaury approached him. It was the sign of a second-rate warrior at best. A true warrior knew to keep his wits about him at all times.

Amaury considered hacking the man down while his back was turned. After all, he and his friends had shown little care for fair play by ganging up on him four to one, but his honor would not allow it, so he roared a warning first. The villain wheeled at once, raising his sword in a desperate bid to fend off the coming blow.

After the impact of crashing into the huge armored man, it took a moment before Emma managed to regain her breath. It was Amaury's roar that did it for her. She suspected that that enraged bellow had scared the breath right back into her lungs. Good Lord, he had a set of lungs on him! Regaining her wits along with her breath, she immediately reached for the dirk at her waist. It was a paltry weapon, good only for stabbing food at mealtimes, but it was all she had. Clutching it in her hand, she pushed herself up slightly away from the man she lay on, and quickly and viciously plunged the dirk at his chest. The damn thing snapped in two as it hit his mail. But it did manage to rouse him. Unfortunately.

The way he stiffened slightly made Emma glance warily up at his face when the dirk broke. The smile he gave her when she met his gaze made her blood run cold.

Pulling his sword free of the man, Amaury didn't even wait to see him collapse to the ground before glancing quickly toward the tree where his wife and the other villain had landed. He frowned when he saw that they were both moving now. From the way they had lain prone moments ago, he had thought them both unconscious, but his wife was even now scrambling off the man, trying to back away from him. As she did, the villain caught the hem of her skirt, holding her in place while he rolled to his feet.

Amaury strode quickly across the clearing and brought his sword down. He had intended on slicing the hand that had dared touch even his wife's clothing, but the man saw his approach out of the corner of his eye and tugged hard on the skirt to get his hand out of the way. Emma was jerked forward into the arm Amaury raised immediately to stop her forward impetus, then bounced backward as the sword sliced through her gown, releasing her like a spring. She collapsed back against a neighboring tree, and Amaury immediately put his back to her, protecting her as he faced the man now on his feet, his sword at the ready.

Emma clutched at the tree to keep her feet beneath her, then glanced sharply toward her husband and his opponent. *Opponents*, she realized as she saw that the second man her mare had gone after had managed to deflect the horse and was now coming to aid his friend. She shouted a warning to her husband, but knew at once that she need not have by the impatient glance he threw her over his shoulder. Then the battle began in earnest. Holding her breath, she waited as Amaury deflected their attackers' blows one after another. His arm moved so swiftly as he fought the two men that it was nearly a blur. There was no question of running. She would not leave his side, but she wished she could help somehow. He appeared to have no trouble deflecting their blows, but should he tire . . .

That thought set up a panic in Emma, and she began hunting the ground. She was looking for a good sturdy rock to throw at the men. It would be of little aid, but might be enough of a distraction to allow her husband to even the odds. She had just spotted a nice-sized stone and picked it up when a scream drew her eyes back to the battle. Her husband's sword was buried deep in the belly of the man she had toppled with her leap from the horse. Her gaze flew to the second man then, fear blooming in her like a bloody rose. While her husband's sword was otherwise occupied, the second man was going in for the kill. Emma shouted a warning and hurled the rock at the villain at the same time.

Amaury grimaced when his wife screeched in his ear. It almost made him miss the rock that flew past his shoulder into the man now bearing down on him. God's breath, he thought grimly, his little wife's lungs must reach all the way down to her knees for her to let loose a sound like that. Part of him was touched by the panic in her voice. It was nice to think she did not wish to see him dead. However, another part of him found it insulting that she thought he might not be aware of what was going on about him, or that he needed her trifling assistance. He was a warrior, he thought irritably. It was his place to guard her. Her place was to rest against the tree and await his pleasure. But then, his wife had shown little evidence of knowing her place to date. After all, had he not sent her back to the castle? Yet here she was, a distraction to him in the midst of a battle, he thought, grasping the impaled man by his shoulder and turning to thrust him into his friend's downward swing even as he pulled his own sword free.

Caught up in the momentum of his swing, the villain was incapable of stopping the death blow he gave his friend. For a moment, his face was a mask of shock. In the next instant that expression was to be his death mask as Amaury thrust his sword into the man's chest.

Emma closed her eyes to the gruesome battle scene and sank weakly back against the tree. A hard hand closing around her upper arm a moment later brought her eyes open to stare at her husband's drawn face. He

187

seemed as tense as a cat on hot coals. Anger along with something else she did not recognize battled on his face.

"I told you to head back to the castle."

"I did try," Emma told him in a pained whisper, thinking of the brief spurt of good sense that had urged her to obey her husband.

Amaury sighed, his shoulders drooping as he recalled the mad way the horse had been rolling its eyes when it had crashed into the clearing. "I must have slapped your mare too hard. I am sorry, wife, you could have been killed. 'Twas lucky she ended running in a circle and returning here, else you may have been cracked against a tree rather than the softer landing that man gave you when she finally threw you."

Emma frowned in confusion over that for a moment. Then understanding suddenly struck and her mouth made a perfect O of amazement as she realized her husband's mistake. He thought her such a ninny that he believed her horse had run away with her, somehow tearing off, then crashing back here to throw her at the villain who had been trying to kill him. For a moment she was almost angry that he thought her so useless. Then she merely shrugged it away. She was too weary to really care right then. Besides, it was probably better than his knowing the truth. That would most likely enrage him.

Her gaze moved around the clearing now, seeking out her mare, but there was no sign of the animal. Worry plucking at her brow, she moved to the center of the clearing to call for the creature, but there was no response.

"She probably returned to the castle," Amaury murmured, moving to her side. "My horse is gone as well. It will bring the men." He paused, pushing her behind him and turning to face the trees at the sound of approaching riders.

When the first of his men broke through into the clearing on horseback, he relaxed at once. Sheathing his sword, Amaury walked forward to meet them as they reined in their horses and dismounted.

Emma started to follow him across the clearing, but paused and glanced down when her foot hit something in the grass. It was her basket. Bending, she picked it up and peered blankly at the drops of blood on the top leaves inside. Quite suddenly she felt rather faint. Emma had never been this close to battle before. Oh, aye, she had seen the men practicing at mock battle in the bailey and then of course there were the few occasions when she had used her bow to save a life by taking one. But letting an arrow fly from a distance was nothing like what she had just witnessed. She had stood a mere foot away, privy to the sounds and smells of death. She could smell it in the air, taste it on her lips, and still heard the sound of a sword crashing through human flesh.

Perhaps it was not surprising then that she felt sick, or that she felt sure today was not a day she would soon forget.

Amaury gave his explanations and orders quickly, commandeered one of the horses, then mounted and walked the beast to his wife to lift her up before him on the saddle. Leaving his men to deal with the bodies, he then headed for home, frowning frequently and worriedly down at his wife as they went. She was oddly silent; not surprising perhaps, but it worried him just the same. Even the news he relayed that her mare had been injured, but not badly, did not elicit a response and that increased his anxiety. It was not like her not to fuss over such things.

Sure that it was shock that was ailing his little wife,

Amaury could only think she should rest. It was the only salve he could think of for what ailed her, and as her husband it was his duty to see that she received it. He had just decided that as they rode into the bailey.

Waving the people with their questions away as he dismounted, Amaury lifted her gently into his arms and carried her up to their chamber. There he set her down beside the bed, took the basket she still held, set it on the floor, and then set about stripping her of her clothes.

Emma stood silent and still as he fussed over her, neither assisting nor deflecting his efforts, and that simply worried him more. Once he had her naked before him, Amaury turned to strip back the bed linens, but when he straightened and turned to urge her into the bed, she suddenly threw herself into his arms. For a moment he simply stood there, his arms at his sides, his expression stunned as she sobbed against his chest, but then he regained himself enough to raise one hand to awkwardly pat her back.

He stood there for what seemed to him to be hours, simply letting her cry as he racked his brain for something he could do to soothe her. Then she suddenly began tugging at his clothes. At first he had no idea what to make of it. She was still sobbing hard enough to make him think her heart was breaking, but she was also setting out most aggressively to strip him of his own clothes. He let her do as she wished, thinking to wait and see what she was about.

Despite the fact that he was positive she could not possibly see through the blur of her tear-filled eyes, Emma made short work of his clothes. When she finished, he was standing at the side of the bed with his chest bare and his hose tangled down around his boots, revealing a rather large erection to her view. Circumstances notwithstanding, having his wife rubbing naked against him as she had worked at his clothes had managed to raise his interest.

He had just opened his mouth to ask what she was attempting to do when Emma gave him a gentle push toward the bed. With his legs tangled up in his hose as they were, that was all the effort it took to send him flat on his back on the bed. His wee wife immediately set about climbing on top of him, impaling herself on his shaft with little warning and no preparation.

Amaury simply lay there for a moment, his eyes wide and shocked. His wife was not shy in their bed, but this was beyond anything so far. Besides, there was no evidence of pleasure or desire on her face, just a grim determination as she continued to sob and ride him. Frowning, he caught her hips and held her still, waiting until she opened her eyes before speaking. "What do you?"

Emma simply blinked at him, her surprise finally stopping the flow of tears she had been unable to halt since they had started. It seemed perfectly obvious to her what she was doing. "I am bedding you." She began to move against him again, but Amaury tightened his grip, impatience flashing across his face.

"Aye, I can see that. Why?"

Emma blinked again. She really had no idea why. She simply felt a need to mate. She wished to feel him in and around her. She wished to share those moments afterward when he held her and cooed sweet words in her ear. She wished to feel alive again. She supposed it had something to do with being so near death that afternoon, but did not see how. She did not feel dead, yet felt a horrible need to feel alive. It made no sense and she knew that. And if it made no sense to her, she felt sure it would not make sense to her husband, so she briefly sought in her mind for a viable reason to give him and ended up with, "We need an heir."

"An heir?"

"Aye."

"Now?" He looked thoroughly flummoxed by her words.

"Aye, now. Afore you go a-dying on me." Anger rose up in her suddenly, and she did not understand that either. She did not truly blame him for the bandits' attack, or for this latest fight. Neither had been his fault, and yet she still went right ahead blaming him for both. "I swear, my lord, never in my days have I known a body who landed himself in so much trouble! Do I not milk your seed and get with child now, you are sure to get yourself killed afore I can! Then I shall be left in the clutches of Bertrand."

Amaury stared up at her blankly for a moment, several feelings rushing through him. Anger, however, was uppermost. Rolling suddenly on the bed, he put her on her back and rose above her, driving a little deeper into her before muttering, "Well, wife, as God is *my* witness, I have never *had* so much trouble in my life afore marrying you. 'Tis the truth I begin to think you are accursed!"

"Accursed!" Emma gasped at that.

"Aye, accursed! You have already put one man in his grave, and the way things are presently traveling along, I have no doubt you shall put me there as well!"

When she opened her mouth to respond to that, Amaury covered it with his own. It was no gentle kiss he gave her, however. It was rough and hard and demanding. Emma gave as good as she got, biting viciously at his lip and bucking her hips upward as he drove ruthlessly into her.

As violent as it was, this mating could not last long. It was only a matter of moments before Amaury stiffened against her, cursing before collapsing atop her. He ay still for less than a heartbeat, then forced himself to rise.

Emma bit her lip as she watched him tug his hose up, then climb into the rest of his clothes. He did not look at her until he was leaving the room. Pausing at the door, he peered back at her, his expression grim. "Let us hope that this time my seed took, wife, for I will not play stud horse for anyone. Not even the king."

Chapter Ten

"Mercenaries?" Blake frowned at him. "Who the devil would send mercenaries out after you?"

Amaury shrugged, a surly expression on his face. "Any number of people."

"Aye. You do have a fair share of enemies, do you not?"

" 'Tis the nature of our business. Our previous business," he corrected himself. Being a hired sword meant always fighting a war against someone, for someone. Not his own war, of course, and that only seemed to anger whoever he was battling even more. He had made many enemies over the years. Any one of them might have set those dogs on him that afternoon.

" 'Tis lucky Lady Emma was not hurt."

"Aye." Amaury frowned as he glanced toward the castle where his wife was no doubt boiling her herbs that very minute.

"I'll have Little George increase the guards," Amaury

said almost to himself. "And I'll tell him Emma is not to leave the castle grounds without at least ten men as escort."

"What about you?"

"Whether I am with her or not. Ten men."

"Nay, I meant that you should take a guard with you as well."

Amaury frowned over that, then sighed and nodded his agreement. "Aye."

Blake was silent for a moment. He had expected more of an argument over that. The fact that he did not get one made him as curious as the fact that Amaury had returned in a dark mood from escorting Emma upstairs. He was dying to ask what had occurred to cause it, and was just working his way toward doing so when Amaury suddenly turned to him.

"She thinks I am a stallion! A stud! Good for nothing more than breeding!" he roared.

Blake's eyes widened at that. "Who?"

"My wife! Who the devil did you think I would speak of?!" He glared at his friend for his obtuseness, before continuing. "All she wants me for is to beget a babe. I am no better than a bull to her! She thinks to have me service her at her whim. To spill my seed 'til she is as full as an overflowing tankard."

"It sounds a horrible chore." Blake grinned his amusement.

Amaury frowned at him for his less than sympathetic attitude. "You may laugh. 'Tis not you she expects to service her night and day, day and night."

"More's the pity."

When a storm began swirling on his face, Blake shook his head. "I do not understand what you are complaining of, my friend. 'Twas just a matter of days ago that you were complaining that your wife enjoyed the joining, which you were sure was not right. Now you are telling me that she thinks of you as only a vessel that holds the seed, which is what the church says is proper for a wife to think, and yet you seem distressed by this as well. Oh . . . aye . . . oh, I think I comprehend."

When Amaury merely scowled at him, Blake nodded. "Aye. It has hurt your manly pride to think that your wife's attentions are based only on begetting an heir and saving herself from Bertrand." He nodded again. "Aye, 'tis. And that suggests to me that your own attentions go beyond thinking of her as just wife."

Amaury looked as if he had been punched by that suggestion, then he immediately began shaking his head.

"Aye." Blake nodded. "Mayhap you even love her."

"Love?!" Amaury looked horrified at the very idea. "She is my wife!"

"Aye, but—"

"Men do not love their wives," he pointed out grimly. "They save that for their lovers. Wives are forborne."

"I do not see you taking a lover, Amaury."

"Nay, but—"

"And while it may be the fashion for lords and ladies to save such flowery emotions for their lovers, Emma is not the average Lady. She would be an easy woman to love," he added sympathetically.

Amaury scowled over that sentiment. "You leave my wife alone. She will not be taking a lover." With that, he turned and stormed across the bailey, leaving Blake staring after him in amazement.

Emma glanced up from the pot she was stirring and smiled at Gytha as she entered. She was the oldest of de Lascey's workers. Old enough to be Emma's own mother. She even reminded her of the deceased Lady Kenwick somewhat. It was in her soothing smile and quiet dignity as she had nipped and tucked the material of one gown after another around Emma's body during the fittings. Emma liked her, and she wasn't the only one. Sebert liked her, as well.

De Lascey and his people had been here no more than four days, and already Gytha and Emma's steward were inseparable. They sat together at mealtimes, and disappeared together after the sup, and Gytha was forever finding some excuse or other to come below stairs during the day in the hopes of catching a glimpse of or a moment alone with Sebert. Emma had come across the pair in lusty clutches all over the castle. The maids and kitchen staff were beginning to giggle about it whenever the pair passed.

Emma herself was not sure what to do about the situation. She found it a bit surprising that a pair of such an age could enjoy the intimacies they seemed to be dabbling in. She also found it touching and a bit amusing as well. Add to that the fact that she had never seen Sebert so happy, and Emma was loath to reprimand them for their behavior, so she had let it go up till now. However, this couldn't continue indefinitely. Something had to end it. She was just afraid of what that might be. Emma was rather hoping that she could persuade Gytha to stay, for she very much feared that should Gytha return to London with de Lascey when he left, her steward might very well choose to follow her. That was not a problem Emma wished to address at the moment. There seemed to be quite enough excitement and difficulties occurring at Eberhart Castle just recently.

Ever since her wedding, in fact, she thought. Then she corrected herself. Nay, everything had started before that. With her husband's death? Or even with her audience at court?

"Is Lord Amaury ailing, my lady?"

Emma gave a start and flushed at the question as Gy
tha moved to stand beside her, peering curiously int
the pot. "N-nay," Emma answered. Her voice came ou
in a hoarse stutter. Clearing her throat, she forced
smile and shook her head. "Nay, he is well."

"Then why do you tonic his ale every night?"

"I . . . 'Tis a new refreshment I am experimenting
with," Emma lied, avoiding looking at the woman.

Gytha frowned slightly now. "But is this not butcher's
broom and—"

"You know your weeds," Emma cut in, eager to
change the topic.

"Aye. My mother taught me." Gytha turned back to
the various herbs laid out on the table beside the fire
Brushing a hand gently over the larger bundle of plants
she appeared surprised, and picked up one of the leaves
to peer at it carefully. "Is that not damiana?"

" 'Tis a general tonic." Emma heard the defensiveness
in her own voice and winced inwardly. "It keeps the
body regular."

Gytha raised one eyebrow slightly, amusement pluck
ing at her lips as she set the aphrodisiac back down
"Oh aye, 'twill keep a body regular right enough."

Emma flushed pink at the suggestion in the woman's
tone, but was saved from responding when the door
beside her opened and Sebert peered in and smiled with
gentle pleasure at Gytha. "The French ferret is kicking
up a fuss about yer prolonged absence, Gytha. Mayhap
ye should—"

"Aye." Gytha sighed and moved toward the door, her
irritation giving way to an intimate smile. "See me back
up?"

Emma's eyes widened with surprise at the suggestive
tone, then widened even further at the way Sebert
flushed, swallowed, then nodded at the suggestion.

"God's gorge," she muttered, shaking her head. She

would have to do something about Gytha and Sebert soon. Very soon, she thought dryly, turning back to the pot she was stirring. It was another batch of damiana. She did seem to be boiling up a new batch nearly every other day. That was because she put so much in his tankards. Emma had hoped that she might soon start cutting back on the amount she gave her husband, but after his threat earlier that afternoon . . .

Not that she truly believed that he would refuse to bed her. He did seem to enjoy it. Besides, she was not quite sure of the reasons for his irritation earlier that day. Still, she was taking precautions. Rather than cut back on the damiana mixture she put into his tankard, she intended to double it. She would stop giving him the other herbs, though. She had to, else there would be no room for his ale. Emma thought it better to be safe and dose him so . . . just in case he had been serious.

Emma opened her eyes, peered at the empty bed beside her and sighed. It appeared Amaury had been serious about his determination not to bed her again. He had taken to drinking at sup the night before, and had not stopped until his head had dropped onto the table-top and great snores had erupted from his chest. Emma had left him sleeping there when she retired to the room they shared.

Despite the fact that she had not only doubled the dosage of damiana in his ale, but doubled that again as well, he had not come to her. Mayhap the effects of the potion lessened as the body adjusted to it. Or mayhap the amount of ale her husband had consumed had merely counteracted the effect. Whatever the case, it had not worked, and she had spent a long, cold night tossing about in their bed alone. It was odd how one could get used to having another about. So much so

199

that his presence was missed when absent.

Sighing, she finally moved herself to get out of bed and set about dressing, considering as she did the idea that her husband might truly intend to refuse to bed her now. It was a concept she did not even wish to consider. 'Twas not just her wish for a babe that made the idea unpalatable either. 'Twas the truth she would miss his very presence.

Amaury had kept to his word, and now consulted her on most matters. He had also taken to actually talking to her of a night, holding her in his arms after loving her and discussing the day's events. It had been awkward at first. She had been more than aware that he had been uncomfortable doing so. Still he had continued and it had become a sort of nightly ritual. A ritual she had missed last eve, Emma admitted to herself as she left their room.

The Great Hall was alive with noise when she reached the bottom of the stairs and headed for the trestle tables where servants and soldiers alike were breaking fast. Her gaze sought out Amaury where he sat hunched at his normal place. He was eyeing the people with discontent, as if resenting their easy smiles and laughter. It seemed his mood had not improved overnight.

Sighing inwardly, Emma dredged up a bright smile to grace him with as she approached, but her steps faltered halfway across the room as her gaze fell on the dogs by the fireplace. Curiosity mingling with worry to pluck at her smooth forehead, she hesitated, then turned her steps in their direction.

The dogs had a pattern to their behavior just as everyone else in the castle did. During the day they hung about outside, either playing with the children or aiding in a hunt were it needed. On rainy days they could be found lolling in the kitchen itself, following the cook with mournful eyes and soft mewls of sound produced in the hopes he might throw them a tidbit. At night they settled before the fire and slept by its warmth, only to awake as the first person entered the Great Hall to break fast. Then they too moved to the tables, where they could be found at every mealtime, snapping up bits of food dropped or tossed down to them.

That was where they should have been now. Yet they appeared to still be sleeping and that made Emma's concern deepen as she neared the beasts. It was almost inconceivable that they could sleep through the noise the diners were creating. Unless they were ill.

Amaury knew the moment his wife entered the room. His body told him with a small tingling sensation that buzzed across his back and up his neck. He always had that sensation when she came around him, though not always across his back. Most often it hit him in front and quite a bit lower. Damned if her very presence wasn't enough to set his nether regions to tingling life. Her smile was enough to make him as hard as the rocks at Stonehenge. The problem was it turned his mind to mush. Blake was right to a certain degree. Amaury was not making any sense. First it had bothered him that his wife enjoyed the bedding; now it bothered him that she seemed mostly interested in the bedding to gain a babe. His feelings were such a mess even he did not understand them. Mush. His mind had become a great mass of cow dung.

His wife was probably just as confused by his behavior as Blake was. No doubt it seemed perfectly reasonable to her that they mate for the purpose of children alone. Enjoying it aside, that was what the Church said the purpose for marital relations was. But . . . he wanted more. He did not simply want to be the one who stood between her and Bertrand. He wanted . . . hell, he did not know what he wanted exactly, and that was the problem.

"Mayhap you even have love for her." Blake's words rang in his mind and Amaury shuddered at the very thought. He had scant experience of that emotion. There had been very little of it in his life. Still, as much as he had lacked the emotion in the past, he did not relish suffering under it now. Especially not for a woman who thought of him as simply a bull in the barn that would save her from Bertrand.

Grimacing, he peered down into the murky liquid of his tankard. His friend was right, however, Emma *was* a special lady. Amaury had been witness to the actions of many a so-called *lady*. His father's wife, for instance. A pretty woman, always ready with a friendly smile— so long as there was someone she deemed worthy around to see it. To the unworthy, such as the servants and her husband's bastard, she was a cruel, heartless, virago.

Then there were the *ladies* at court, he thought cynically. It had seemed to him that the women there ran their pursuit of a husband much as the men ran their wars. Coldly, brutally, and with much plotting and sneakiness.

He saw none of these qualities in his wife. Her people, whether servants or men-at-arms, seemed to truly like and respect her. That was made obvious by the way they responded promptly to her softly spoken requests. Even to the point of seeing that every article of cloth in the castle was blackened when she wished it, including their own clothes. When Amaury had asked the steward, Sebert, why they all wore such bleak raiments, he had answered simply, "Her ladyship requested it. She is in mourning. Or she was. I suppose that ended on her remarriage." As he had stood contemplating the etiquette of the matter, Amaury had asked, "And you did it?"

"Aye, my lord."

"Why?"

"Why?" He had seemed perplexed by the question. "Why, to please her."

A simple enough answer that said much more than the words themselves. To please her. Not out of fear. Not out of duty. Not even because she was their mistress, but to please her. Her people worked hard to please their lady. And in turn, she fussed over them. Fretting over their health, seeing to their meals, caring for their needs. She had even taken his men under her wing, tending their countless wounds and ailments and fussing over their health.

An exclamation of dismay drew his eyes to the fireplace. His wife was kneeling by the dogs, horror on her face. Frowning, he stood to move toward her, then paused as Little George burst into the castle and hurried to his side.

"A party approaches."

"Who?"

"I could not see their banner. They are too far away."

Amaury frowned. "A war party?"

"Nay. Too few."

"Mayhap Lord Rolfe returns," Amaury suggested with a shrug, then continued on to stand behind his wife. "What is it, wife?"

Emma sat back on her heels and stared blankly at the animals lying so still. "They are dead."

"Dead!? All of them?" His exclamation caught the attention of the rest of the people in the Great Hall, and many of them began to drift toward the fireplace.

Emma sighed at the disbelief in his voice. She could hardly believe it herself, though she had touched each one and felt the cold stiff bodies beneath the fur of the three animals. They were dead, and had been so for hours. "Aye, husband all three of them."

"Is it the plague, my lady?" Maude asked in a bare whisper, kneeling beside her to peer at the animals herself.

"Nay," Emma muttered grimly, throwing her a reproving look for the suggestion. Just mentioning the word "plague" was enough to cause a panic nowadays. Turning away from the woman, she lifted one of the poor animals' heads in her hands to examine the eyes and mouth, a frown furrowing her brow.

"Is it the spotted fever?" Maude asked.

"Nay!" She snapped as a murmur of fear rippled through the crowded hall and people began moving a step or so away again. " 'Twas poison."

"Poison!" the servant gasped, eyes askance.

"Poison?" Amaury's gaze moved over the animals. They ate only the food from the tables, scraps tossed to them from the diners. No one else was sick. Other than that, the only offering given to them was a large bowl of water that was set out by the kitchen door each morning. His gaze slid slowly to that bowl now.

"Aye, poison." Emma got grimly to her feet and turned toward him.

"You killed them!" The accusation exploded into the silent room, nearly knocking Emma over with the shock of it.

"What?" she asked in a whisper of amazement.

"You killed them. Poisoned them with those herbs of yours."

She stiffened indignantly at that. "Are you mad? Why would I poison the dogs?"

His gaze turned down to the poor animals. "Me."

"What?"

"Me. You were trying to poison me!" he exclaimed as if just realizing it.

"My lord husband," Emma said with exasperation, stepping toward him.

"Nay!" He took a step back, holding up his hand as if holding off a witch. "Did you or did you not put a potion in my drink at sup last eve?"

When she merely glared at him silently, Amaury closed the distance between them to grab her by the arms and give her a shake. "Did you?!"

"Aye!" she spat, and he released her at once, almost throwing her away.

"I poured that drink into the pot you set out for the dogs last night. Now they are dead . . . of poisoning. 'Twas poison in my cup."

Even Emma went still at that damning news. The entire hall seemed to hold its breath as it awaited her response, but before she could speak, Alden hurried to her side.

"Mayhap 'twas an accident," Amaury's squire suggested in her defense. " 'Tis fair true, my lord, those weeds look very similar. I cannot tell them apart. Mayhap . . ." He paused, searching for a way his beloved mistress might have accidentally almost killed her husband.

Emma wanted to cuff him. The mere fact that the boy was seeking an excuse told her he too thought her potion was the source of the poison. One glance around the room showed confusion on the others' faces as well. Emma felt as though she had been kicked in the stomach.

"I made no mistake and I did not poison my husband!" she bellowed furiously.

There was dismay on every face at her unladylike display, but Emma cared little for their opinion at that moment. They all thought her a killer, for goodness sake. Even her own people were looking uncertain. Disgusted with the lot of them, she turned on her heel to leave, but Amaury grabbed her arm, bringing her to an abrupt halt.

"You will not simply walk away from this, wife."

Emma glared pointedly at the hand grasping her arm, then raised cold eyes to his angry face. "Husband?"

She said it so sweetly and in such contrast to the icy fury on her face that his eyes narrowed warily. "Aye?"

"*S'neck up!*" The entire room seemed to gasp as she roared that. Glaring over them in cold satisfaction, Emma tore her arm away and swept toward the stairs. She had no intention of standing about listening to such tripe. Next they would be calling her a witch and preparing to burn her at the stake.

Amaury stared at his wife's retreating back in amazement, then turned to his friend. "What did she say to me?

"I believe she said *s'neck up.*"

"Aye." Amaury nodded, his eyes narrowing to slits. "She did."

He started to follow her then with murder in his eyes, but Blake caught him back quickly. "Nay, friend. Let her go for now. She is angry and—"

"*She* is angry!?" Amaury bellowed, turning on him. "My wife just told me to go hang myself! And in the *lowest* terms! She is no lady, Blake. I tell you, she is no lady! I suspected as much when she enjoyed the joining, but now I am sure. No lady would use such common language. Nor would they enjoy the marital act. And they sure as hell would *not* try to *poison their husbands!*" he roared toward Emma's retreating back, then turned to his own men. "Damn ye to hell, think ye to let her try to kill me then just walk away?! Stop her!"

"Now, Amaury, we must think this through," Blake cautioned desperately.

"What is there to think of? 'Tis not bad enough that

I have bandits and mercenaries determined to do the deed, but now *my wife tries to kill me!*" He bellowed the last toward his wife's departing back. " *'Tis no wonder Fulk killed himself!"*

Emma froze at those words and whirled to spit an opinion or two at her husband, but her attention was distracted by the four men hurrying toward her. Her eyes widened in dismay as she began to recognize the seriousness of her predicament. What was happening was a great deal more than a simple insult to her person. She had been dosing her husband with those blasted herbs, as everyone appeared to be aware. He had poured his ale into the dogs' dish the night afore, and now, this morn, they were dead . . . poison. It was damning evidence no matter the insult. Evidence of murder. An offense punishable by death.

The castle doors suddenly burst open, drawing all eyes in surprise. That surprise deepened when Lord Bertrand entered. Emma must have made a sound of surprise, for his eyes immediately flew to where she stood and he smiled brightly enough to near blind her.

"Lady Emmalene, I came soon as I heard!" Hurrying to her side, he reached for her hands.

"Heard what?" she asked, taking a nervous step backward from his presence. Her gaze flew to her would-be captors to see that they had paused and now stood uncertain whether to take her into custody or not. Her eyes were drawn abruptly back to Bertrand when he took her hands warmly in both of his and squeezed them gently. Confusion immediately set up a riot inside her. His demeanor and greeting were all wrong. He should not be so happy to see her. She had married another, vexing his plans. His parting scowl when he had last been here had hardly led her to expect such a warmhearted welcome now. And warmhearted it most definitely was, she thought with dismay as he drew her

---

---

unwilling body toward him.

"Unhand my wife!"

Both of them were startled at Amaury's thunderous words. Emma took a relieved breath as Bertrand released her. Then she turned a scowl on her husband for his capricious behavior. One moment he was accusing her of trying to kill him, and the next he was barking possessively at another for touching her.

Amaury frowned at his wife's reaction, then took note of Bertrand's.

The man looked more than startled, he looked shocked. He also looked slightly sick as he murmured, "But you are supposed to be—"

"Bertrand!"

Emma cringed at that harsh, high-pitched voice. Turning to the doorway, she eyed the woman standing there warily. Tall, thin, and cadaver-like, the hard-faced woman stared coldly back. This time Bertrand had not come alone. More's the pity, Emma thought grimly as she met the cold hatred in Lady Ascot's eyes.

Amaury bore the silent war of wills between his wife and Bertrand's mother for as long as he could, then shifted impatiently, drawing both women's attention to himself. "I take it you have come for a reason?"

Lady Ascot arched an eyebrow at his rudeness, but Amaury did not care. He had no time to humor the old nag and her mewling son just now. He had three dead dogs and his wife to deal with.

"We were on our way to court and thought to stop and offer our congratulations," Lady Ascot said after a moment of silence. Then stamping her cane on the hard floor, she snapped, "Did we not, Bertrand?"

"Aye." He cleared his throat and moved closer to his mother in a sidling move that smacked of cowardice. "Congratulations."

Amaury's gaze narrowed on the twosome. They were

like snakes, the both of them, slithering about his hall and flicking their honeyed lies off narrow forked tongues. He knew they had been staying at Chesterford's keep since his wedding. Chesterford had sent him news of that himself. And Eberhart would not be out of the way on their way to court, but if they had come to congratulate, then he was King Richard's dead wife. He had not missed Bertrand's words on entering. "I came soon as I heard." Heard what, pray tell? Of the dogs' deaths? Or something else? His gaze slid to his wife as he rolled things over in his head. She was eyeing the twosome by the door with unsavory suspicion. Then she peered back toward the unfortunate beasts frozen in their last moments of life by the fireplace, before glancing finally to him. Understanding slid across her face. Then her lips twisted bitterly. Amaury flinched under that look, guilt rising in him, a wraith that wrapped itself around his innards and gave a gleeful squeeze.

"We shall not tarry for refreshments," Lady Ascot announced arrogantly now, as if some had actually been offered. "We go to join court. Come, Bertrand." Whirling imperiously on the doorstep, she swept back out of the keep and out of sight, her son scurrying to keep up with her.

Amaury turned to the four men he had originally set after his wife. "Follow them. Ensure they leave my lands."

The four men left at once.

He glanced toward his wife then to see that she had turned on her heels and was hurrying above stairs.

"Shall I fetch her back?"

Sighing, Amaury shook his head at Little George's question, his gaze returning to his wife's backside as she mounted the last step and disappeared out of sight.

"I take it you have decided your wife may not be responsible for the poison in your tankard?" Blake murmured, relief obvious in his voice.

Amaury glanced to his friend, then moved back to the head table and sank wearily onto the bench. Picking up his tankard he peered into it as the two men joined him. "I have had a streak of very bad luck lately."

"Aye," Blake agreed slowly. "I have never noticed you to have such bad luck. You have nearly died three times now in but a few short weeks."

"Hmm." Amaury frowned.

"What are you thinking?"

"I am thinking 'tis odd that the bandits attacked me. According to Emma's men-at-arms, they have never attacked anyone afore. Robbed? Aye. But not tried to kill. They did not demand my purse. So why did they attack?"

"Mayhap they feared that as the new lord you would force them out of the woods," Little George rumbled the words.

"But their attacking made me do just that, and would have forced such an occurrence no matter the outcome."

Blake nodded. "They were set on killing you."

"Aye, just like the mercenaries."

Little George's eyebrows rose. "You no longer think the mercenaries were hired by someone connected with your past employment?"

"Nay."

"And you no longer think your wife tried to poison you?"

He shook his head wearily and pointed out what had occurred to him only moments before. "She is the one who said 'twas poison. Else we would have thought it just sickness."

Both men nodded at the truth of that. Then Blake took in his expression and frowned slightly. "You do not seem pleased at that realization, my friend."

" 'Tis the truth I am not sure I am," Amaury admitted ruefully. "While I am glad my wife would not see me dead . . . I do not look forward to the cost of my incorrect accusation."

"She will forgive you," Blake assured him, a hand on his shoulder. "In truth, I think she has great affection for you."

Little George rumbled his agreement to that and Amaury straightened in his seat. "You do?" The hope on his face faded to be replaced by a grimace as he recalled the expression on her face when she had last looked at him. She had not looked to have any affection for him then.

"You are thinking the three occurrences are connected? The bandits, the mercenaries, and the poisoning?" Blake drew his attention back to the conversation at hand.

"Four."

"Four?"

"Aye. The wedding, the two attacks, and the poison." He let that sink in for a moment. "The attacks did not start till the day after the wedding. Who would gain should I die?"

Blake pursed his lips grimly. "Bertrand."

"Aye. 'Twas his words on greeting Emma that made me think it."

"I came soon as I heard?" Little George murmured the words now, then raised his eyebrows. "What did he mean?"

"Most likely he meant that he had heard of my death."

"But how? You are not dead."

"Aye, but all he would know is that his agent applied the poison and Amaury drank his drink. That being the case, this morn he should have been dead," Blake explained as he caught the drift of Amaury's thoughts. "Amaury was careful to ensure no one saw him dump

Lynsay Sands

his drink in the dogs' bowl, he did not wish to hurt his wife's feelings."

"Mayhap ye should send word to the king. He will take care of Bertrand."

Amaury shook his head at his first's suggestion. "There is no proof. He could do nothing without proof."

Blake nodded at that, then glanced up with surprise when Amaury got to his feet. "Where go you?"

"I must speak to my wife."

"But we must decide what to do."

"Double the guards, watch all coming and going, and see if anyone saw a stranger around, or someone besides my wife near my tankard, then check to see if anyone is missing."

"Missing?" Little George raised his eyebrows at that.

"Someone placed the poison in my tankard. 'Twould not be an easy feat for just anyone. It was most likely someone from the castle. If 'twas, they had to have gotten a message to Bertrand that the deed was done for him to have arrived this morn. Hopefully they took the message personally. Else we have a—"

"Traitor in our midst?!" Blake cut in, cursing at the realization.

Little George frowned over that. "But if they were from here, they would have known that Lady Emma was dosing you and should have realized that she would have been accused as the culprit."

"Aye," Amaury agreed dryly. "It's enough to make you think that someone doesn't want *her* around either, isn't it?"

Both men seemed surprised at that. Then Little George muttered, "It cannot be Bertrand then. 'Tis more than obvious that he wants her to wife."

"Aye, but mayhap Lady Ascot does not," Amaury pointed out.

"Mayhap you are right," Blake murmured thoughtfully. "Lady Ascot is a bully, and I do not think Emma would take to that very well. She has too much pride and temper to allow herself to be mistreated. Look how she handled Fulk's neglect. She put up with it for only so long, then took her complaint to the king. Nay, Lady Ascot most likely would not wish to have her about."

Amaury nodded his agreement to that, but his concentration was on the one sentence. *She has too much pride and temper to allow herself to be mistreated.* Aye, she did, and he very much feared he had roused both of those traits with his foolish accusation.

Chapter Eleven

"Cook and his helpers swear that the only people in the kitchen yesterday afternoon besides Lady Emma were two of the tailor's women."

Blake glanced at Little George sharply at that news. "Two of de Lascey's women?"

Amaury's first nodded grimly.

"Damn!" Lifting his sword over his head, Blake slammed it into the post he had been practicing at when Amaury's first had approached him. "Which two?"

"The young one with yellow hair and the one Sebert is sweet on."

Tugging his sword free, Blake considered that as he swung his blade into the post again. "Were either of them near Amaury's tankard or Emma's potion?"

"He cannot recall if the yellow-haired one was, but Sebert's sweetheart was talking to Lady Emma while she was making her potion."

Blake's expression thinned at that. "Have you told Amaury this?"

"Nay, he was still above stairs when I . . . Sweet Saint Simeon," Little George breathed the words in dismay.

Leaving his sword in the post, Blake turned to peer about at those muttered words. A laugh immediately launched itself upward from his gullet when he followed the other man's gaze to see Amaury approaching. It seemed the tailor had finished some of his new outfits. Amaury's ragged hose and braies had been traded in for a fine new pair. His worn old tunic had been replaced by a spanking new doublet of forest green with sleeves so long they trailed on the ground. And on his head was a turban-style hat with an overlarge plume that stuck out and waved in the wind as he approached. But that wasn't what made Blake want to laugh. It was the way his friend was walking. Amaury was stomping toward them, lifting each leg high in the air and slamming it down in an exaggerated march. Disgust was clear on his face as he cursed, muttered, and snorted his way across the bailey.

"Good morrow, friend," Blake murmured as Amaury reached them.

Little George went to the heart of the matter. "I see you have decided to don some of your new finery."

"Aye," Amaury snarled in disgust. "Have you ever seen such frippery?"

Little George chose diplomatic silence, leaving it up to Blake to tell the lie. " 'Tis fine. Finer than fine. You look most lordly in the new doublet."

"Lordly? My sleeves drag on the ground like a lady's gown. And just look you at this hat," he complained. Rolling his eyes upward, he grabbed at the foolish looking feather, giving it a disgusted flick with his hand. Then he glared down at his feet. "And see you these crakows?"

"I have been trying not to," Blake admitted wryly, glancing down at his friend's feet once more. He was unable to hold back his laughter any longer, and a small burst of it exploded from his chest before he caught his friend's dejected look and controlled himself enough to force the lie. " 'Tis not so bad."

" 'Tis not so bad?!" Amaury glared at him. "The toes are so long they near reach my thighs!"

"Well, nay, not that long," Little George said honestly. In truth the turned-up toes of the jester-like shoes reached only to his knees where they were held by gold chains.

Blake frowned over the sight and shook his head. "Could you not have him make another pair? Shorter mayhap?"

Amaury sighed his misery. " 'Tis the latest fashion at court."

"Aye, but—"

"I'll not embarrass Emma by looking odd at court."

Little George shrugged. "If you ask me, you'll look most odd indeed slapping around like you've two fish tied to the bottoms of your feet."

"I know," Amaury moaned. "What am I to do?"

Blake scratched his head. "I would have the popinjay take the shoes in a bit. And the sleeves. And mayhap try a different style of hat."

Biting his lip, Amaury frowned miserably down at his feet.

Deciding a change of subject might be helpful, Blake stuck his blade back in its scabbard and asked, "Did you set things to right with Emma?"

"What? Oh, nay." Propping his hands on his hips, he glared blindly at the activity in the bailey. "She would not speak with me. She is in the bedchamber with the door barred."

Blake and Little George both nodded. They, along

with most of the castle occupants, had stayed in the Great Hall for quite a while listening to him blustering above stairs to his wife, demanding she listen to his apology and forgive him. Blake had considered going up and giving him some advice on how to deal with the situation, but while he knew bellowing at her through the door would not work, he was not sure what would, and had stayed out of it.

"What will you do?" Little George asked now, gaining a scowl for his trouble.

"I am doing it."

When both men merely stared at him blankly, he gestured impatiently to his attire. "I am wearing these. She wished me to wear fine fashionable clothes and I am wearing them." He glanced down at himself with distaste, then sighed and asked, "Think you she will be pleased?"

Blake shook his head. "I fear 'twill take a bit more than donning your new finery to make her forget you accused her of trying to kill you."

Amaury grimaced. " 'Twas stupid of me. I must have misplaced my faculties in that moment to even consider such a thing. My wee wife trying to kill me? Nay. 'Twas the height of foolishness. Bertrand is behind all this. Or more likely his mother. Now there is a she wolf if ever I saw one. Not like Emma." He sighed her name, his expression softening. "She is far too gentle for such base behavior. I have never met a more kindhearted woman. Why, I doubt she could bring herself to swat a fly. She—" Amaury's dissertation on the softer qualities of his wife came to an abrupt end when a hissing whoosh of air sounded just above his ear. It was followed by a sensation of sudden coolness that made him reach up to feel that his hat was missing.

All three men turned to stare at the post beside them, a comical look of horror on their faces as they stared at

217

the befeathered article, now dangling from an arrow embedded in it. A mere inch above his head.

"What the-" Dazed, Amaury whirled to peer in the direction the arrow had come from, jaw dropping as his gaze fell on his 'gentle' wife standing at the top of the castle steps, a bow and arrow in hand. A choked sound emitted from his throat, drawing his friend's attention away from the post as she released a second arrow.

The hiss of the coming missile focused his attention on the mini spear, and Amaury watched as it sailed between his parted legs. Less than a heartbeat later, he heard it hit the post behind him.

"God damn," Blake breathed at the near miss, speaking the words Amaury could not seem to get out between his parched lips. The entire bailey seemed rooted where they stood as Lady de Aneford then calmly descended the keep steps and crossed the hundred feet that separated her from her husband.

Emma had stayed locked up in their bedchamber for over an hour. She had spent most of that time pacing the floor and muttering under her breath. She had done so throughout Amaury's demands that she unbar the door and hear him out, then for another half hour after he had finally realized she would not do so and had left her in peace to fulminate over it all. It had not taken much soul searching to realize why she was so upset. It was not just anger she was experiencing, but hurt. It hurt that the man she thought she might be in love with believed her capable and cold enough to try to kill him.

Love?! Good God! Surely she was not falling in love with him? 'Twas a wife's duty to love her husband, but not be "in love." There was a distinct difference between the two. It was not possible. How could she be in love with the great oaf? Nay. She could not. Not a man whose face scowled as if in pain at the mere thought of talking to her. True, she enjoyed his attentions in bed, but Emma was heartily sick of having to drug him to get him there and last night was proof that it was only her drugging him that brought him to her bed. She had put too much damiana into his drink, and he had tasted it and dumped out the liquid, then proceeded to drink himself into a stupor rather than join her above stairs. To her that seemed irrefutable proof that her husband had no desire to bed her without her potion.

Her thoughts had run around in circles thusly, until she had realized that she had quite forgotten the entire reason for her own anger. The man had accused her of trying to kill him. Imagine! She had saved his life twice now in their short marriage and he thought her a killer. She would see to that! she had thought, and had gathered her bow and arrow and set out for the bailey.

Now, as she paused before him and took in his pallor, she smiled her satisfaction. "I merely thought to show you that had I wished you dead, it would be so. I need no trickery to kill you. All I needed to do was leave you to the bandits. Or to the mercenaries, for that matter."

"Lord Darion!" Blake breathed suddenly.

Emma remained silent, her cool gaze on her husband.

Swallowing, he glanced at the arrows sticking up from the carrier on her back. There was no mistaking their flights as the same as those that had been recovered from the bandits. They were very distinctive with their red feathers. There was no doubt in his mind they were hers. Her comment regarding the mercenaries, however, caught his attention more, for it seemed she was claiming it had been no accident that she had come pounding back into the clearing, evening the odds somewhat by trampling one man and crashing into another. Replaying the scene in his head, he saw that it had only been his own blindness that had allowed him to convince himself otherwise.

Emma's expression hardened at his continued silence. "No doubt you shall now turn away from me as Fulk did as soon as he learned of my unladylike capabilities. But then, 'tis not as if I am losing much in the way of a husband, is it? You informed me yesterday of your intent to refuse me my rights as wife."

On that note, she turned and strode back across the bailey.

"You were saying?" Blake commented dryly.

Amaury's amazed gaze turned to his friend then, and he finally recalled the necessity of closing his mouth and swallowing.

"I think," Little George suddenly murmured, " 'Twill take a bit more than your new finery to draw her out of her temper."

Emma's anger was still riding high as she returned to the Great Hall. She had intended to return to her room and bar the door once more. She was more than sure that once Amaury got over his shock, he would wish to express his opinion regarding her precipitous actions of a moment ago. However, Sebert stopped her as she headed for the stairs, requesting her keys so that he might inventory the spices. She had barely handed them over and turned to continue on her way, when Maude stepped into her path.

"I be thinking ye might like to have a little nibble now that ye've spent your anger. Ye did not break fast this morning, me lady, and Cook made up some pastries special for ye. A little sweet treat will help right your day."

The expression on the woman's face was contrite as she spoke. Emma supposed this was her way of apologizing for whatever traitorous thoughts she had had that morning during all the furor. Cook's too. The man hated making pastries. Before she could accept or reject the peace offering, the Great Hall doors crashed open, drawing her reluctantly around.

"Bring me the tailor and his women!"

Emma grimaced at the fury on her husband's face as Little George moved away to fulfill his order. Amaury then turned in her direction.

Silently cursing the delay that had caused her to still be in the hall, Emma braced herself for an earful of his wrath, then noticed the odd slapping, stuttering step he used as he hurried toward her. Eyes focusing on his feet, she stared in horror at the odd contraptions flopping on them.

"Wife?"

Emma's eyes raised at once at that, and she finally noticed that he had that ridiculous hat back on his head. She had noticed the foolish thing when she had shot it off his head. Now it was back there, perched precariously on his dark hair, looking more absurd than ever with its bent plume and the hole through it. Her eyes dropped to his furious face beneath it then, and despite her anger with him, she could not contain the bubble of laughter that ballooned upward from her stomach and burst out.

Amaury reddened at her laughter, his disgruntled expression deepening. That only managed to make him look more idiotic. A furious court jester. Emma began to shake as she tried to restrain the giggles that wished to follow the ones that had escaped. Trying desperately to contain herself, she dropped her eyes at once, only to find herself staring at his feet again and the chains attached to his knees to hold the toes up. She immediately wondered how much of the shoes were filled by his feet and how much by air. Surely it was mostly air? Else she would have noticed his great feet. They would have made a tent of the bed linens when they were abed, she was sure. On that thought, Emma lost the battle to contain her amusement and it was wrung from her in dismayed peels of laughter.

Amaury felt his chest squeeze painfully. He had worn the outfit to please *her*, dammit. "You find my vestments amusing, wife?"

The cold anger in his tone reminded her of her own anger with him and Emma's lips tightened, all signs of amusement gone. "Nay, husband. They are fine . . . if 'tis a court jester you strive to be."

Amaury stiffened. " 'Tis the latest fashion at court."

Emma's eyebrows rose. "No doubt that amuses King Richard no end. No wonder minstrels are becoming de rigeur. Who would have need of them?"

Amaury looked ready to explode at that, and Blake grabbed his arm, dragging him a few steps away. "Apologize to her," he told him in a hiss.

"Apologize!?" he exploded. "She has just called me a court jester."

"Nay. She is simply angry. Rightfully angry, Amaury. Think you on how you would feel had she accused you of trying to kill her."

"Aye." Shifting uncomfortably, he started to turn back to his wife, then paused and tugged his hat off. Shoving it into Blake's hands with a mutter, he turned once again, only to find that his little wife had moved away. She now sat at the trestle table, a fare of sweet treats before her, gentilely nibbling at them and sipping at a tankard of mead. Sighing, he moved to the table, easing onto the bench beside her and collecting his thoughts before turning to face her. "Wife, 'tis sorry I am that I accused you of trying to kill me."

Emma turned to arch one eyebrow at him, only to pause as her gaze was caught by his sleeve. She had noted the overlong length of them earlier and thought nothing of it. She had seen many men wearing them at court. In truth she had seen many men with crakows on too, some even with toes as long as his, but somehow they had not appeared as amusing on others as on her husband. Perhaps because the other men had had enough practice walking in them not to appear to be fish-marching. She had not found the overlong sleeves amusing either, but then none of the people at court had had theirs hanging down into her tankard of mead.

Amaury frowned over his wife's response. At first she had simply peered at him with that slightly arrogant tipping up of one eyebrow he was beginning to detest, but just now she was beginning to tremble, her lips working in a way that gave him the very nasty suspicion she was about to burst out laughing at him again. Following her gaze, he glanced down at his arm, and jumped up from the table with a curse, grabbing at the sopping sleeve.

"Here." Blake was at his side at once, helping him to wring the liquid out of his sleeve and ushering him a little away to say, " 'Tis not going well."

"Nay. She thinks me the veriest buffoon."

"Nay," his friend lied reassuringly.

"Aye. She is laughing at me."

"Nay." Stiffening, Blake straightened and held up the tip of his sleeve. "This doublet is not finished. The sleeves are unsewn."

Amaury sighed. "Aye. I rushed de Lascey to have it done enough that I could wear it to impress my wife," he admitted bitterly. " 'Tis just the hem of the sleeve. He will finish it later."

"Hmm." Blake dropped the cloth and peered at him. "Mayhap she would warm a bit if you explained why you believed she had poisoned you."

Nodding, Amaury straightened his shoulders and turned toward the table, then paused and turned back.

"What reason should I give?"

Blake rolled his eyes. " 'Twas due to all the potions she was putting in—"

"Oh, aye." Turning abruptly, he stepped back up to the table and dropped onto the seat beside his wife, careful to avoid dunking his sleeve this time as he faced her. "I believed you had done the poisoning due to the fact that you were forever sneaking those potions into my ale."

Emma's amusement fled. "Those *potions* were for your health."

"Aye," he agreed soothingly at once. "And 'tis sure I am the dogs have not been healthier . . . until they died of course." Amaury shifted uncomfortably, his gaze dropping. Then it suddenly flew up again, brightening as he thought to add, "And they did aid my health, wife. Think on it. Had you not been sneaking those potions into my drink since my head injury, I would not have been dumping my ale in the dogs' bowl and might have been the one to die last night of poison."

Emma opened her mouth on an angry retort, then paused and blinked. "Would not have been dumping . . . How long have you been dumping your ale out in the dogs' dish?"

"Since the first night I was up from my sickbed," Amaury admitted after a hesitation, bracing himself for her anger. Instead of anger, Emma looked completely bemused.

"Then 'twas not the damiana that brought you to my bed?"

Amaury frowned over her faintly spoken words. "What? Damiana?"

A commotion drew his gaze toward the stairs, and he sighed impatiently as he saw that Little George was returning with de Lascey and his people. "We shall finish this discussion later," he announced, getting to his feet.

224

to face the group as they approached.

Catching the coldness in his voice, Emma glanced at him curiously, then at the people moving toward them. She stood slowly. "What is occurring, my lord?"

Amaury glanced at her warily. His wife did not appear angry any more, simply concerned, so he allowed himself to relax somewhat. "Little George questioned the cook and his helpers about anyone being near my tankard, and learned that two of de Lascey's women were the only ones in the kitchen besides yourself yesterday before sup."

Emma nodded at that. "Gytha and Sylvie. Gytha came in to fetch a beverage and spoke to me while I made the potion, and Sylvie was entering the kitchen as I left." She peered up at him. "Surely you do not suspect either of them?"

Amaury grimaced. "I only wish to question them, wife. 'Tis the only clue we have so far." He frowned as he glanced over the seamstresses. "There are only five here. Which one is missing?"

"Sylvie," Emma admitted reluctantly. Sylvie was the youngest of the seamstresses, a mere slip of a girl, not yet sixteen. Emma could not imagine the girl poisoning anyone, and feared her absence would make him judge her harshly.

Little George led the group to stand before them, then stepped aside. Amaury glared over them, his gaze going over each face. The women looked confused and anxious, but nothing more. De Lascey was doing his best to cower behind the women without appearing to. "Where is the one called Sylvie?"

There was a moment of silence as the women glanced at each other; then de Lascey stepped forward long enough to say, "I zent her to zee kitchens to get me zome vine." Then he stepped quickly back behind the women again.

Amaury turned a glance to Little George at that, but he needn't have bothered. His first was already moving toward the kitchen door.

A moment later he was back with the news that she had been and gone, and was supposed to have returned above stairs. A nod from Amaury then sent the man sprinting up the stairs to seek out the missing girl.

"Might I ask what ees 'appening, my lord?"

Emma's surprise showed when the tailor found the nerve to step out from behind his women long enough to ask that question. Amaury merely seemed annoyed. He glared at the man, then continued his slow study of each of their faces as he awaited his first's return. He wanted to see if anyone betrayed guilt by expression. All of these people were strangers to the castle and therefore any of them could have been the guilty party.

Emma nearly sighed in relief when Little George finally hurried down the stairs. The tension in the Great Hall was unbearable. That relief turned to concern, however, when he whispered something in her husband's ear that made Amaury take her arm and lead her toward the stairs.

"What is it, husband?"

"Little George found the wench." He paused at the top of the stairs and turned to her to add grimly, "She is dead. It appears to be poison. I wish to know if 'twas the same poison that killed the dogs."

Emma nodded her understanding. He wished her to view the body and look for the same signs she had found on the dogs.

"Thank you," Amaury murmured, then led her down the hall to the room de Lascey had chosen to store the fabric in. It was crowded with bolts of fabric stacked haphazardly in any space not taken up by the two makeshift, blanket-covered straw beds on the floor and the large draped bed in the center of it all.

The Deed

It was the large bed where the girl in the plain home-spun dress was. She was draped across the bottom of it on her back, an empty vial clutched in one hand. Her legs hung off the edge as if she had sat down to rest. She had never gotten back up. In this last sleep Sylvie appeared even younger than she had in life.

Sadness welling up inside her at this waste, Emma moved to sit carefully beside the reed-thin body and bent to peer on her eyes and mouth. She then lifted the hand holding the vial, peered at her nails, then took the vial and gave a sniff.

" 'Tis the same?"

"Aye."

Amaury grunted. "Bring me de Lascey and his women."

Emma sat staring at the dead girl, wondering what had brought her to this pass in her life, then glanced to the door as the rustle of clothing and several small gasps announced the arrival of de Lascey and his women. Straightening her shoulders, she stood and moved to her husband's side.

"What is zis?" De Lascey peered at his seamstress in dismay.

"She is dead," Amaury announced grimly. Then, before they could quite accept that, he asked, "How long has she been in your employ?"

"I hired her just before coming here." He looked truly taken aback by these events . . . as his missing accent suggested.

"How did that come about?"

De Lascey shook his head. "One of my other women did not appear on the day we were to leave. Sylvie arrived at the door just as we were about to depart. She claimed she was accomplished at sewing. It seemed a blessing."

Amaury grimaced at his choice of words. De Lascey's

blessing had very nearly been his own funeral. "Where are her belongings?"

The tailor looked blank at that, then glanced to his workers questioningly, and one of them hurried to one of the makeshift beds and retrieved a small sack. "This was hers, my lord."

Accepting the small bag, Amaury turned it over, dumping its contents on the bed. He and Emma both stared sadly at the contents. A wooden comb with many teeth missing, a plain brown gown with several holes, a small sack, and another vial. Picking up the vial, Amaury opened it and took a whiff, then handed it to Emma for her to sniff as he reached for the sack.

The vial was empty, but there was still the faint bitter smell she had noted in the first vial, and Emma shook her head with a sigh.

"Is it not also poison?"

"Aye," she admitted reluctantly. " 'Tis the same as the one she held. But I do not believe it. Why would she—" Her voice came to an abrupt halt when Amaury tipped up the sack he held and poured out a handful of coins.

"There is your reason," he said.

" 'Twould seem so," Emma agreed, still with some difficulty. It was a paltry sum to her, but she knew it would have seemed a fortune to the young girl on the bed. Still, it just did not seem possible that the girl who looked so sweet in death had been capable of murder. There were too many unanswered questions. "Then why did she kill herself? Why take the poison?"

Shrugging, Amaury poured the coins back into the sack. "Guilt. Fear of being caught. Who can tell." His gaze lifted to de Lascey, who stood behind his women once more, an anxious look on his face. When he noticed Amaury peering at him, he took a nervous step back.

"I did not know," he babbled. " 'Twas not my fault. I

never would have brought her had I realized."

Emma grimaced at his pathetic words.

"You brought this wench into our midst," Amaury accused. "I should bring you up on charges."

"Nay!" The tailor looked horrified at the thought. "But I did not know."

"You should better check your people."

"Aye, of course, but—I will make it up to you, my lord."

"How could you possibly make it up?"

"I will give you a discount on your wardrobes," he said desperately.

Amaury merely arched an eyebrow at that.

"Half the price I meant to charge you. Half. And I will not charge you for my having to travel out here."

Amaury pursed his lips briefly over that, then nodded. De Lascey sagged in relief, then stiffened once more when Amaury added, "However, you will make no more of these contraptions." Bending, he undid the chains at his knees and removed his crakows, throwing them at the man with disgust. "And you shall shorten the sleeves on this doublet and make the others so as well." He shrugged off the doublet and tossed that across the room at the man as well. "And no more of those ridiculous feathers in my hats."

"Aye, my lord." His relief was palpable.

"And if I see anything so foolish on my wife . . ." He let the threat trail away, leaving it to the tailor's imagination.

"Aye, my lord. Thank you, my lord." Bowing repeatedly, he backed out of the room, gesturing for his women to follow.

Amaury watched them go, then shook his head, muttering an unflattering description of the man under his breath.

Emma remained silent. She did not blame de Lascey

for Sylvie's actions, but was not going to argue over his agreement to halve his fee. He had inflated the cost enough to begin with that, at half the price, he was still getting a more than fair deal. Her gaze moved to Amaury as he peered at himself with a frown.

"I shall have to dress again." Taking her arm, he led her toward the door. "Take care of the girl, Little George," he ordered, then ushered Emma out as she added, "Give her a proper burial, please."

She then remained silent until they had reached their room. As sad as the morning's events had been, she had hardly known the dead child and her mind was already turning to other events. Her discovery, for instance, that Amaury had not been taking her potions in all the time since their marriage. If it was true, then—

"What is damiana?"

Tipping her head, she peered at her husband wide-eyed. It was as if he had read her mind.

"Wife?" He frowned at her impatiently when she remained silent.

Emma hesitated as he dug his old green doublet out of the chest at the foot of the bed and proceeded to put it on. Sighing, she sank down on the side of their bed. "You said you have been dumping your ale in the dogs' dish since regaining your feet?" she asked carefully.

"Aye." He tugged the worn old doublet over his head, then glanced at her unhappy face and sighed. "I am sorry, wife. But those potions of yours are fair bitter in a man's mouth. 'Sides, I did not need them."

"Nay. 'Twould seem not," Emma said faintly, thinking of the active love life they had enjoyed. Until last night.

Eyeing her thoughtfully, he moved to sit on the bed beside her. "Tell me."

Emma peered up at him uncertainly, wondering if he would be angry at her for drugging him, then decided to delay a bit longer. "Why did you not come to bed last night, my lord?"

Grimacing, he avoided her eyes briefly before admitting, " 'Tis foolish."

"Nay. Tell me."

Shrugging, he peered at the window of their room. "My thoughts were confused. In truth they still are."

"You became angry with me when I said 'twas for an heir I was . . ." She colored faintly, unwilling to even think of her shameless behavior the day before, let alone put a name to it.

Amaury nodded wryly.

"And yet, is that not why a wife is supposed to wish to . . . you know?" When he remained silent at that, it was Emma's turn to sigh. "In truth I did not tell all regarding why I was so . . . aggressive. 'Twas not simply for an heir. I know not a better way to explain it than that, after the violence in the woods, I wished to be held by you and to feel alive. The joining with you makes me feel so."

"Truly?" He appeared bemused by her words.

"Aye. And more," she admitted almost with shame, then added in a hurried rush, "Damiana is an herb said to increase a man's ardor."

Amaury blinked over that. He had been about to pursue the "And more" she had mentioned, but now was thoroughly distracted by her admission. "Increase a man's . . . ?"

"Aye." Emma peered down at her hands, grimacing over the fact that they were now twisting a portion of her skirts into a crumpled heap. "I feared 'twas the only way to bring you to my bed."

"Nay!?" Amaury peered at her wide-eyed. Had he not shown the depths of his passion for her by his attentions? Good God, but he was like a dog in heat at every turn, even going so far as to jump upon her in the woods. Then understanding struck. She had most like thought that as a result of her potions, he realized and immediately began working at the lacing of her gown.

"My lord? What do you?" Emma grabbed at his hands to still them.

"Proving my ardor, wife. I have had no damiana this day, nor any other. God's truth, had I drank those potions, I most like would not have let you leave the bed this last week," he added wryly, undoing the last of her ties and pushing the gown quickly off her shoulders.

"But . . . what of my skill with the bow?" Fulk had turned from her in disgust on learning of that. Surely he would as well.

Amaury paused, irritation flashing across his face. "Oh, aye." Picking her up beneath the arms, he stood and held her before him until her gown slid off. Once it hit the floor, he sat back down, laid her across his lap, and gave her behind a sharp whack as he ordered in an almost bored voice, "You are never to shoot an arrow at me again, wife. 'Twas sinful of you to do so. I am your husband and lord." Shifting her again, he laid her on the bed.

"Is that it?" Emma asked with dismay as he came down on top of her.

Pausing, Amaury raised one eyebrow. "You wish more?"

Emma blinked. "Nay, but . . . I am fair skilled with the bow," she pointed out.

"Aye. I did notice, wife." Finishing with her ties, he tugged her into a sitting position and slid the tunic off her shoulders as well, his eyes lighting up when her breasts were revealed.

"You do not mind?" Emma watched his face doubtfully.

"Mind?" Pausing again, he glanced at her quizzically. "Nay, wife. In truth I am fair grateful for that skill. As is my manhood. Had your shot been even the littlest bit off, not even your potions could help my ardor."

"But—" Emma paused to gasp as he finally cupped the breasts he had worked so hard to disrobe.

" 'Sides," Amaury murmured, pressing a kiss to one breast, then turning to the other. "Without that ability, the bandits may have got the best of me. 'Tis a valuable skill, wife. Now, shut up and help me shed my clothes, else I shall have some damiana put in *your* tankard."

Chapter Twelve

"We should be stopping soon," Blake murmured encouragingly, slowing his mount to ride beside a rather wilted Emma on her mare.

Nearly sagging with relief, she smiled gratefully at the fair-haired man.

They were on their way to court. It was two weeks since the incident with the poison. Things had changed a great deal since then. Amaury, like herself, had concluded that Bertrand was behind the poor luck they had been having of late and fully expected those attempts on his life to continue. But he had taken what precautions he could to guard against it. Despite the fact that Emma herself had never been targeted in the attacks, he had included her in those precautions. Until now, neither of them had been outside the keep walls, both of them now had guards following them about throughout the day, and both of their tankards were dunked in boiling water before each use.

The tail of the veil attached to Emma's conical hat slid across her face. Lifting a hand, she pushed it aside as she rode. De Lascey had finished the last of their wardrobe just two days before they had decided to leave for court. There were no long-toed crakows, no dragging sleeves, and no huge plumes drooping out of hats. In truth he had done a fine job on their vestments. There would be no shaming titters behind hands, or jokes this time, she thought with a smile that faded quickly. It was hard to find pleasure in anything when her behind felt as though it had been scalded and left to fester.

Emma was not used to riding for so long. She had been in her saddle since first light that morning with only one short respite when they had stopped for a nooning meal. The sun was crawling downward and still they rode. Emma had just decided that Amaury meant to ride them through the night when Blake had dropped back to where she rode.

"Did my husband say so?" Emma asked now, her spirits dropping when Blake grimaced and shook his head.

"Nay, but—" He paused as Amaury suddenly shouted the order Emma had been awaiting, then turned to beam at her. "You see?"

Emma could not help but smile back at his grin as she drew her mount to a halt, but that smile vanished, replaced by a gasp of surprise, as she was suddenly grasped about the waist and swung off her horse into her husband's arms.

Clutching anxiously at his shoulders, she glanced back to see Blake laughing softly as her husband carted her off into the woods. She also saw that he had not forgotten the need for a guard. Little George and one of the other men were following at a discreet distance.

"Where are we going?" she asked as the trees closed around them.

Amaury was silent so long, she began to think he would not answer her. Then he suddenly paused, a smile of satisfaction spreading across his face. "Here."

Turning, Emma stared silently around the clearing stretching before them. It was at the side of the river. A small glen with sweet-smelling grass and flowering bushes that were just coming into bloom. It was lovely, even in the falling dusk.

" 'Tis beautiful, is it not?"

"Aye," she agreed in a whisper, almost afraid to disturb the peace here by speaking with her full voice.

" 'Tis why I wished to camp here. I thought to share this with you."

Emma's eyes widened at the sweetness behind that thought. It explained his inconsiderateness in making them travel so late and in her mind at least, excused it completely. Her thoughts were scattered when he suddenly set her down and began tugging at her clothes. "Husband, what—"

"We shall bathe away the day's travels here. You must undress to do so."

"Aye, but what of Little George and—"

"I ordered them to wait a hundred feet back. They are near enough to come running if there is any trouble, but cannot see. Do not fret. How do you undo this blasted—"

"Here, my lord." Emma pushed his hands away with exasperation and took over the deed of undressing herself. Amaury paused to watch her for a moment, then turned his attention to his own clothes. He was naked and rushing into the water before she had even sat down on a fallen log at the edge of the river to remove her hose.

Laughing at his shout at the coldness of the river,

Emma paused to watch him dunk himself.

"You are dallying," he accused her when he resurfaced and saw her simply sitting on the dead tree watching him.

"Nay." Emma smiled and lifted her under-tunic above one thigh so that she could work at her hose. At his sudden silence, she glanced back to the water, eyebrows rising at the way he had gone still as he watched her. Eyes twinkling with devilment, she slowed her actions and raised her leg into the air, stretching it like a cat as she undid her hose and rolled it along her leg. Dropping it to the ground, she then repeated the action with her other leg before getting languidly to her feet and reaching for the hem of her under-tunic. She paused briefly then, a blush coming to her cheeks at what she was about to do, then slowly lifted the hem of her gown, revealing her hips, her stomach, and finally her breasts before she slid the tunic over her head.

Growling deep in his throat, Amaury headed for shore at once, but Emma quickly held the gown up to shield herself. "Nay. I would bathe, husband. I have been riding all day and must smell of horses."

His steps faltered and he hesitated, then sank back into the water, simply watching her. Emma cast him a slow smile, then raced toward the water, tossing her under-tunic over her head as she rushed in. The water was cool on her heated skin, startlingly so, and Emma squealed as she floundered toward the deeper water at the center of the river.

"Cold, wife?" Amaury moved slowly toward her as she finally began to adjust to the temperature.

"Aye."

"Shall I warm you?' he murmured, catching her hand and tugging her closer.

"Nay." Emma turned away, trying to move out of his reach, but he caught her from behind and drew her back until her behind rubbed against his lower belly. Purring in her ear, he shifted his hands from her arms to cup her breasts, playing with them shamelessly beneath the water as he fitted her more firmly against himself. "Hmm. You *are* cold. Feel those goosebumps."

Giving a half laugh, half gasp, Emma slapped at his hands as he gently pinched her erect nipples. "You are shameless, husband."

"Aye, it must be those potions of yours," he teased, and Emma tried to elbow him. He had teased her just so at every turn since she had revealed her attempt to drug him. Rather than being angry, her husband had found her admittance vastly amusing, much to her annoyance. Unfortunately, her attempt to elbow him was foiled easily by Amaury, and only managed to maneuver her lower in the water so that she rubbed against his erect manhood.

Swiveling quickly in the water, she grabbed his rigid member firmly, blushing brightly at the startled expression on his face, even as she teased right back, "I am cold? Feel this goosebump."

"Who is shameless now, wife?" he asked with a wicked grin, and reached for her, but she caught her feet on his knees and launched herself backward, swimming swiftly away. Laughing as he struck out after her, Emma swam for shore, then hurried quickly out of the water and grabbed up her discarded tunic as she turned to confront him. He was just reaching for her when the beginnings of a startled shout reached them through the trees even as it was silenced.

Stiffening, Amaury changed direction, reaching for his braies and sword. "Get dressed."

He did not need to give her the order twice. Tugging the under-tunic over her head, she rushed to the log she had laid the rest of her clothes over and quickly snatched up her gown. She had the dress over her head when the sound of breaking branches warned her of trouble and had her tugging the gown quickly over her torso, freeing her vision.

Amaury had managed to don his braies, but that was all before the first attacker broke from the trees. Seeing his half-clothed and apparently unarmed state, the man rushed forward for the kill, but Amaury had been bent over, reaching for his sword. He straightened and thrust that sword forward, through the oncomer's chest, as he approached. He had barely pulled his sword free when at least a dozen more seemed to explode from the woods all about them.

Stopping, he gaped at the uneven odds, then straightened grimly and raised his sword. That was when Emma suddenly hurtled herself at him, throwing them both backward into the water. She was back on her feet at once. Turning her back on him, she faced the men narrowing the space between them as Amaury floundered to regain his feet in the shallow water.

"Will you kill me?"

The attackers stilled at that. Even Amaury froze in the water behind her as she hissed those words.

"Will you?! For you will have to kill me to get at my husband, and I fear Bertrand will not be pleased at my death. He loses all should I die." Even as she said the words, she recognized the lie in them. Bertrand could most likely still claim Eberhart should she die. He simply would not gain her dowry. That would have to be returned to Rolfe. Still, she doubted these louts would know that. "I suggest you give it up and save yourselves. For if we heard your approach, no doubt our men did too, and they will cut you down like the dogs you are should you be here when they arrive."

The last words had barely left her mouth when the shouts of approaching men could be heard. Emma was just sagging in relief when Amaury regained his feet, pushed her to the side, and threw himself into the middle of the men now standing uncertainly before them even as Blake and the others flew into the clearing to aid him with the rest.

Emma had always known her husband was a warrior and good in battle. Now, however, she learned that when enraged, he was a force to be reckoned with. And he was most definitely enraged, she thought as she noted the grim satisfaction on his face as he dispatched one of their attackers. And she very much feared some of his anger would be with her for her interference. She supposed she had hurt some of his manly pride by shielding him with her own body. She also supposed she would hear about that anger once he and his men were finished here.

Sighing, she sank onto the log she had sat on to take off her hose and calmly set about putting the hose back on as she waited. It did not take more than a few moments for Amaury and his men to finish off the attackers. When they were through, all but one was dead. The one still alive was badly injured, however. Amaury ordered him taken back to camp for questioning, then turned to peer at his wife. She had just finished donning her clothes, and now sat primly on the fallen log, eyeing him warily.

He took a moment to try to settle his temper somewhat, then moved to stand in front of her. "Wife."

"I never should have put myself before you," she blurted hurriedly, jumping to her feet. "You most like had everything under control and 'twas most dangerous. I am very lucky I did not get myself killed and I shall never *ever* risk myself so again. I swear it."

Amaury rolled his eyes at that. "You should never make a promise you cannot keep, wife. I have no doubt that you shall risk yourself again. 'Tis in your nature.

However," he added grimly when she began to relax at his words. "The next time . . . and I do mean the *very next time* you do something so foolish again, I shall take you across my knee and—" His words came to an abrupt end as his wee wife threw herself against his chest, wrapping her arms about his waist.

"You are a very generous and forbearing husband, husband. I am very lucky."

"Aye . . . well . . ." Clearing his throat, he reached a hand up to pat her back. "Just try not to be so impulsive in future."

"Aye, husband. 'Twill be so, I swear it." Tipping her head back, she smiled up at him sweetly, relaxing in relief when he bent to press a kiss to her soft lips. Well, it was not so bad, she decided as the kiss deepened. Her husband's temper was not so horrid. Most husbands would have blistered at least her ears, if not some other part of her body, for what she had done.

Ending the kiss, Amaury straightened and tried not to frown. In truth he felt like something had gone wrong. He had intended on shouting her ears off with his anger and yet oddly, that anger had fled like a bird before the storm under her smile. Shaking his head, he stepped away and retrieved the rest of his clothes. Quickly donning his tunic and doublet, he belted his sword back on and spared a glance at the bodies lying strewn about the clearing. "I shall have to have Little George and some men see to them."

Emma frowned at that. "Did you send anyone to check on Little George and the other fellow? They did not join the battle."

"Damn." Slapping one hand to his leg in irritation, he strode off toward the trees. Emma hurried after him to lend her aid in finding the men.

It was growing darker quickly now. Soon it would be full night and impossible to find the two men if they were unable to call for help, so it was with some relief that Emma cried out to her husband as she spied a hand sticking out from a bush to the side of the path. It was Little George. Unconscious, he was sprawled on the ground like an abandoned doll, a great bruising bump on his noggin telling the story of how he came to be that way.

After assuring himself that the man was alive, Amaury left Emma to try to wake him, and headed out in search of the second man. He found him twenty feet away, his throat slit.

Little George was just stirring to life when Amaury returned. The fact that he carried his fallen man over his shoulder did not tell her he was dead so much as her husband's expression did. Emma cast him a sympathetic glance, then turned her attention back to the man now coming to grumbling life in her lap.

Amaury's first cursed a blue streak as his aching head forced him back into consciousness. Then realizing whose lap his head rested in, he apologized tersely and sat up, one hand going to rub the knot on his forehead. "Damn me, that hurt."

"Aye, it looks fair sore," Emma murmured, rising slowly to her feet. "Did you cry out afore you were hit?"

"Nay. I had no chance. I heard a sound behind me. Turned . . ." He shook his head. " 'Tis all I recall."

"Then it must have been Edsel," Amaury murmured grimly.

Little George stiffened. "Is he all—?" The question died in his throat as he finally glanced up and saw his comrade draped over his shoulders. Little George's expression fell, and his shoulders slumped wearily.

"Come," Amaury murmured, offering his man his free hand. "We shall return to camp and see if our prisoner talks."

The first's eyebrows rose as he got to his feet. "You caught one?"

"Nay. We caught them all. . . . but only one lives."

Rolling her eyes at the arrogance in her husband's voice, Emma moved past him to lead the way back to camp.

Blake met them on the edge of the clearing with the news that their captive had died and he had dispatched men to tend to the dead. Amaury was silent and grim over the news. Emma knew he had been hoping to gain a confession from the man that he had been sent by Bertrand so that he could present this proof to the king. She watched helplessly as he stalked away, still bearing his fallen man across his shoulders, then moved to where Maude sat by the fire in the clearing, silently hoping that the rest of the trip would be less eventful.

She should have known it was too much to hope for.

They managed two days of uneventful travel. On the second night after the attack, Amaury chose a spot along the river again. When he urged her to join him at the river for a swim, she was reluctant to chance it. It did seem to be pushing their luck a bit, but she was hot and sweaty from the trip and gave in in the end. Still, she held her breath throughout, not relaxing until they had returned safely to camp and the dinner of rabbit cooked over an open fire that Maude had helped prepare.

No one tarried long by the fire after eating. It was a lovely night with a star-studded black velvet sky, but three days of hard riding was beginning to tell on everyone. Emma herself was so tired she nearly dozed off where she sat.

Scooping her up easily in his arms when she started to topple toward the fire as she dozed off, Amaury got to his feet, shaking his head at Maude when she stood to follow to help her lady undress, then carried her to the tent.

"Hmm." Emma leaned her head wearily against her husband's chest as he carried her. "Thank you, husband. I fear I was getting quite tired."

"I noticed, wife."

"Did you?"

Amaury smiled slightly at the faint surprise in her voice. "Aye, you were about to topple into the fire as you dozed."

She blinked awake at that. "Nay. I was not."

"Aye, ye were." His chest rumbled with the answer as he pressed her closer and bent to enter the tent. Turning back, he instructed her to close the flap, then turned back to face the interior of the small tent once she had.

"You may set me down now, husband. I am awake now."

Ignoring her, Amaury stepped forward and set her on the bottom of the makeshift bed, then set about undressing her. Recognizing the look in his eyes, Emma simply smiled and began working on his clothes as well. Long day or not, her husband had retained some energy for his nightly duties. Or mayhap the dip in the river had helped revive him earlier. Whatever the case, his attentions revived her quickly enough, and once he had satisfied the fires that always seemed to burn just below the surface for him, she was wide awake and frisky.

Hugging him close as she lay half sprawled across him afterward, Emma purred and rubbed her face against the small soft hairs on his chest, then tangled one finger languorously in those hairs before asking softly, "Husband, when is Little George's wife going to join him?" She had asked that question repeatedly since Little George's arrival and did wonder at the delay. She was curious to see what kind of woman the man had married. So much so, that she hoped to convince her husband that they should stop and collect the woman on the way back from court. Hence the reason for her question. She had thought it a good lead in to the suggestion.

Realizing that he was not answering her, Emma tipped her head up to glance at him, and smiled when she saw that he was sleeping. Leaning up, she kissed him briefly on the cheek, then pulled the blankets up to cover them both and snuggled down to go to sleep.

Tired as she had been earlier, it took quite a while for her to doze off for the night. It seemed she had just managed to do so when something jarred her back to wakefulness.

Opening her eyes slowly, she waited for them to adjust to the darkness in the tent, her ears straining to catch the small whisper of sound that had awakened her to begin with, but all there was was silence now. Frowning as she began to distinguish shapes and shadows in the dark, she moved her eyes around. She was no longer sleeping with her head on her husband's chest. Now her legs were tangled with his, and her head was lying several inches away from his own. She had just realized that when she recognized that the large, dark shape looming on her husband's side of the bed was not the far wall of the tent as she had at first presumed, but the shadow of someone standing over him.

Stiffening where she lay, Emma took a moment to consider the situation, then spotted the glint of metal in his hand as the shadow moved. Recognizing it as a knife, she tugged her legs free of her husband's, placed them on his behind, and gave him a powerful shove even as she let loose a shrill scream.

Amaury rolled from the makeshift bed, knocking into the legs of the would-be assassin and sending him crashing to the floor as he rolled atop him.

In the next moment, the tent was filled with cursing

and shouting as the twosome began rolling about the floor.

Standing on the bed, Emma screamed at the top of her lungs again for assistance, then threw herself onto the rolling mass of male arms and legs.

"What the bloody hell?!" Blake lifted the torch he held a bit higher and gaped at the threesome struggling about on the floor. Amaury and Emma—naked as the day they had been born—and a fully clothed Little George were all rolling about the floor kicking and hitting. Or to be more honest, wee Lady Emma appeared to be the only one kicking and hitting. The two men seemed to be more concerned with blocking her blows as she leaped about between, atop, and beneath them all at the same time. Mayhap if Lady Emma would open her eyes, which were squinted closed at the moment, she might realize it and give up the battle, for she was the only one fighting it, Blake thought with amusement. Then he waved away the men who had followed him into the tent, before bellowing, "What goes on here?"

Lady Emma stilled at once at his words, much to everyone's relief. Opening her eyes to find the tent as bright as a sunny morning, she clambered quickly out of the tangle of arms and legs on the floor and scampered to the bed to grab up the bedclothes to cover herself as she turned to face the fracas she had left behind. Unfortunately, everything was a blur just then, and she reached up fretfully to rub at her eye. She had received a fist to the eye on first joining the fray. It was the reason she had kept her eyes closed after that. Now she scowled in the direction of the two men raising themselves from the floor, and pointed accusingly at the one who was dressed. Or at least, he appeared to be dressed. Emma's eyes had not yet adjusted to the light. For all she knew she might be pointing at her husband, but presumed Blake would know who she meant as she exclaimed, "He tried to kill us!"

Blake cocked one eye as he turned to peer at Amaury and Little George. He thought surely she must be joking, until he saw the shamefaced look on the man's face. "Little George?" he said uncertainly.

Emma frowned at that. Squinting harder, she tried to make out the man she had pointed at. Surely it could not be Amaury's own man?

"He did not try to kill me," her husband announced wearily, much to both Blake and Emma's relief, but that relief died on dismay when he added, "I was awake. He stood there a good ten minutes and could not bring himself to it."

Blake saw Emma drop weakly to the bed at that, and would dearly have loved to join her in doing so as he tried to sort out the muddle before him. "Nay. Not Little George. Tell me 'tis not so," he demanded, anger beginning to rise within him.

Avoiding his eyes, Little George stared guiltily at the ground.

"But why? Amaury has been good to you. He—"

"Where is your wife?"

Emma turned to her husband in surprise at that question. It was the same one she had asked him earlier, though she knew he had been asleep then. It seemed he too had wondered at the delay keeping the newlyweds apart.

Understanding coming to his face, Blake slumped slightly where he stood. "She is not with relatives, is she."

"Nay," Little George admitted unhappily.

"Where is she?"

"Taken." That one word was filled with a wealth of grief. "We were on our way to Eberhart. An hour from the castle she asked me to stop so she might relieve herself. She went a little ways into the woods. She never returned. A stranger came instead. He said they held her and would kill her should I try to find her. He said she would be safe . . . so long as I did as I was told."

"What did they want?" Amaury asked when he grew silent.

"Very little at first. I was simply to wait and listen and tell what I learned when asked."

"Who were you to tell?"

"I did not know at first. So I watched and listened, and then de Lascey and his women came."

"Sylvie." Blake murmured on a sigh.

"Nay. Gytha."

"Gytha?" Emma peered at him in horror. It had been bad enough when she had thought it was the young girl Sylvie, but Emma had liked Gytha.

"Aye." Little George nodded. "She used Sebert to find out things I could not tell her."

Amaury's eyebrows rose at that. "What would Sebert know that you do not?"

"A great many things just lately, it seems," Little George told him with a brief flash of amusement that soon died. Sighing, he shook his head. "Sebert has been spending his time since your wedding bouncing between doing his duties and trailing Lady Emma about, trying to be privy to any and all conversations in which she partook. 'Twas at your order," Little George added when Emma began to look upset at that.

"Mine?!"

"Aye. He told Gytha that you ordered him to listen at doors and make himself privy to any and all conversations so that you did not have to waste time explaining things to him."

She nearly groaned aloud as she recalled her panic on the day of her wedding and the stupid orders she had been bellowing about.

The Deed

"You did that?" Amaury stared at her wide-eyed.

Waving the question irritably away, Emma turned back to Little George. "So she was the one to put the poison in Amaury's tankard?"

"Aye."

"Why did she kill Sylvie?"

"The girl saw her put the potion in the tankard. That morning when they went down to break fast, Gytha slipped some into her ale. I do not know what happened after that, but when I went up to fetch de Lascey and his women, Gytha trailed behind to speak to me. She slipped an empty vial to me and told me to put it in the girl's hand. She must have already put the other in her bag."

"Did you know that we would be attacked when we went to the river on the first day of our travels?" Amaury asked now.

"Nay. Not until I was approached in the woods standing guard," he admitted reluctantly.

"Who was it approached you in the woods?"

"Gytha."

"She was there?" Emma asked in dismay.

Little George nodded. "Edsel had stepped a little distance away to . . . er . . . relieve himself." He grimaced apologetically at Emma as he said that. "I heard him cry out and started to follow him. Gytha stepped into my path. She told me my wife was alive and well, so far, but would only stay so if I continued to do as asked. Should her men fail this time, I was to kill you before we reached court, else my wife would die. Then she koshed me over the head."

"So you planned to kill me tonight," Amaury murmured.

"I tried," Little George said grimly.

"And could not."

His first shrugged uncomfortably. "As Blake said, you

249

have been good to me. We have been friends for years. And I do not know if my wife still lives or if they have already killed her. I simply could not bring myself to—"

"Who is Gytha working for. Is it Bertrand? If so, we can go find your wife right now," Blake said urgently, but the other man shook his head.

"I do not know. I have never known. Had I known, I would have gone to get her long ago and refused all their orders."

Silence filled the tent. When it had stretched out as taut as a bow, George shifted uncomfortably. "What will you do now?"

Amaury shrugged unhappily. He had been awakened by the faint breeze that had entered the tent with Little George. Had heard the faint rustle as Little George had approached the bed, and had stiffened in preparation of defending himself, only to freeze when his eyes had adjusted and he recognized his first. It had taken a few moments for him to recognize the weapon he had then unsheathed and stood over him holding. Hardly able to believe what he was witnessing, Amaury had waited tensely to see if the man could really go through with it. After a good ten minutes had passed with Little George simply standing there, seemingly unable to do the deed, and at the same time unable to walk away, Amaury had been about to speak up and let him know he knew of his presence. Unfortunately, his wife had awakened and preceded him, he thought wryly, recalling the boot to the behind that had sent him sprawling into his would-be attacker.

"I will do nothing, Little George," he said now with a sigh. "I am sure had I been in your position, I would have plunged the knife home for Emma."

Little George shrugged. "I thought I could too until I stood over you."

Grimacing, Amaury moved to peer out the entrance

of the tent. The first faint rays of dawn were streaking across the sky in ribbons of pink that underlined the inky black of night. " 'Tis almost dawn. We will reach court today."

"And they, whoever they are, will know I failed," George said unhappily, misery taking shape on his homely face.

"Not if Amaury is dead."

All three men turned on Emma in horror at her words. She rolled her eyes at their expressions. "Not really dead. We shall pretend he is. No one but the three of us know what happened in this tent. Who is to say that Little George did not succeed?"

"Well . . ." Blake shifted uncomfortably. "There are more than the three of us," he admitted wryly after a moment. When Emma raised her eyebrows at that, he grimaced. "Half the camp followed me in here when you started screaming. I sent them away when I realized you were . . ." He gestured to where she now sat wrapped in the bedclothes and Emma flushed. It appeared as if half the camp had seen her thrashing about naked on the floor with her husband and Little George. A damned embarrassing bit of knowledge, but she really did not have time to worry on it overmuch.

"Did they get enough of a look to see if he was wounded or nay?"

Blake thought on it a moment, then shook his head slowly. "Nay, I do not think they would have."

"Well, then, 'tis settled. You are dead, husband." Emma smiled at her own cleverness. "That will keep Little George's wife safe until you can save her."

His eyebrows rose at that. "I am to save her, am I?"

"Surely. Being dead gives you a great deal of freedom. We can put you in a disguise. You can sneak into Bertrand's castle, snoop about, find out where she is and . . . Why are you shaking your head at me?"

251

"You have read too many books, wife," he told her grimly, then shared a glance between Blake and Little George. "I do not think it a good thing that some fathers allow their daughters to read now. It does seem to addle them somewhat."

Emma narrowed her eyes on him and snapped, " 'Tis a sound plan!"

"Mayhap if we were characters in one of Chaucer's—"

"Husband!"

Amaury sighed. "You forget one thing, wife. Should I be considered dead, 'twould leave you unprotected. Bertrand would force a marriage."

Emma frowned over that, then brightened. "I shall claim that I am pregnant. I would be safe then."

Amaury shook his head at that. Rather than keep her safe, such a claim might simply put her in graver danger. He had no doubt that to Bertrand, a child would simply be an inconvenience. He'd either arrange for her to suffer a miscarriage or kill her outright, depending on how great his desire was for her. Amaury tended to think he would try to cause her to miscarry, for in his eyes, his wife was a very desirable woman. He did not bother to mention this to her, however, for his thoughts were taken up with plotting of his own.

"Nay, I will not be dead," he announced, moving to finally don his braies. "But I shall be dying."

Chapter Thirteen

"Oh, my lady. 'Tis so unfair!"

Putting a hand to her maid's shoulder, Emma patted it soothingly. "Aye, fate is a fickle witch," she murmured, adding a dramatic sigh for good measure.

Amaury grimaced slightly at his wife's poor acting, then silently cursed his forgetting himself when Maude gasped.

"Look, my lady! He appears to be coming around. He is in pain."

Emma glanced down with a start, and frowned at her husband as she caught the expression that Maude had noticed just before he eased it back into the expressionless mask he had been feigning since shortly after explaining his plan that morning. It was to look as if he had been attacked in his sleep and stabbed. He was to be at death's door, but lingering before stepping over the threshold. The official story was that Emma had awakened as her husband was stabbed and thrown herself at the adversary, so that she and her husband became tangled up with him, but when Blake had arrived with the torch, they had found Little George.

Amaury's first was to claim he had arrived before Blake and, unable to see in the dark, had joined the tussle, but that the villain had somehow escaped before the others had arrived. Bertrand and Lady Ascot, however, would know that they had commissioned no one else to attack her husband, and would assume that Little George had simply done the deed they had set before him. Her husband was hoping this plot would keep both Emma and Little George's wife safe until they could figure some way to find the woman.

Emma thought her plan would have worked better, but the men had not agreed, so she had had to bow to the majority. And had fretted over it ever since. There had been a myriad of problems that day. First they had had to convince the others that they had not raised a hue and cry and set them to searching the woods for the phantom attacker because they had been busy trying to save her husband's sorry hide. Then there had been the problem of Maude. Amaury, being near death, had had to lay, supposedly unconscious, in the wagon for the remainder of the trip. Her husband had not handled real illness well, so she should not have been surprised that he bore this feigned illness even worse. He had whined and complained over the need to ride in the wagon like a baby at every opportunity.

He had gotten that opportunity often. To prevent Maude from trying to change Amaury's bandages or do something else that would allow her to learn that he was not injured after all, Emma had been forced to ride in the wagon as well, playing the concerned wife. She had spent most of that last day of traveling attempting to keep Maude from overhearing her husband's complaining. Especially at the nooning meal when all she could offer her deathly ill and supposedly unconscious husband was an apple. It would not have done for her to be taking food to her supposedly weak and dying husband, but try to explain that to a hungry man who had had naught but a corner of bread that she had managed to sneak away for him to break fast with.

It had got worse after that, for it had begun to drizzle. In an attempt to keep her "poor" husband dry in the uncovered wagon, Emma had taken up a blanket and crouched over him for the remainder of the ride. That had merely allowed him to complain more, for they were sheltered somewhat by the blanket. Between his complaining and the fact that her back had felt near to cracking from being in such a bent position for so long, Emma had been ready to stab her husband herself.

It had been a great relief when they had finally arrived at Leicestershire, where Richard was holding temporary court. Amaury too had seemed relieved. At least he had stopped his infernal complaining for a bit as they had seen to carrying him up to this room where they were to remain during their stay. But then, there was no longer the creak of wood and the whirring of the wagon wheels to cover any complaints he might have made, and Maude was no longer separated from them by the length of the wagon and a blanket. Emma suspected that was the only thing that kept him silent, and was in no rush to see the servant go. However, she was beginning to think she might have to. For her husband was obviously having difficulty maintaining his role. All he really had to do was lie silent and rest, yet it seemed even that was too difficult for him to accomplish.

Emma was about to give in and send Maude away when a knock sounded at the door. The servant immediately hurried to answer it, and stepped aside with a small gasp when the king entered followed by Blake.

Moving directly to the bed, King Richard peered down at his fallen warrior, his shoulders immediately slumping. "So 'tis true," he murmured glumly, and Amaury issued a low moan.

As she glanced at him, Emma's lips tightened vexedly. He was to be at death's door, for goodness sake. Did he keep moaning and frowning, people would think him on the mend. Damn! It was his own plan. He could at least have the decency to keep to it.

Richard took in the glare she was gracing her husband with and frowned. "I think he is trying to say something, madam," he snapped sharply.

"Nay," Emma murmured, managing a mournful look. "Nay, Your Majesty. He is beyond words now. Death is his companion, and has ever demanded silence of those he courts. He will linger some, I am sure, bu 'tis all a matter of—ouch!" Glancing down, she scowled sharply at Amaury. He'd pinched her, the bloody ogre! He'd slid his hand out from beneath the blankets and pinched her! He was just lucky no one saw him.

"Is something amiss?" Richard asked.

Emma glanced sharply at the suspicion on the king's face and shook her head. "Nay, Your Majesty. I just— 'tis my new shoes," she prevaricated. "They are new enough to pinch." Her gaze happened to slide to Blake then, and noting the fact that he was making faces at her and nodding toward Maude, she hesitated, confusion covering her expression. She was just grasping the fact that he thought she should have Maude leave, when the door burst open and Little George stormed in with the king's guard on his heels trying to catch his arms and drag him back.

"She is dead!" he roared disconsolately. " 'Twas all for naught! She is dead." The last word sank away on misery as he came to a halt. The guards immediately caught him and tried to wrestle him from the room.

"He is Amaury's man," Blake explained quickly to the
ing, who nodded and turned to the three men strug-
ling at the door. In truth, only his guards were strug-
ling. Little George was slumped where he stood, not
ghting, but as immovable as a castle wall.

"Leave him be! Leave us!" As soon as the door had
losed on his men, King Richard turned to survey the
nhabitants of the room. He could feel a storm of secrets
lowing about him, and was beginning to suspect he
vas the only one who did not understand what was
appening. "What is the meaning of this? What goes on
ere?"

There was silence for a moment. Then Amaury sat up
n bed with a sigh. " 'Twas my idea, Your Majesty," he
nnounced apologetically, rising from the bed.

"Oh, sweet Saint Christopher, 'tis a miracle!" Maude
ried, dropping to her knees to offer a prayer of thank-
ulness.

Sighing, Emma moved to her servant's side. "Aye,
Maude. 'Tis wondrous." Her voice hardly sounded
leased as she took the woman's arm and urged her
ack to her feet, but the servant did not notice. She was
oo busy sobbing with joy. Ushering her to the door,
Emma patted her back. "No doubt his lordship would
ppreciate some refreshments and food after his illness.
After you have refreshed yourself, mayhap you could
ring him a repast."

"Aye, my lady. 'Twill be good for him."

"Aye," Emma agreed, and closed the door.

Amaury turned to where Little George stood so stiff
nd silent, despair his only expression. "Tell me," he
rdered.

King Richard opened his mouth to countermand that
rder and demand his own explanations, then decided
gainst it as the man began to speak.

"I was helping Wesley to see to the horses at the sta-

bles when he struck up a conversation with Lord Woo
sey's first," Little George told them dully. "I overhear
him commiserating with him over your injury, and te
ing him that they too had suffered several misadven
tures on their way here."

Aye." King Richard nodded at that. "Woolsey told m
all about it when he arrived at court earlier this month
His favored horse went lame and had to be put dowr
one of his men became ill, and they came across
woman floating in the river one of the nights when the
made camp." The king paused to frown when Amaury
man winced over that last bit of information, his fac
transfixed with agony. "But they knew not who th
woman was," he added after a moment.

"Nay, they did not. Nor did I, until he showed m
this." Holding his hand out, Little George opened it t
reveal a small circular band.

"Your wife's?" Amaury asked reluctantly.

He nodded. "It has our initials."

Amaury crossed the few feet that separated them an
took the ring. Peering at it closely, he looked for thos
initials, then sighed when he espied them. Handing th
ring back, he clasped his first's shoulder. "She has bee
dead all this time?"

"They found her two days after she was taken, bu
said she looked to have been in the water for at least
day."

Thinking he had been patient long enough, King
Richard crossed his arms and frowned on them all
"What goes on here? Amaury, explain yourself. You are
obviously not injured. Why was I told you were?"

"I am sorry, Your Majesty, and I do appreciate you
forbearance so far," Amaury murmured, squeezing hi
first's shoulder before turning to face his king. It was a
breach of protocol, Emma was sure. One was not sup
posed to show the king one's back, but Richard did no

ppear upset. In truth he was so tangled up in intrigue
t the moment, she suspected he had not even noticed.

"We have had some difficulties since the wedding,"
er husband announced now. "I was beset by bandits,
hen mercenaries in two separate attacks, and my dogs
vere killed by poison meant for me. My wife and I were
ttacked on the journey here. Then we learned that my
irst's wife had been kidnapped a few days after the
vedding in an attempt to force him to aid in seeing to
ny demise."

The king digested all of this, then quirked one eye-
row. "Bertrand?"

"That is my guess."

"And this injury you supposedly suffered?"

Amaury cast a glance at Little George, then sighed. "
Twas for George's wife. He was ordered to kill me if
he last attack failed. At threat of her death. We hoped
ny being on death's door would protect her and Emma
t the same time. There was also the hope that they
vould grow impatient with my lingering, try again to
ill me here, and be caught in the act."

"And now?"

Amaury hesitated, then shrugged. "It may still work
s a trap."

"You forget your maid. By now she has no doubt told
ne and all that you are recovered. Up and about, in
act."

"Aye," Amaury agreed wryly. "But that may be to our
advantage. Aye, 'twill work," he decided. "You and
Blake can explain that I am still weak, but definitely on
he mend. 'Twill force them to make another attempt."

The king considered that, then nodded. "I will have
my own men posted at the door and—"

"Nay! My apologies, Your Majesty, but I would not
have you do anything to put off my assassins. Guards
may frighten them away entirely. Then I shall just have

259

to deal with them later. I need no guards. I have an advantage in that I am not ill. I shall be waiting for them."

"I will not have that, de Aneford. Bertrand may be a coward, but his mother is clever. They may see right through this ruse of yours. I would have at least one guard with you. Here in the room."

Amaury considered that, then nodded.

"I will be that guard." When everyone peered at him, Little George tightened his hand on the ring he held. "I have an interest in seeing justice done."

"It shall be so," King Richard decided.

Emma paused on the path and tipped her head up, closing her eyes as she inhaled the sweet scent of the flowered trees about her.

It was the second morning after their arrival at the king's temporary court at Leicestershire, and for Emma the last day and a half had been a nightmare of anxiety. Waiting was not one of her favorite activities on the best of occasions, but waiting for someone to try to kill her husband was unbearable. Even Amaury, who had seemed to relish the idea at first, was beginning to show the wear of wasted hours lying abed awaiting assassins who were definitely taking their time. It was one of the reasons she had delayed returning to their room. Her husband was growing short-tempered in his impatience. A few moments alone in the garden had seemed a lovely treat. It was so fresh here, clean. Truly, court was foreign to her. Everyone seemed so cold, uncaring, and quite debauched. It made her mind spin to think of how many wives were sleeping with other wives' husbands. But that was only one of the infractions going on here, she thought, grimly recalling a conversation she had had at table.

Emma had been seated next to Lady Magdalyn, a

rather cold and caustic creature who seemed to delight in shocking people. When she had noticed Emma staring warily at Lady Ascot as she had entered the hall, Magdalyn had leaned closer and murmured, "She is a nasty old bitch, is she not? 'Tis lucky you escaped marrying her son." Then after a silence, "I wonder where her *maid* is? I have never seen them apart until this visit."

Curious at the way Magdalyn drawled the word maid with such sarcasm, Emma had murmured, "Her lady's maid?"

"Hm. She is much more than maid. If court gossip is to be believed, she is Lady Ascot's lover. Though of course, for propriety's sake she is called maid."

"Lover?" Emma had gaped in amazement at the very idea. Being a woman herself, she was positive the maid would not have that odd appendage that was needed for the joining. How could they possibly be lovers then, she had wondered with confusion. But when she had stated these thoughts aloud, Lady Magdalyn had laughed and shaken her head in amazed disgust.

"You *are* naive, are you not?" she had drawled, then stood and moved to another seat. Moments later, loud laughter had drawn Emma's eyes along the table to find Magdalyn and the woman next to her laughing openly as they eyed her.

The snapping of a twig brought Emma's eyes open with a start to stare at the man before her. "Bertrand." She eyed him warily, discomfort creeping up her back when he smiled at her.

"Good morning, Lady Emmalene. I see you like gardens as well. We have something in common then."

Shifting carefully to the side to move around him, she nodded stiltedly. "I must return to my husband. I have been remiss in neglecting him so. He will be fraught." More than fraught, she thought grimly. Her husband

261

would be livid should he learn that she had put hersel
in a position to be caught alone and unawares by Ber
trand. He had ordered her to stay in the room where he
could protect her at all but mealtimes. Then she was to
travel directly to the hall to dine, then return directly
In fact, he had taxed Blake with the chore of seeing her
back and forth. But on arriving at the table that morn
ing, King Richard had announced his wish to have a
word with him.

When her husband's friend had hesitated, Emma had
assured him that she would be fine and would return
directly to her husband once she had finished breaking
fast. Only then had he reluctantly stood to join his king.
One did not refuse royalty.

Emma truly had meant her promise when she had
made it, but after Magdalyn had left her alone, a servant
had placed some greasy cheese and a chunk of brown
bread before her and Emma had felt her stomach roll
in protest. For a moment she had feared she might be
ill, then had managed to swallow the bile in her throat
She did not think she was coming down with anything
In truth she blamed her jumpy stomach on the constant
tension of anxiety she had been suffering, not only this
last day, but for weeks now. Her stomach had always
been the first to react to troubles. Her head was usually
second, and she could already feel the beginnings of the
aching gathering in her head.

"Is he often fraught?" Bertrand asked, and was not
surprised by the startled confusion on her face. He
knew her thoughts had been far away. He had watched
the play of emotions cross her face for the last several
moments, his heart lifting with hope as he noted that
each expression seemed to be a negative one. A frown,
a sigh, a grimace. Aye, Lady Emma was not happy in
her marriage. He had suspected such would be the case.
De Aneford was a great buffoon with beefy hands and

little between the ears but wood. How could anyone prefer a man like that over himself? Impossible. Bertrand was aware of his attractiveness to women.

Nay. Lady Emmalene did not love her husband, Bertrand decided now. He had feared it might be otherwise when Gytha had told him that she cried out at night with her passion, but now he decided those cries had been pain-filled sobs. Nay, they had not been cries of pleasure the wench had heard. Women did not do such things. It was only men who shouted their victory as they succumbed to the pleasures of the flesh. He ought to know. Had he not bedded a hundred women at least? And not one of them had cried out with pleasure.

Emma frowned over his question, and rubbed her forehead in a vain attempt to ease the aching that was beginning there. "I must return to my husband."

"Wait!" Catching her arm, he drew her back to his side. "I heard of Lord Amaury's misfortune and wished to express my sympathies."

Emma's mouth tightened at his words. It was more likely he wished to gloat than sympathize.

Noting her displeasure, Bertrand nearly clapped his hands with glee. To him it meant that truly she was not happy in her marriage. It was impossible that she might see through his words and be aware that it was he and his mother behind the many misfortunes her husband had experienced of late. His mother was too clever.

"Your husband is most fortunate to have you for a wife," he told her passionately now, with the first iota of truth he had spared in this conversation. He did think Amaury lucky, and it was a luck he hoped to have soon.

Emma's stomach rolled again at the covetous calculation in the face of the man before her. She knew he was savoring the possibility of gaining all he wanted once her husband was gone, was relishing the idea of possessing all he now held.

"Aye, he is fortunate," Emma agreed impulsively. "He is a grand duke now, with a large estate, many retainers, and an heir on the way."

Emma would forever savor Bertrand's reaction to that. He looked pole-axed. Taking advantage of his stunned state, she turned abruptly and moved back through the garden. Her headache was already easing, as was her anxiety. There would be no more attempts on her husband now. Lady Ascot and Bertrand would believe it a waste of effort. They could not force a marriage were there an heir. It was just a shame that it was not true, she thought with a sigh.

She had nearly reached the doors leading back into the castle when Lady Ascot stepped through them and started down the path toward her. Her steps faltering, Emma slowed as she came abreast of the woman, but other than a cold nod, Lady Ascot did nothing.

Walking at a much slower pace Emma continued forward through the doors, then paused and peered back. Bertrand still stood where she had left him. He stayed there until his mother reached him. Lady Ascot paused, and they exchanged a few words, then glanced furtively around before moving further along the garden path and disappearing from sight.

Biting her lip, Emma hesitated a moment, then cursed under her breath and moved back into the garden. Pausing on the edge of the trees, she glanced nervously around, then stepped cautiously into the trees, following the faint murmur of their voices.

"What do you mean?"

"Pregnant, Mother. Surely you know what that means," Bertrand snapped.

"Do not be smart with me, boy!" The words were followed by a sharp crack. Pushing a branch of leaves aside, Emma saw Bertrand holding one very red cheek. His mother was just setting her cane back on the ground.

"I am sorry." He peered at her woefully. " 'Tis just that I am distraught. All our work and planning has been for naught."

"Nonsense. We shall continue as planned."

"But she is with child. She cannot be forced to wed if there is an heir."

"She can if she miscarries," Lady Ascot said coldly. "And that should not be too difficult to arrange."

Emma's eyes widened in horror at that. Would they stop at nothing?

"Oh Mother, you are clever."

"And do not forget it."

Emma grimaced at that, but it was only a halfhearted effort. She was distracted by the thought that it was already the end of June. She had had her last woman's time directly after the wedding, over a month ago. It was late, was all, she assured herself, but with little belief. She was usually as regular as the sun's rising and falling. But then she had been under a great deal of stress of late and had heard that could affect such things.

You were nauseous this morning when you sat down to break fast, some nasty part of her mind reminded her, and Emma's hand clenched over her stomach. It was stress, she tried to reassure herself. Stress always affected her stomach.

What about the constant need to relieve yourself? Was that not a symptom? Emma winced. She knew the symptoms of pregnancy backward and forward. She had memorized them in the first month of her marriage to Fulk. A weak bladder was often a symptom and it was true that she had had to make water more often than usual lately. She had not noticed until they had headed for court, for it was when it was most inconvenient to stop and find a spot to take care of such matters that they had become most noticeable.

Good God! She could not be with child! It was ironic that the one thing she had yearned for for so long suddenly terrified the breath out of her. But if her foolish impulsiveness in claiming a pregnancy she had not thought to be real put the longed-for child in danger . . .

"How shall we do it? 'Twill not put her life in danger, will it?"

"Nay. Gytha will know a way. Where the devil is that woman anyway? You did tell her to meet us here, did you not?"

"Aye, of course. She is probably late a purpose. She is an arrogant bitch. I do not know why you put up with her as lady's maid."

Emma stiffened at that. Gytha was Lady Ascot's maid? The one said to be her lover? It was the proof they had been looking for. She must tell Amaury. The king would have Bertrand and his mother in the tower before the nooning meal. Emma had straightened to hurry away with this news when pain exploded inside her head. Stumbling under the blow, she turned shakily, and just managed to make out Gytha's coldly smiling face before darkness rushed in on a roar to overtake her.

"Where the devil did my wife get to?" Tossing the bed linens aside, Amaury stood and began to pace the floor.

Little George raised an eyebrow at his lord's impatience, but had no answer.

Scowling at him for his silence, Amaury moved to the window and stared blindly out. He detested this inactivity, and he detested the fact that his wife had to leave for meals. In his mind it put her in danger and he did not like it, but Blake and King Richard had agreed that she must leave. It was to give the assassin a chance to strike. Besides, they had assured him, Bertrand and his mother could hardly harm his wife in public. While he had agreed with that at the time, the fact that she was late now was gnawing at his innards like a pack of hungry rats.

He was about to send his first to search for her when a trio of riders leaving the bailey caught his attention. Distracted briefly, he narrowed his eyes on the man traveling with two women, suddenly sure it was Bertrand. The rider had the same carriage and diminutive shape. Added to that, one of the females with him bore a striking resemblance to Lady Ascot. Amaury's gaze slid to the last rider and he frowned. She looked familiar, but from this distance he could not see her face, all he knew was she was too big to be his wee wife.

His gaze slid back to the man, narrowing as he noted the tapestry across his lap. It was a damned strange thing to be riding about with. It was big too, overflowing his lap and hanging down both sides of the horse, Amaury noted. Then he stiffened, his blood running cold as he glimpsed a small gold item slip from the folds of the rolled material and drop to the ground.

Whirling away from the window, he grabbed his sword from beneath the bed linens and rushed to the door.

"My lord!" Little George cried, leaping from his seat to follow.

"What the devil?!"

Amaury heard that exclamation seconds before the man coming down the hall suddenly stepped into his path and caught his arms to stop him. "What are you doing? You risk everything!"

It took a moment for those hissed words to sink in enough to make Amaury peer at the face of his obstacle.

Recognizing Blake, he grabbed the front of his doublet urgently. "Where is she?"

"Who?"

"Emma. Where is she? You were to return her to the room."

"The king wished me to . . ." He paused. "She should have finished breaking her fast at least half an hour ago," he admitted grimly.

Cursing, Amaury pushed past him and continued down the hall.

Muttering some unpleasant descriptive words himself, Blake hurried after him, whipping off his cloak as he did.

"At least put this on," Blake hissed, draping it over him and tugging the hood up to cover his face. Glancing back at Little George, he snapped, "Go back and close the chamber door, man! Would you let all and sundry know he is up?"

Skidding to a halt, the first retraced his steps to fulfill that order, then caught up to the two men again as Blake said, "You must not rush about like this, Amaury. You will draw attention to yourself. Where the devil are you going?!" he added when they reached the bottom of the stairs and Amaury suddenly turned toward the outer doors.

"Lord Blake?!"

Sliding to a halt, Blake whirled quickly and made a bow as the king approached from a side door of the hall. A glance over his shoulder showed Amaury escaping out the door.

"Rise. What is happening?"

Straightening from his bent position, Blake glanced briefly around the empty hall, then murmured, "Lady Emma is missing."

"What?" King Richard stared at him in stunned horror for a moment. Then his gaze slid to the open door and the cloaked figure crossing the bailey toward the stables. "Is that—?"

"Aye."

"Good God!" Richard started after him at once, Blake, Little George and the king's liveried men-at-arms now following.

They had just reached the stables when Amaury came riding out.

The king raised a hand and opened his mouth to call him to a halt, but it was too late. Amaury rode out like the Devil was on his tail.

"Damn! He must be on to something. Where is the stable master?! I need horses, man! Bring me horses!"

It took only a few short moments for Amaury to reach the spot where he had seen the small golden item slip from beneath the tapestry, but to him it seemed to take forever. He recognized it as a tiny single slipper before he had even dismounted to pick it up, but once he held it in his hand, his fear became a reality and he was lost for a moment in grief.

"What is it, de Aneford? What have you there?"

Amaury gazed up at King Richard as he and the others reined in beside him. He was silent as he held the slipper up for them to see.

Blake immediately blanched. "Emma wore gold this morning."

"Aye." Hand closing on the slipper, Amaury quickly remounted. "Bertrand has her. I saw him ride away with his mother and another woman from my chamber window."

"And she left a slipper behind to let you know 'twas her!" the king guessed excitedly.

"Nay. Bertrand had a tapestry rolled up and strapped over the horse before him. This fell out of one end."

King Richard grimaced at that. Being carted off in a

269

rolled-up old carpet was not nearly as romantic as riding away under force and dropping bits of clothing as a trail to a lover. Richard liked romances.

"Hold!" The king ordered when he turned his horse to chase Bertrand.

Amaury hesitated. By law he could not ignore an order by the king, but he wanted to just then. Frustration churning inside him, he paused.

"You do not know where they head," Richard pointed out calmly. "You cannot race about heedlessly. We must think on this."

"There is nothing to think on. They went in this direction. I will catch them up afore they go far . . . if I hurry."

The last few words definitely carried a message for him, King Richard thought with amusement. "What if they did not go straight? What if they turned in one direction or another soon as they were under the cover of the trees? Do you not think they would have realized they could be seen from the castle by anyone who cared to look? Do you not think they know they would be the first under suspicion when 'twas discovered Lady Emmalene was missing?"

"Aye," Amaury admitted bitterly, recognizing the wisdom behind the words and the fact that he himself should have thought of that himself, and most likely would have had he not all but panicked. Panic was what got men killed. Not panicking was why he had survived so long as a warrior. Odd that he had lived with himself for twenty some years, yet had never panicked over his own health, but now that Emma's was in jeopardy, he could seem to do little else.

"He could be headed for his demesne," Blake suggested. " 'Tis not that far from here, though as I recall, 'tis in that direction." He gestured to the north.

"Aye, but he may have cut off that way as soon as he

hit the trees," Richard commented thoughtfully.

"Aye," Amaury decided after a moment. " 'Tis most like he headed for there. 'Tis the only land he holds, and he could not risk taking Emma elsewhere when he holds her against her will."

Turning to one of his men-at-arms, the king gestured, bringing the man immediately to his side. "Return to the castle. Gather a hundred men. Nay, two hundred, then follow us. Bring Amaury's men as well."

"If we hurry we will not need the men," Amaury muttered impatiently as the soldier rode back toward the castle at once.

"His keep is only a day's ride from here and he may know a shortcut we do not," the king pointed out. "If so, we are prepared. Ride on, de Aneford."

Turning his horse with relief, Amaury set out after his wife.

Chapter Fourteen

Emma awoke to find that she could not breathe or see, her head pained her something horrible, she was hot and sweaty, and she seemed to ache everywhere. She was also wrapped in something decidely old and dusty and hanging over what she guessed was a horse by the way she was being bounced about so.

Ten minutes later she was still soundly berating herself for getting into this mess when the jarring motion beneath her halted abruptly. A moment later, she felt hands grasp her through the thick, hard material about her as she was shifted, jostled and carted about briefly. Then the covering about her was ripped open and she found herself lying upon a bed in a small stone room.

"You are awake."

Emma was having some difficulty seeing after the sudden change from dark to light, but did not need her eyes to recognize the speaker: Bertrand. And he sounded damnably pleased. She opened her mouth to share her feelings on the subject of being cracked over the head and kidnapped, but all that came out was a disappointing croak before her throat closed up with dryness.

"A beverage." Bertrand got to his feet and moved toward the door. "I shall fetch you one. You just rest now. 'Twas a long ride."

Emma glared at his departing figure, then sighed unhappily and eased to sit on the edge of the bed and peer around. There was not much to see. The cot she sat on was the only piece of furniture in the room. Aside from that, her prison boasted one window and a small fireplace. Grimacing, she eased herself forward, got awkwardly to her feet, and staggered toward the window. It was not very far, but it seemed she had traveled miles by the time she reached the square opening.

Sagging against the ledge, she drank in deep breaths of the sweet fresh air coming through the window, then tipped her face up to the kiss of the afternoon sun. Both of nature's blessings were energizing after the hours she had spent in what she now saw had been a tapestry. Within moments her aches and pains began to ease, and she was able to concentrate on the problem at hand.

She was being held captive in a tower by people who wished to see her husband dead. And her child dead as well, if she were indeed carrying one.

Moving a hand to her stomach, Emma probed it gently. There was no pain or tenderness. Surely there would be both if she were with child and the ride had knocked it loose? And surely that ride had been enough to knock the most determined baby loose? Mayhap she was not with child after all. She grasped at that possibility eagerly, then shook her head. She could not be sure either way just now. Looking back, she saw that she had had a couple of the symptoms, but they might have simply been due to stress. She could not discount the possibility that she might be however, and that if she was, she had put that child in grave jeopardy by her words to Bertrand. His mother now wished to see her miscarry.

She had to get out of here, Emma thought grimly, focusing her gaze on the landscape outside the window. It was an old keep. Much smaller than Eberhart. The window of the tower she was in looked out of the side of the keep.

Leaning out and turning her head to the right, she could see the side of the wall that surrounded the bailey and one of the watchtowers that stood on either side of the drawbridge. The watchtower was manned by two men. She eased her head back inside lest they spot her peering about, then turned to glance at the ground below her window.

It was a long way down. A great long way. There was one thin ribbon of dirt in front of the wall, then a moat that presumably surrounded the whole keep. Beyond that was a clearing that stretched for a good hundred feet before the trees began. She would not escape this way, she decided grimly. She could not fly.

Sighing, she turned and peered about her prison. Dull stone walls, bare stone floor, the cot, and the door. It seemed the door and the window were the only two exits. If she could not leave through the window, then she must escape through the door. Only, she already knew the door was locked. She had heard Bertrand bar it on leaving.

Then she must get him to unbar it, she thought determinedly. Mayhap she could even get him to take her below stairs. She would have to gain his trust first, of course. The easiest way to do that was to convince him that she would prefer marriage to him over marriage to Amaury. It would not be a difficult task, she thought.

Bertrand, from what she could tell, seemed to have a rather high opinion of himself. She had witnessed it both at her wedding to Fulk and at court this last day or so. Aye, he would be easily convinced. If she could stomach the convincing.

"You shall have to," she told herself firmly. "Else they kill your husband and the child you may be carrying."

Amaury slowed his horse, then stopped and turned to peer at Blake and the king as they reined in their animals beside his. "They cannot be headed for their keep. Bertrand's horse is carrying two people. He could not possibly outrun our animals. Were he heading home, we should have overtaken them hours ago."

The king was silent for a moment, his gaze moving over the forest ahead of them before he turned to peer at the path they had already traversed. Squinting slightly, he could just make out a long red stream flowing over a small hill some distance back. It was his men. With the speed Amaury had been traveling, the army he had sent for had not been able to catch up to them yet. From this distance, they looked like one long body. A bright red caterpillar creeping over a bump in the lane. "Mayhap he knows of a shortcut that saves time," Richard said.

"Think you 'tis possible?" Amaury frowned at the idea.

King Richard shrugged. "As I recall on the map, his demesne is closer as the crow flies, but a deep river causes a detour of several hours."

Blake nodded at that. "Aye. I recall a sharp turn to the path when we reached the river. 'Twas several hours back."

Richard turned to Amaury now. "There may be a spot near there that can be forged during some parts of the

275

year. If so, only someone who traveled this way often would know of it."

Amaury's face creased with worry. "But what if 'tis no such spot? What if he simply did not go this way, but headed somewhere else?"

The king frowned impatiently at him. He had ridden into battle with this man several times, and had never known him to be so indecisive and uncertain. What the hell was the matter with the man? "His keep is only about an hour from here, Amaury." There was a decided snap to his voice as the king pointed that out. "Why do we not finish what we have started, make our way there, and find out?"

"Aye, of course you are right."

"Hmm." Richard peered at him narrowly for a moment, then shook his head. The man was in no state to think clearly. Should they arrive at Bertrand's demesne to discover Lady Emmalene there, he would no doubt charge right up and get himself killed. If given the chance. He would not give him the chance then, Richard decided. "You will follow me from here," he announced abruptly, and urged his horse forward again.

She was seated on the bed again when Bertrand returned. A servant followed him in, carrying a tankard of mead. Emma smiled gratefully at the woman as she accepted the refreshment, doing her best not to wince at the scars and marks she also carried. Lady Ascot's treatment of her retainers showed well.

"Drink," Bertrand urged her as the woman left. "You must be parched."

Forcing a smile, she raised the tankard, only to pause with it at her mouth as she recalled the poison in her husband's ale. She did not fear being killed by poison, but there was always the possibility that one of those *ways* Lady Ascot had thought Gytha might know of to get rid of a child was through a potion of some sort. There were potions for everything else. Why not for miscarriages?

When she saw Bertrand frown over her hesitation, Emma continued to raise the tankard, taking a surreptitious sniff of its contents before pretending to sip from the container. She did not smell anything out of the ordinary in the liquid, but decided it was better to be cautious.

Faking a swallow, she lowered the tankard and smiled at him. "You look fair pleased with yourself, my lord."

Bertrand broke into a grin, his body visibly relaxing at her winsome smile. "I should be. I am this far from gaining everything I dreamed of." He held his thumb and forefinger a hair's breadth apart before her.

Emma felt herself flush from the tip of her forehead to her toes. She knew it was from anger, but could only hope Bertrand thought it a blush as she ducked her head in feigned shyness and murmured, "I must look awful."

"Aye."

Charm was not one of his failings, she decided, raising a hand to try to straighten her hair somewhat. She could feel that it had fallen loose and now lay in curly ringlets about her face. Her gown too had suffered, she saw with irritation, taking in its dusty wrinkled state. The gold material looked more of a mustard color now. No doubt her face was a sight as well, she thought impatiently. If she wished to succeed at her plan, she must look attractive to him.

Bertrand watched Emma straighten her appearance, and knew it was for his benefit. Women always primped when around him. Most often it annoyed him, but it had quite the opposite effect just now. His heart took flight. Lady Emmalene wanted him. He had thought she must, for most women did, but to have his hopes proved true was just wondrous. He wanted . . . he wanted . . . her.

Emma was taken by surprise when Bertrand suddenly launched himself at her. She was so unprepared, all she managed was a small squeak of protest as he tumbled her backward onto the bed, knocking the tankard from her hand.

They surveyed the castle from the cover of the trees in the dim twilight.

"They hold her here."

"Aye," Blake agreed with the king. "Just look, they have the drawbridge up. The keep is locked up tight as a drum."

Amaury started to urge his horse forward at that, but Richard and Blake both caught his reins and held him back. "Nay, Amaury. Wait," Blake urged him.

"Wait?! They hold my wife."

"What would you? Ride up and knock at the gate?" Blake asked grimly.

"Blake is right. We must wait for our men. Their size will aid us. Come." Richard turned his horse, then paused to glance back at Amaury where he hesitated. "We shall rest and plot our course as we wait."

Slumping in his saddle, Amaury nodded at that. It made sense. One never went riding heedlessly into a fray. One planned and plotted, and in the end won. He knew that. It was why he had never lost a battle . . . and yet he had nearly rushed headlong into this one. It almost made him sick. He could have gotten himself, or worse yet Emma, killed. He had been rushing about so since seeing her crakow drop from the tapestry. He had known it was something of his wife's before he had even seen it properly. Amaury had never had such premonitions before, but then no one he had loved had been in danger before.

Then he swallowed as he heard his own thoughts. Love. Damn! There was that word again. Such a little word for such a strong and tormenting emotion. Did he really love his wife? He certainly felt lust for her. His blood had seemed to be bubbling for weeks now, always threatening to boil over with his want of her. Mayhap he even liked her. She was fair smart. He liked that. She was charming too. Many was the time she had made him laugh in the last month, sometimes without even meaning too. It was hard to recall what his life had been like before marrying her. It seemed to him to be just a mass of gray days.

Just as his future would be should she die, he thought suddenly and felt pain stab through him. Nay, he could not lose her. Love or not, he liked having her around. In truth, he might even need her. He would give his life to save her, but would rather not have to. He looked forward to many long years with the temperamental wench. She could not die.

Amaury peered toward the keep again. Where was she? And what was happening to her? If Bertrand or his old witch mother harmed Emma, he would kill them both. Slowly.

"De Aneford!"

Sighing, Amaury turned his horse to follow the king. He must settle down some. Calm himself enough to come up with a plan. His wife would not die. Nor would he. Bertrand could not have her.

"Nay, my lord! Prithee, control thyself!" Emma muttered, pushing at Bertrand's chest as his lips slobbered a passionate circle by her ear. "We cannot!"

"We cannot?" He pulled back to frown at her. "You do not wish to?"

279

Emma blinked at that. She would rather—well, it was of no matter. Just then she could not afford to be honest. She needed his favor were she to escape. "Aye, of course, but I—pray, my Lord, forbear. We must forbear."

"Why?"

"Why?" Biting her lip, she thought frantically. "I—'tis my woman's time."

"Your . . ." He swallowed at that, distaste flashing across his features briefly, then he suddenly frowned. "But you are with child."

"Oh, well, I . . ." Emma stared at him blankly for a moment, then saw a way to save the child that might be growing within her, and smiled at him coyly. "Now my lord, do not tell me that you believed that?"

"What?"

"Well . . . Clever as you are, you must have realized that that was all a ploy?"

"A ploy?"

"Aye. My husband thought 'twould get you to leave him be."

His eyebrows rose slightly at that. "He did?"

"Oh, aye. But surely you realized that? That last attack near killed him. He was lucky to survive. He fears that the next might succeed." She silently sent up a quick prayer that her husband would forgive her such slander.

"He does?"

"Aye. So he insisted I say I was with child. I did not wish to, of course."

"You didn't?"

"Oh, nay, my lord. What? And give up the opportunity to have you for husband? A fine . . . er . . . handsome . . . intelligent man such as yourself?"

He preened briefly, then narrowed his eyes. "Then why did you lie?"

"Why?"

"Aye. He was not in the garden. You could have told me the truth there."

"Um, well . . . Aye, 'tis so, but had he found out he would have beat me."

"Beat you?" His eyes widened.

"Aye. He threatened to beat me." Emma marveled even as she said that. It did seem she was quite adept at this new skill of weaving tales. She was actually even beginning to enjoy it somewhat.

"He did not?"

"Oh, aye," she told him airily. "And he is such a large man, I feared one beating would kill me."

"Oh, aye, 'twould," he agreed when she tried to look pathetic. Then he grimaced as he admitted, "My mother is over-fond of using her cane, but of course her beatings merely hurt. They could not kill you."

Emma did not know what to say to that, so she merely nodded with a sympathetic expression.

"Oh, my love!" Bertrand suddenly cried, catching her to his chest. "We have more in common than I had ever hoped. We shall be so happy together. I swear, I shall do my utmost to make it so." He emphasized that remark with a kiss that made Emma shudder inwardly.

"My lord, please," she gasped as soon as he released her lips to trail his mouth wetly down her throat. "My woman's time."

"Oh, aye." Releasing her at once, he put a goodly space between them. "I am sorry. I forget myself. 'Tis just that I am so happy."

"Aye, of course," Emma murmured with relief.

"I can hardly wait to consummate our feelings. I will be a tender lover, my dear. You shall never suffer under great clumsy paws such as Amaury's again."

"I cannot say how that news affects me," Emma murmured archly, then forced a smile. "Might I have another refreshment, my lord? The last seems to have spilled." She picked up the fallen tankard for proof as she spoke.

"Oh, aye. Of course." Turning, he moved to the door and tugged it open to yell down the hall after a servant.

"I thought mayhap we could go below stairs to have one," she murmured as he closed the door.

"Oh, no. Mother said you must stay locked up until . . ." His voice died at Emma's frown. "I am sorry, my love, but Mother will have her way. 'Twill not be for long. As soon as Amaury is dead, we shall be married and you shall be free."

Emma tried to withhold the groan that rose to her lips at that. She had hoped to be allowed some free movement. At least enough that she might find a way to escape. It looked as if she had failed somewhat.

Sighing, she moved to the window, peering down at the forest beyond the clearing. It was not that far between the moat and the trees. If the room they had chosen for her prison were only a little lower . . . On the first floor for instance, she could have jumped down and . . . But it was not lower, she thought with a sigh.

Seeing her despondency, Bertrand frowned himself. "I am sorry," he offered after a moment. "Is there anything I might gain you that would make your confinement more bearable? A needle and thread to embroider with? Or a book?"

When Emma remained silent, he sighed unhappily, longing on his face as he peered at her outline in the dusty golden gown. Then he perked up suddenly. "Mayhap you would like a change of clothes? I had a gown made for you."

When she turned on him sharply, he shifted uncomfortably. " 'Twas in case something like this ever occurred."

Emma turned away with a sigh at his explanation,

and sensed him shifting uncertainly behind her.

" 'Tis yellow," he tried. "You would look lovely in it."

She would look jaundiced in it, Emma thought with a grimace. Yellow was not a favored color on her, though gold was quite nice. It made little difference, however. Were she naked, she would not have worn anything he had had made for her. The arrogance of the action alone would have forced her to refuse it. She would rip any dress he brought her to shreds and make a meal of the strips before donning the thing. She would sooner make a rope of it and hang herself fr—

"Rope?" she breathed, her gaze dropping to the ground below the window.

"What?"

Turning abruptly, she smiled at him sweetly. "Aye. A change of clothes would be nice." But not nice enough to get her to the ground. What else could she ask for that they might supply? "Rags."

Bertrand blinked. "Excuse me?"

"I will need linens, my lord. A great many of them."

"Linens?"

"Aye. For my woman's time." When he frowned slightly, her smile widened. "I fear 'tis a terrible trial. It lasts a great length of time and flows as freely as the Thames River. I will need a great many linens. A great many."

"A great many." His gaze dropped below her waist briefly and he actually began to look a bit sickly. Emma was almost embarrassed by the enjoyment she suddenly experienced at his discomfort.

"Aye, I fear 'tis heavy enough I near drowned Amaury one night. Why, my maid says she has never known a woman to bleed so much. She is amazed that I do not bleed to death each time I . . . Is there anything amiss, my lord? You are looking fairly green just now."

"Nay. Nay." Swallowing, he backed toward the door.

"Nay. I shall have some linens sent to you at once." Stumbling out the door, he slammed it heavily behind him, and Emma smiled widely as she turned back and leaned out the window to survey the wall of the castle and the surrounding area. It was not completely unguarded. There was a man posted on the corner, and another where the wall of the keep met the wall surrounding the bailey, but she hoped that a combination of darkness and boredom might work in her favor if she waited until night.

Moments after he left her, the door was opened again. The servant was returning with a beverage to replace the one spilled. She also brought a lit candle. It was only then Emma realized how late in the day it was getting. She would need the candle to work by soon, she thought as another servant entered carrying a yellow gown and the clean linens. As he had promised, Bertrand had sent a great many of the cloth strips. More than she had dared hoped for, she saw as the woman set the gown and linens on the bed.

Relaxing as the servants left and the door was barred once more, Emma picked the yellow gown up and examined it. It was a frilly, fluffy thing. Far too young for her and ugly as sin, but it would make good rope if ripped into strips. She turned to sort through the linens then, amusement quirking her lips as she counted them. It seemed Bertrand had taken her at her word. She really would have to flow like a river to need as many as he had sent her.

Shrugging wryly, she sat back upon the bed and set to work ripping the gown into long strips that she tied end to end. It took her much longer than she had expected, and her hands began to ache with the effort, but once she was finished, she turned immediately to the linens, unfolding, twisting, and knotting them to the end of her makeshift rope.

The sun was beginning to set when she heard the door being unbarred. Her heart skipping a beat, Emma scrambled to quickly stuff the evidence of her escape efforts under a blanket, then folded her hands in her lap as the door opened.

She was not terribly surprised to see Lady Ascot enter, but she was not terribly happy either. Bracing herself inwardly, she tried for a pleasant expression as the woman surveyed her.

"My son says you are not pregnant."

Emma tried not to wince at the hard words. "Aye."

"You lied."

"I already explained to Bertrand that Lord Amaury ordered me to—"

"He told me."

Emma fell silent and waited.

"He also told me that you love him. Bertrand."

She swallowed. This was the tricky part. "I fear I have not known him long enough to lay claim to that emotion, but 'tis true that I favor him over—"

"You lie again."

Emma went still at that. "I—"

"Gytha told me."

Emma raised her eyebrows, her body tense. "Told you what?"

"He fawns over you like a starry-eyed fool."

"Amaury? Nay. He—"

"He subjected himself to de Lascey's arrogance purely to please you."

She blinked at that.

"He did not wish to shame you at court. Gytha heard him and Blake talking about it."

Emma's eyes widened at that. He had told her that he had decided to do it because his one tunic had been ruined in the attack by the bandits.

"She also said you enjoyed mating with him."

Emma flushed beet red at that. "I—"

"Set up a caterwauling every night and some mornings."

Her mouth dropped open. Good God, had they made so much noise? Had the whole castle heard them then? She would have to discuss this with Amaury. She would never be able to enjoy his touch again if she thought the whole castle was listening.

"Yet you told my son you loved him. Why?" Before she could even think of something to say to that, Lady Ascot continued. "No doubt you were hoping for a chance to use him to escape. He is conceited and foolish enough that it might work," she said thoughtfully, then stabbed Emma with a stare. "Were it not for me. But there is me, girl, so take heed. 'Twill not happen. You will remain right here until de Aneford is dead. Then you will marry my son."

"Not so long as there is breath in my body," Emma snapped furiously, giving up the pretense. It seemed useless anyway.

"Then you shall be killed."

She clamped her mouth shut at that.

"Either way, my son shall have Eberhart Castle. 'Tis only right. It belongs to him. It should have passed to him on Fulk's death." She smiled suddenly. "Now that we understand one another, I shall leave you be. I doubt you have much appetite just now, so I shall tell the servants not to bother with the tray they were arranging." Turning, she swept out of the room.

Emma glared at the door grimly for several minutes, then tugged the linens back out from under the blanket and continued determinedly at her work. Hours passed as she laboured. She was about to attach the last of the strips of cloth when there was a light tap, followed by the scraping of the bar being removed once more.

Cursing under her breath, she quickly stashed her

makeshift rope beneath the covers again as the door opened. It was Bertrand this time. Emma peered at him warily, unsure whether his mother had told him of discovering her ruse. When he smiled slightly before turning to close the door, she knew she had not.

Turning back to her, he opened his mouth, then paused as he took note of her dusty gown. "You are not wearing the gown I sent. Did you not like it?"

Emma froze at that, cursing her own stupidity and pride, then forced a smile and lied, "I am such a fright I feared I might sully the gown just now. I thought to wear it on the morrow after I bathe."

"Oh. How clever of you." Relaxing, he moved forward. "I heard Mother order the servants not to bring you any supper, so I brought you something to eat." Reaching into his pocket, he tugged an apple and a chicken leg from its depths, and offered them to her as he took a seat on the bed beside her.

The apple looked lovely, but the chicken leg was a little less than edible. There were bits of lint and threads caught on it from resting in his pocket. Emma managed a smile of thanks anyway and bit into the apple. She hadn't realized that she was hungry until she spied the offering. Now she considered the fact that she had a long arduous journey ahead of her. She had no food and no horse, yet meant to find her way back to court, or at least a neighboring castle or keep, on foot.

Realistically, it was doubtful she would make it. On the other hand, sitting about waiting for news of her husband's death and her imminent marriage to the useless creature before her did not seem a viable alternative. Besides, there was always the possibility that she would stumble into the midst of some bandits. If that happened and she were allowed to plead her case, she might succeed at gaining thier protection and an escort back to court in exchange for a reward.

"What did you say that pleased Mother so?"

Emma pulled the apple away from her mouth to peer at him doubtfully. "Your mother told the servants not to feed me because she was pleased?"

"Oh, nay. That was just to show you she was boss. She does that to me as well. Orders me to bed without my supper. But she has been smiling ever since speaking with you."

She digested that with some difficulty. It was hard to believe that a man of his age would allow anyone, mother or not, to order him to bed without his supper. But then Bertrand had proven himself to be a coward and somewhat less than intelligent. Shrugging those thoughts away, she considered his question. No doubt his mother was happy at the way her plans were working rather than at anything Emma had done. Still, she thought it better to keep that to herself.

"Mayhap she is pleased that we have affection for each other," she murmured, avoiding his eyes as she spoke the lie.

Bertrand perked up at that. "Aye, mayhap she is."

Emma took another bite of her apple. "How do you intend to kill my husband?" She tried to ask the question as nonchalantly as possible, but knew there was a thread of tension in her voice. Bertrand did not seem to notice it.

"Chancellor Arundel will see to it."

Emma nearly choked on the apple in her mouth at that. "The archbishop?"

"Oh, aye. He is a friend of Mother's. He plans to poison him at court. He most like has already done so. We should receive news any time now. Then we can be married." He smiled at her as he said that, then sighed. "I should leave now before Mother notices I am missing. She would not be pleased that I am visiting. She ordered that no one was to see you again tonight."

288

Standing as he said that, he bent as if to grace her with a kiss, then spotted the last of the linens lying on the bed beside her and backed away, a pained smile on his face. "No doubt we shall have to wait a day or two to be wed. 'Twill make the wedding night sweeter."

Emma managed to contain her grimace until the door had closed behind him. Then she dropped the rest of the apple onto the bed and pulled her rope out again. She had completely lost her appetite at the last bit of information Bertrand had imparted. The very thought that her husband might be dead was enough to make her stomach roil with fear. Determined not to think of it, she knotted the last linen onto the end of the rope, then stood and moved to the window.

It was full dark out now. So dark she could no longer tell where the wall ended and the ground began. It looked to be an abyss outside her window.

Grimacing, she turned and quickly stripped the linens off the bed, adding them to the end of her rope. Then she hurriedly checked each knot to make sure they were firm. That done, she paused to take a deep breath to bolster her courage, then stooped to tie the end of her makeshift rope around the bedpost before moving back to the window and leaning out to peer toward the guards. They were busy yelling at each other across the distance separating them. Emma waited a moment, but they did not glance away from each other so, giving her shoulders a shrug, she dropped her rope. It disappeared into the darkness even as it slapped against the wall. 'Twas not a very loud sound, but made her glance nervously toward the guards again anyway. They did not appear to have noticed.

She waited a moment just to be sure, then started to lift a leg onto the window ledge. There was every possibility that one or the other of them would glance over and spot her golden gown in the darkness. It was something she had thought of as she was making the ropes, but there was little she could do about that. It was a terrible shame she did not have on a gown of a darker color, but Amaury had insisted he did not wish to see her in anything even vaguely resembling black. She would give him hell for that the first chance that she got, she decided, refusing to consider the idea that he might already be dead. He simply could not be. She would not have it. She simply could not be widowed by him. And not just because she did not wish to marry Bertrand. Damned if she hadn't become used to having her husband about. Why, she was even becoming used to the idea of being in love with the great lug. Truly, her knees went weak whenever he touched her, and his smile somehow seemed to make the morning brighter. It would be a gray world without him in it.

Her thoughts managed to distract her from what she was doing as she sat on the ledge and eased to its edge, preparing to shimmy down her rope. A quick glance to the side assured her that she had not been noticed yet. It also helped to delay her descent. She was not sure what she would do if she were spotted. She supposed she could simply push herself out from the side of the castle and drop into the moat in the hope that she could get out and avoid her pursuers long enough to lose herself in the woods. On that thought, she wrapped the top of the rope around one arm, grasped it with both hands, and pushed herself off the ledge.

Chapter Fifteen

Emma did not have far to drop with the rope wrapped around her as it was, but she realized her mistake in doing so the moment the rope jerked tight around her arm. The pain was excruciating. She managed to bite back a shout of agony and hold on as she swung just below the window ledge. Forcing herself to concentrate on the solid stone wall before her, she tried to ignore the pain in her arm. It felt as if that limb were afire.

After a moment of time in which she waited to see if the pain would lessen any, she glanced nervously to the side to see the guards. They were still talking, but she knew she could not count on their continuing their conversation forever.

Biting her lip to keep back the whimper of pain and fear that wanted to escape, Emma shifted her hold and allowed herself to lower a hand's span down the rope. She paused again then before lowering herself the same amount once more. Then again. She traversed most of the wall like that, inch by painful inch, every second expecting a shout to call the warning that she was trying to escape. She was halfway down the wall, the muscles in her arms and shoulders aching so badly she feared she could hear them screaming in her head, before she stopped worrying about that. It seemed that in the dark the guards could not see her.

Emma discovered she had arrived at the end of the rope when she reached down to grab it a bit lower and grasped nothing but air. Holding still, she glanced down, squinting in an effort to see the ground. After a moment she was just able to make it out. From what she could tell she was a little over two thirds of the way down the wall. That still left a third of the way to traverse. With no rope. She felt panic rise up in her briefly, then stomped down on it determinedly as she tried to consider her options.

Climbing back up the wall to her prison was one.

"Not bloody likely," she muttered under her breath.

Jumping to the ground was another option, but it carried the possibility of breaking her legs with it. It would be difficult to escape on broken legs.

She surveyed the ground again, then glanced at the moat. She could always make a jump for that. Her nose wrinkled at the idea. She had begun to smell the moat before she had traversed a quarter of the distance down. Right now the scent was almost unbearably strong. Diving into the source of that smell was not the most appealing option. Unless she put it next to seeing her husband dead, she thought grimly and peered below again. She would have to move quickly. Her splashing into the moat would no doubt be heard. It would at least be enough to have the guards send someone to look about. She would have to pull herself out and reach the woods before being caught, but there was no help for it, she decided. Yet she still hesitated.

A sudden shout from above brought her head up. She could just see Bertrand's silhouette in the window of the tower, framed there by the candlelight in the room. It seemed he had come for another unapproved visit. He did have the damnedest timing.

Grimacing, Emma turned to face the wall, took a deep breath, pushed herself out with her feet, and released her hold on the rope.

She dropped like a stone, her skirts flying up over her face as she slammed into the stinking water of the moat. It was deeper than she had expected. It seemed to take forever for her to plummet to the bottom, though she supposed that at the moment, as she imagined guards pouring out of the gate to search her out, everything seemed to take too long. Feeling slightly uneven ground beneath her feet, she pushed upward, only to reach the surface and barely manage a gasp of putrid air before her skirts dragged her down again.

She struggled briefly, attempting to reach the surface anyway, but it was impossible. When her lungs began to burn from lack of air, she started to tug desperately at her gown, shedding it as quickly as she could before struggling back to the surface again. As fetid as the air that she drew into her lungs then was, it was about as sweet as the scent of a rose to Emma.

Gasping more air into her lungs, she struggled through the foul stew toward the outer edge of the moat, aware of the shouting above her head as the guards on the wall tried to pinpoint her in the dark. She could also hear the rattle of the drawbridge being lowered.

Emma had almost reached her goal when she felt something brush up against one of her legs. Images of what might actually be alive, or even dead, in the moat exploding in her head, she grasped desperately at the turf on the far side, and quickly pulled her shuddering body out of the water. She would have liked to do a little dance of disgust as she drew herself to her feet on the grass, but there was no time for it. Gaining her feet, she glanced over her shoulder at the men pouring over the drawbridge after her, then sprinted for the woods.

Emma had almost reached the trees when a solid wall of men stepped from them, barring her path. She paused in astonishment, then turned to flee to the side.

"Emmalene!"

Freezing at that voice, she whirled, peering in the direction it had come from. But all she could see were the dark shapes of soldiers. Until one stepped forward. He had the vague outline of her husband and she truly wanted to believe that it was him, but it was so dark . . . Then someone lit a torch, holding it aloft as the men pursuing her began to slow in confusion. The man bearing the torch was Blake. Beside him stood Amaury, and beside him was King Richard. On either side of them stood a line of men that seemed to go on forever.

Sobbing her relief, Emma raced forward and threw herself against Amaury's chest.

Amaury raised his arms automatically to catch his little wife to his heart. He had never been more relieved in his life than when he had spotted her at the tower window. The soldiers who had trailed them all day had just caught up to them when she had appeared. They had all stood silent as they stared at her. His relief to know that she was at least alive had been nearly enough to make his legs collapse beneath him as he had recognized her gold gown in the candlelight.

Then she had leapt from that window and his heart had stopped dead. When she had been brought up short in her downward flight and he had realized that she was hanging from a rope, his legs *had* given out. Only Blake and the king's speed in catching his arms had kept him on his feet. The following few minutes had been sheer hell as they had watched her descend inch by painful inch toward the ground. All of them, every last man, had seemed to hold their breath as they watched his wife do what few of them would have dared. And all of them had felt completely useless from their position on the edge of the woods.

Sweat had beaded Amaury's brow and his hands had ached from clenching them by the time she had reached little more than halfway down and suddenly stopped. He had known right away there was a problem. Still, none of them had been prepared for her sudden plummet down into the moat. They had all stood frozen to the spot briefly. Then she had pulled herself from the water and charged across the grass as if nothing had happened. At first she had headed straight for them. Almost as if she knew they were there. It wasn't until she had suddenly changed her course that he had realized that she did not know it was them.

Now, he lowered his face to press a tender kiss to the top of her head, only to stiffen, dismay crossing his features as he got a whiff of her. A glance to the side showed the king taking a hasty step back, waving one hand frantically before his nose as he too caught a sniff. Blake had taken two decidedly large steps to the side, taking the torch with him and nearly casting them in darkness again.

The sound of hoofbeats drew Amaury's attention to Lady Ascot as she crossed the bridge on a horse, her son behind her on another. The men who had stopped in their pursuit of his wife, and now hesitated uncertainly a few feet behind their quarry, immediately made way for their mistress as she rode up before them.

"Ah, de Aneford. I see you saved us the trouble of hunting down both your wife and yourself," she drawled, then glanced toward her son. "Kill him."

Bertrand looked nonplussed for a moment, then turned to the men standing on the ground before his horse. "Kill him. But do not harm Emma."

The men simply stood there with expressions of uncertainty. They had seen the king. They had also had time for their eyes to adjust to the darkness, and now saw the number of men they faced. None were willing to act.

"Did you not hear my son?" Lady Ascot snapped impatiently. "Why do you hesitate? Kill the man!"

"I fear it may have something to do with my presence." Richard stepped briefly back into the torchlight, wrinkled his nose, then hurriedly moved around to Blake's other side, as far from Amaury and his aromatic little wife as he could before relaxing again and smiling at Lady Ascot. A smile that became decidedly predatory as his soldiers made their numbers known by circling Lady Ascot's men.

To her credit, the woman paled, but retained enough of her wits to try to protect herself. "Your Majesty, what a . . . lovely surprise. We were just . . ."

"Attempting to recapture your prisoner?" Richard finished for her archly.

"Nay. Never. Nonsense. Lady Emma was our guest."

"Do many of your guests leave by the window?" Blake asked dryly.

"Only the more adventurous," Lady Ascot snapped.

Thinking he had most definitely comforted his wife more than enough, Amaury barked over his shoulder for his squire. "See your lady to the horses."

"Nay," Emma protested, pulling back to peer at him. "Amaury—"

"Aye, wife. We will tend to Bertrand and his mother," he insisted, grimacing as a fresh whiff of moat reached his nose.

"But I must tell you, Gytha is her maid. And they

296

knocked me out and held me captive. And Arundel was supposed to poison you at court. Then they were going to force me to marry *him*." She gestured toward Bertrand, who was doing his best to appear invisible at the moment.

"Aye, wife. Now go with Alden. You are barely dressed." He gave her a gentle push toward the boy, then turned back to face Ascot and her son.

Emma frowned at his back, then turned reluctantly toward the squire.

"Come, my lady." Alden stepped forward to take her arm, then immediately stepped back as far as he politely could and still lead her by the arm into the woods.

Bertrand watched the woman he had coveted disappear into the woods, and took a moment to wonder at the unfairness of a bastard son of a village maid having gained everything he sought. Then he sighed and slid off his mount. It was apparent to him what he must do now.

Both Amaury and Blake drew their swords, crossing them before their king when he suddenly hurried toward him. The action brought him to an abrupt halt, but did not stop his saying, "I beg your leave, Your Majesty. It must be obvious to you that I had nothing to do with this? 'Twas all her doing."

"Bertrand!" Lady Ascot roared furiously when he waved vaguely in her direction, but her son ignored her.

"I was a mere pawn! A victim as surely as Lady Emmalene herself!"

Blake and Amaury glanced at each other, sharing a look of amused disgust at this display. The king was less than entertained, however.

"Quit your sniveling, man! Yer in this up to your neck." A quick gesture was enough to bring two of his men forward to collect Bertrand as the king faced Lady

Ascot. Blake and Amaury lowered their swords and turned to glare at her as well.

She lasted a moment or two longer under their combined accusing scowls than her son, but it was only a moment or two.

" 'Twas Gytha!" she screeched at last. " 'Twas all her idea. I only told her to get her cousin, that fop de Lascey, to take her with him so that she might spy on you. She took it upon herself to poison you. 'Twas she who knocked your wife out as well. She caught her listening to us—" Lady Ascot's panicky babbling came to an abrupt end when the servant she was accusing pushed her way through the horses and yanked the woman off her horse by the skirt. Before anyone could move, the maid had her mistress before her, a dirk at her throat.

" 'Tis glad I am that loyalty works both ways in our relationship," she muttered bitterly to her betrayer, then pressed the knife closer until a bead of blood appeared at its tip when Amaury made to move forward. "Nay, de Aneford. While you may have nine lives, I much fear her Ladyship here does not."

Amaury stopped, but shrugged at the intended threat. "Kill her then."

Lady Ascot released a choked squawking noise at that, and he turned his gaze to her, adding, "Why should I care? She has been working hard enough to do just that to myself. 'Sides, once she is dead, you will have no shield."

Gytha's mouth twisted bitterly at that, and she began moving backward, pulling her mistress with her as Lady Ascot's men stepped out of the way. "It seems I made a mistake again," Gytha said. "The first was in backing this old bitch as a victor."

"The second was in underestimating me," Amaury told her arrogantly, following her retreat.

"Aye. I will not do that again," she muttered, glancing

behind her and pausing when she saw that she had backed up to the moat. Gytha started to turn back, spied the rush of movement out of the corner of her eye as Amaury hurried forward, then stumbled off balance as Lady Ascot began to struggle. Her mistress's struggles stopped the moment the knife pierced her neck, but it was too late. Off balance and already falling, Gytha was unable to stop them both from tumbling backward into the moat.

Amaury shouted in warning as the two women began to fall. The nearest of her men stepped forward at once, intent on catching at least their mistress, but none were close enough to be able to grab at her before both women plummeted into the moat. Once they had disappeared beneath its dark surface, the men all simply stood about, grimacing as they watched for one or the other of the women to resurface.

Amaury reached the half circle of men and burst through to the front. Grabbing a torch from the nearest man, he crouched down on his haunches and held it out over the moat. It looked like black pudding. There was not a bubble or circle of disturbance on the top. It was as if it had just swallowed the women up.

"Phew!" Blake muttered, reaching his side. "Think you some one should dive in there and fetch them out?"

Lady Ascot's men peered at him as if he were mad.

"Her ladyship is dead," one of them said. "The maid slit her throat wide open as they fell."

"Aye," another agreed. "And I'll not be diving into that mess to save the woman who killed her."

As the others murmured agreement to that, Amaury straightened, his frowning gaze still on the surface of the moat.

"Their gowns will keep them down there," the king murmured, stepping through the crowd to Amaury's

Lynsay Sands

side and surveying the fetid water. "And good riddance too. I'll not make a man risk his life swimming in that muck to save a murderer."

" 'Tis amazing Emma survived her plunge in there," Blake muttered.

"Aye," Amaury agreed grimly, then glanced at the king as he spoke again.

"Post a guard here until the bodies surface."

"What of Bertrand?" Amaury asked.

"I shall banish him. Put a guard on him as well for now. Tomorrow he can be taken on a boat and sent to France, or mayhap Italy." He shrugged. "Whatever the case, he will no longer be a threat. Without lands, riches, or courage, he shall not bother us again."

Amaury nodded at that. "And what will you do about Arundel?"

He pursed his lips. "Nothing. He will stay on as lord chancellor," he decided, a grim tinge to his voice. Then spying their dismay, he explained, " 'Tis better to keep Arundel, whom I know I cannot trust and can therefore guard myself against, than to have a new chancellor whom I may trust mistakenly." He let them think on that briefly, then added, " 'Sides, Arundel has many friends. Most of them much like Lady Ascot and her son. 'Twould take more than hearsay to oust him without a battle, and that is all we have. Hearsay from Bertrand to Lady Emma and from her to me. He did not get the chance to try his trick. Therefore we have no proof."

Blake nodded solemnly at that, then glanced toward Amaury, only to find the man gone. No doubt to find his wife, he realized, and smiled to himself as the king began barking his orders.

"They are sure that they are dead, are they not?"

Emma glanced at her cousin with surprise. It was

300

nearly three weeks since the events that had ended in Lady Ascot's and her maid's death. She and Amaury had returned to court the morning following the escapade. Emma had thought they would simply collect their things and return home. However, the king had insisted they should stay at court for a few days to be sure Emma was recovered from her excitement and had not collected a chill from her dip in the moat.

Those few days had dragged into weeks before they had managed to extricate themselves and start home. They had arrived back at Eberhart Castle only the day before. Just in time, it had seemed, for Emma had awoken that morning to the news that her cousin and Bishop Wykeham were riding up to the castle.

It had taken her longer than expected to make her way below stairs. Rolfe and the bishop had already been seated at the table enjoying a repast when she joined them. Emma had greeted them warmly, then spent the first little bit updating her two guests on court gossip. Rolfe and the bishop had not been at court during the time she and her husband had. "In Scotland on court business" had been all the king had told her when she had asked.

Once she had exhausted what little gossip she had bothered to listen to at court, Emma had turned to the tale of their woes with Bertrand and his mother. Now she smiled gently at her cousin's concerned expression.

"Aye. Lady Ascot floated to the surface of the moat the day after we left the demesne for court and Gytha . . ." Emma paused, her lips pulling down with concern as she saw Sebert enter the castle and head toward them. The expression on his face was oddly determined and miserable all at the same time.

Emma let the conversation with her cousin drop at once. Sebert had been miserable over Gytha's involvement in the plot since hearing of it on their return from

301

court. He had decided the woman had been using him all along, and blamed himself for not having noticed how most of the subjects they had discussed had focused on Emma and Amaury. She had tried telling him it was not his fault, but nothing would console him. She only hoped that with time, his wounds and this unnecessary guilt would heal.

Sebert moved directly to the table, but rather than approach her as she had expected, he stopped beside the bishop. "My lord bishop, I know you are retired, but Father Gumpter is away just now and you did take confessions when you were here last. I hoped you might be willing to hear my confession . . . again?"

"Of course, of course." The bishop was on his feet in an instant. "Mayhap there are one or two others who might like me to hear their confessions as well," he suggested happily, clapping Sebert on the back as they moved off.

Rolfe watched them go, then got to his feet as well. "Excuse me, Em. I must find Blake."

Emma stared after him with some surprise, wondering why he would seek her husband's friend. As far as she knew, until her wedding to Amaury, her cousin had never even met Blake. Curious, she thought, then shrugged inwardly and stood to seek out Maude. Emma had need of some more weeds that were not available in her garden. Weeds that would help ward off morning sickness.

She smiled to herself as she thought that, her hand moving to rest on her still flat stomach. She knew now that she was indeed pregnant. It was a blessing and even a miracle in a way. A miracle that the babe had survived her journey in the tapestry. It was the morning sickness that had convinced her. She had been suffering the ailment for three weeks now. But Amaury had been up and about early every morning at court, attending the king's pleasure. This morn was the first time that he had still been there to witness her bout with the malady when she rose. Gravely concerned, he had cursed a blue streak as he had held her in her throes. By the time her stomach had settled, he had been determined she should stay abed. It had taken a great deal of arguing to get him to allow her to move down to the Great Hall to greet their guests. She supposed he would have relaxed soon enough had she confessed it was just the morning sickness, but Emma found herself oddly resistant to that idea.

It was the bedding of course. May the Good Lord save her soul, but she did not wish to give it up. It was one thing to enjoy the bedding that ladies were said not to enjoy, for the bedding was necessary to beget a child. However, it was another thing entirely to seek out the bedding when there was no need for it. She feared her husband would not agree with that and she would suffer the next seven months without his body to cuddle and his loving to comfort her. She was not willing to give that up just yet, so she intended on keeping her pregnancy a secret for as long as she could. Hence the need for the weeds. Should she wake up every morning with the sickness, he was sure to catch on.

Finding Maude in the kitchens, she told her what she wished to do and sent her to have the horses saddled, then headed up to her room to fetch her bow and arrow. It was not for her protection. Amaury would insist she take a guard, but now that her husband knew of her ability with the weapon, she thought it might be nice to practice a bit.

Entering her room, Emma crossed to the chest at the foot of the bed and began rummaging inside. She had just uncovered the bow when the bedroom door clicked closed behind her. Still on her knees, she glanced over her shoulder curiously to see who it was, then paled sickly.

"My lady."

The bow clutched in her hand, Emma got slowly to her feet at those sarcastic words, and faced the woman eyeing her with cold hatred. "You did not drown."

Gytha raised an eyebrow. "You do not appear surprised, my lady."

"I survived my time in the moat. Why should you not have?"

"And yet you *are* surprised to see me."

Emma nodded. "I thought you too intelligent to bother coming here. I thought you would be more concerned with your own survival."

"Survival?!" Gytha spat the word bitterly, her right hand jerking at her side and drawing Emma's eyes to the ugly-looking blade she held there. "I may as well be dead. You ruined everything. Everything!"

Emma scooted quickly back against the wall, then to the side as the woman moved toward her. Coming up against the edge of a chest, she faced her pursuer, waited until she was within striking distance, then swung the bow at her.

The weapon hit Gytha flat on the side of her face. Reeling from the blow, she stumbled a couple of steps backward, just far enough for Emma to escape the corner she had been backed into and flee for the bed. It was the only path open to her. Gytha barred her way around the bed, so Emma tugged the curtains open and started over it to the other side. She had nearly reached the second set of curtains on the opposite side of the bed when she was brought up short by a sharp tug on the back of her skirt.

Crying out, she glanced around. Emma took one look at the mad rage on Gytha's face and swung at her with the bow again.

The Deed

Letting go of her skirt, the maid caught the bow before it struck and tugged at it.

Giving up the sorry weapon, Emma finished her hurtle across the bed, lunged through the second set of curtains, and ran right under Amaury's arm as he opened the bedroom door and stepped inside.

Pausing in the hall, she whirled and screamed her warning. She need not have bothered. Gytha was already coming through the curtains of the bed and Amaury was drawing his sword. The maid did not even hesitate. It seemed to Emma that there was a look of satisfaction on the other woman's face as she spied Amaury and hurtled herself forward, right into the end of his blade.

Chapter Sixteen

It was an odious scent that roused Emma. Blinking her eyes open, she choked and gasped, raising a hand to push away the horrible odor that was tormenting her. God's truth, it was worse than the moat at Bertrand's demesne.

"Thank the Lord," Maude sighed, removing the noxious brew she had been waving beneath her nose.

Frowning, Emma watched her set the bowl aside, then sighed and peered at the people crowded about her bed eyeing her so anxiously. It reminded her of her wedding night. Once again every possible person who could cram themselves into the room had done so, and the rest were struggling to peer over each other from the door.

"What happened?"

"You fainted," Amaury told her worriedly.

"Nay. Did I?" She raised a hand to her head with confusion, then recalled exactly what had happened before she had fainted. "Gytha!"

"She is dead, wife," Amaury assured her at once.

Her gaze slid to the spot by the door where the woman had died. He added, "I had her taken away."

"Oh."

"You told me she had drowned," Rolfe accused her now. "You said her body was found."

"Nay," Emma denied at once. "I said Lady Ascot was recovered. We were interrupted ere I could tell you Gytha had not been." Sighing, she tried to push herself into a sitting position. "I should get up."

"Nay. You will rest," Amaury said firmly, pushing her back on the bed. "You are ill."

"I am not ill," Emma reassured him quietly as she sat up again.

Amaury pushed her back down. "You were retching this morning. Mayhap all this excitement these last weeks has weakened you."

"I am not weakened," she said with exasperation, once again attempting to sit up, only to be pushed back down, this time by Rolfe as he glanced at her husband sharply.

"She was retching?" Rolfe asked.

Amaury nodded grimly. "Aye. Retching and weaving. I thought she was fit to die. 'Twas why I came up here when I heard Maude order the stable master to saddle her horse." He turned to Emma now. "You will not go riding. You are ill."

"I am not ill!" Emma insisted, sitting up again.

"You are upsetting her, Amaury," Blake pointed out, worry on his face as well now. " 'Tis the worst thing to do if she is ailing. She should rest."

"He's right, my lord," Little George rumbled. "Rest'll mend her."

"Ye can see I am trying to get her to do so, can ye

not?!" Amaury roared at them, then pushed his wife back on the bed again and snapped, "You are ill and will stay abed."

"I am not ill!" Emma roared.

"Do not argue, wife. You are ill and will stay abed until you are better."

"I will not," she said indignantly, imagining being confined to the bed for seven and a half months. That was how long it would be until the baby came and that was all that was wrong with her. A little morning sickness, dizzy spells . . . She was not laying abed for seven months.

"If I say you will remain abed, you will," Amaury told her firmly, a grim glare adding strength to his words. "Even do I have to set guards on you and—"

"I am pregnant," she confessed in desperation.

The people around the bed itself, the only ones who had been able to hear her confession, went quite silent and still of a sudden.

"What did she say?" the cook asked from the door.

Sebert craned his head slightly to peer over the crowd. "Lady Emma said we're to have a child among us soon."

"What was that?" one of Amaury's men barked from the hall.

The cook turned to beam on the man. "We're pregnant!" he shouted.

There was a mingled reaction to that of both pleasure and worry from the people on the fringe of the room and in the hall.

"Well, tell 'er she cannot be runnin' about and shimmyin' down walls anymore then," one of the men yelled back, drawing a nod from everyone in the room.

"She should rest," was another's suggestion.

Emma finally turned away from Amaury's stunned expression and peered pleadingly at Rolfe after that comment. Her cousin looked about as stunned as her husband, but caught her expression and understood it.

"Mayhap . . ." Pausing, he cleared his throat. "We should leave them alone," he announced firmly.

Cook was the first to move. Beaming at Emma from his position by the door, he clapped his hands and turned toward the hall. "I shall make a special meal to celebrate."

"I'll fetch some extra ale," the alewife announced, following on his heels.

"I need a drink," Blake muttered, moving toward the door.

"Aye," Rolfe, Little George, and Sebert agreed as one and followed him.

" 'Twould not go amiss, I think," the bishop murmured, moving after them.

Sighing as the door closed, leaving her and her husband alone, Emma peered down at the bed linens she sat on and began to pluck at them nervously. "You are not happy about the babe?"

"Aye." Amaury dropped weakly onto the side of the bed, a hand going to his head as if he were dizzy.

Emma frowned. "Nay. You are not."

"Aye. 'Tis just . . . You are so small," he complained worriedly.

"Oh, my lord." She reached to cover his hand with hers as she realized he feared for her health. Many women died in childbirth. " 'Tis true I am short, but 'tis not the height that is significant. 'Tis the width of the hips that are important for birthing babies," she said reassuringly.

Amaury's gaze dropped to her hips. His anxiety did not ease. "They are small hips, wife."

"Nay!" Sliding off the bed, she stood in front of him and brought his hands to rest on either side of those

309

hips. "They are wide, husband. Certainly wide enough for a babe."

"You are sure?" He raised worried eyes to hers.

"Positive, my lord. All will be well." Leaning forward, she kissed him gently on the lips.

"Ah, Emma," he moaned, pulling her into his arms and holding her tightly for a moment. "You make me so happy I am afeared to lose you."

"You will not," Emma murmured softly against his chest, reveling in his embrace. At least he would not keep those from her during the pregnancy. It would have to be enough, she thought with a dismal sigh, then forced a smile when he pulled back slightly to peer at her before bending his head to plant a passionate kiss on her lips.

Winding her arms around his neck, she held him close and kissed him back, then quickly set about pushing him away in surprise when his hands began roaming over her body through her gown.

"What do you?" she asked in confusion.

His eyebrows rose at that. "Is it not obvious, wife?"

"But I am with child, husband," she protested at once.

Amaury stilled at that, worry crossing his features. " 'Twill not harm the babe, will it?"

"Nay, but . . ." She flushed uncomfortably. "The Church does say that the . . . er . . . marital act is to be performed only to gain children, and as we are already with child . . ."

Amaury smiled as her voice faded. Her choice of words in saying that "we are already with child" made him feel warm inside. It was their child. Theirs. Their child, their castle, their people. A whole world of things was theirs, he thought, and suddenly realized that the possession of those things was not really what he had wanted at all. He had wanted simply to belong. And he did. He belonged with Emma.

"I love you," he said suddenly, and Emma stopped batting at his hands to peer at him wide-eyed.

"You do?" she asked with awe.

"Aye," he said solemnly.

"Wh—" Emma paused to lick her lips, then managed to ask. "Why?"

Amaury's eyebrows rose at that, and she flushed bright red.

"I mean, what do you love about me?"

Easing his embrace, he sat back to eye her thoughtfully, then gave a wry smile. " 'Twould be easier to tell you what I do not love."

Her eyes narrowed at that. "What do you not love?" she asked suspiciously.

"Your temper," he admitted promptly. "But only when it is directed at me. Else I love even that." When she peered at him doubtfully, he pulled her close again and hugged her. "I think you know I love your body."

Emma blushed and nodded shyly.

"I also love your mind. 'Tis as fine as any man's I have met."

Her lips tipped up with pleasure at that.

"But mostly, I love how you make me feel," he admitted quietly. "I am happy with you. I feel at home."

Tears shining in her eyes, Emma hugged him closer when he would have pulled away, and admitted, "I love you too. Sometimes I feel I was not even really alive until you came into my life. I . . ." Her voice trailed away as she realized he wasn't listening, but was intent on touching seemingly every part of her. "Husband, I love you, but the Church says—"

"I know." Amaury pulled back again to smile at her. Contrary to what she thought, he had been listening to her, and the fact that she loved him back made him so happy he wanted to explode. Preferably inside of her. His smile deepening, Amaury suddenly turned her in

311

his arms, his hands moving to work busily at her stays.

"The Church is made up of men, wife," he began his lecture. "And men, even holy men, are not infallible. For instance, they believe that ladies do not enjoy the joining." The stays undone, he slid her gown off her shoulders to fall in a pool at her feet, then turned her in his arms again. "Did you know that?"

"N-nay," Emma gasped as his lips closed over one nipple through her chemise.

"Nay?" he asked with surprise, pulling his head away from her breasts to lift her under-tunic over her head now.

"I mean, aye," she corrected quickly as she briefly regained her senses now that his lips were not torturing her. "Aye, I knew that. Mayhap there is something wrong with me. Or mayhap I am not a true lady."

About to drop the under-gown to the ground, Amaury paused, anger flashing across his face. "Never say that, wife. You are every inch a lady. But you are also a woman." He turned to lay her gown over the chest by the bed, then turned back, his eyes alight as they traveled over her. "With a woman's body." He reached for that body now, running his hands freely over it as he whispered huskily, "And a woman's desires."

Emma moaned against his lips as he finally kissed her, her own hands moving to tug at his clothes. She hadn't even managed to get his sword buckle undone when he ended the kiss to help her.

" 'Sides, 'tis my fault."

In the process of tugging his shirt up over his chest, Emma paused to peer at him in confusion. "What is your fault, husband?"

"Your enjoyment of the mating," he explained, tugging his tunic over his head himself. " 'Tis my touch that sets you so afire. Is it not? Without that, you no doubt would not enjoy the joining at all. Unfortunately, I like

The Deed

it when you like it, so I make sure you like it."

He paused to peer at her, a lecherous grin on his face. " 'Tis the sounds you make. Moans and groans and high-pitched wails. And you writhe beneath me. I like that too." He kissed her then until she began to shudder against him and make some of those sounds. Then he pulled back and drew her hand down to cover his manhood through his braies. "You see? It fires me up. 'Tis all my fault."

He released her then to remove those braies, and Emma let her eyes drift over his body, taking in the wide strong chest, the hard-muscled legs, and everything in between. She was not surprised at the wave of heat that rolled up through her, or the fact that her toes were curling into the rushes beneath her feet. Just looking at her husband was enough to set her afire, but he did not need to know that, she decided.

"Oh, aye, husband," she breathed huskily, stepping into his arms as he straightened from removing the last of his clothes. " 'Tis your fault. 'Tis your touch that fires me so." She caught a glimpse of his satisfied smile before his lips covered hers, and she thought how lucky she was to have a husband like him. And soon they would have a child too. Then she stopped thinking altogether as he swept her into his arms and carried her to the bed.

THE ROSELYNDE CHRONICLES

JOANNA

Roberta Gellis

"A superb storyteller of extraordinary talent!"
—John Jakes

Beautiful, iron-willed heiress to power, Joanna secretly burns with an explosive inner passion as wild and radiant as her flaming red hair. But her deepest emotions are tragically frozen by the cold fear of a man's tender love.

Ensnared in the violent lusts and dangerous intrigues of King John's decadent court, the tempestuous noblewoman defies every outward peril—only to come face-to-face with Geoffrey, the knight whose very presence unleashes terror in her heart. Caught between willful pride and consuming desire, Joanna struggles hopelessly to avoid surrendering herself to the irresistible fires raging within her.

_3631-2 $5.99 US/$6.99 CAN

ᴛʜᴇ ROSELYNDE CHRONICLES

ROSELYNDE

Roberta Gellis

"A superb storyteller of extraordinary talent!"
—John Jakes

In an era made for men, Alinor is at no man's mercy. Beautiful, proud and strong willed, she is mistress of Roselynde and her own heart as well—until she meets Simon, the battle-scarred knight whose passion and wit match her own. Their struggle to be united against the political obstacles in their path sweep them from the royal court to a daring crusade through exotic Byzantium and into the Holy Land. They endure bloody battles, dangerous treacheries and heartrending separations before their love conquers time and destiny to live forever.

_3559-6 $5.99 US/$6.99 CAN

The Rose of Ravenscrag

PATRICIA PHILLIPS

Bestselling Author Of *The Constant Flame*

The daughter of a nobleman and a common peasant, Rosamund believes she is doomed to marry a simple swineherd. Then a desperate ruse sweeps the feisty lass from her rustic English village to a faraway castle. And even as Rosamund poses as the betrothed of a wealthy lord, she cannot deny the desire he rouses in her soul. A warrior in battle, and a conqueror in love, Henry of Ravenscrag is all she has ever dreamed of in a husband. But the more Rosamund's passion flares for the gallant who has captured her spirited heart, the more she dreads he will cast her aside if he ever discovers the truth about her.

_3905-2 $4.99 US/$6.99 CAN